For

Flight officer James Lyman Eagleson R.C.A.F.

1923-1944

CHAPTER I

Going Back

"He's all but dead."

"Will they disconnect?"

"I don't know; there's a legal squabble. Not my business. Until I'm told differently, my job is to keep him alive, even if the best he gets is the life of a turnip."

The resident physician read the monitors and noted her charts. "I hate this floor; it's nothing but machines and barely breathing corpses. I've been on this rotation for three days and already want out. I should have done a residency in family practice." She stood over the patient. "I have to wonder what his life was like before."

"Aren't you the sensitive one. I wouldn't have expected something like this with him though. From what I'm told he knew his way around up there. I can't imagine why he was where he was. And speaking of the Adirondacks, how about Lake Placid in two weeks for a weekend? We'll sneak away like we used to."

"Philip, Doctor, you know I'm trying to hold my marriage together."

"You said he'd be out of town, and it's not like we don't have a little history of our own. Come on."

"No, I don't think so. My phone is vibrating, I have to answer it. Doctor Webber speaking ... yes, doctor ... yes ... the straight protocol for these machines ... morphine, yes ... yes, sir, all of those. No sir, the prognosis is clear on that, no recovery."

The resident answered more questions and suggested, "Doctor Carter is the attending physician. He's here if you would like to talk to—OK sir. Thank you, too."

She flipped the phone closed and looked down.

"What's the problem?"

"It's just strange. I told him as much as I could. But when he had the chance to talk to you he got off the phone."

"Who was it?"

"Doctor Charbonneau."

"Doctor Charbonneau is on vacation in Alaska. He's been there for over a week. Said he'd be fishing where no one could find him. Why in hell would he call about this guy? It couldn't have been him."

"Who then?"

"I don't know. Are you sure he was a doctor?"

"He asked all the right questions."

"Huh. Well, right now we have something more important to attend to. How about Lake Placid? You know you love it up there, and no strings."

"I don't think so. I'm really trying to make things work."

"Come on, just you and me, our secret, no one knows, no one's hurt."

"I don't know."

"Just think about it, all right, just that much?"

The resident paused. "I'll think about it. Philip?"

"Yeah?"

"Why did that doctor call?"

* * *

Stosh sped down Route 614 weaving in and out of the mid-morning Tampa Bay traffic. He casually held the steering wheel of his bright red F-250 at its bottom and gazed in deep thought as the fresh Florida air blew on his sun-damaged face from the open window. Stosh was obsessed with his business and seldom took the time to reminisce. Driving Jimmy to the airport gave him a chance to look back awhile. His thoughts were interrupted by the "tat-pist" of an opening beer can. Jimmy took a long leisurely sip. "Beer, Stosh?" he asked.

Stosh looked at his watch, and then at his friend. "Jesum Crow, Jimmy; it's 10:30 in the mornin'."

Jimmy took another long slow sip. "The sun must be over the yardarm somewhere, Stosh."

Stosh shook his head and returned to his zone. His mind popped up snippets of his childhood with Jimmy. He met Jimmy in third grade when his family moved to Plattsburgh from a small hamlet in the Adirondacks so his father could look for work. Some kids thought he was a hick because of his shabby clothes and the way he spoke, but Jimmy knew different, and they quickly became friends. When he saw how little Stosh brought in his beat-up lunch box, Jimmy started packing extra sandwiches and snacks. Stosh never forgot and always had Jimmy's back.

Stosh was a big guy with a big name. Yashu Stanislaus Stoshowicz. Soon after they met Jimmy condensed the whole thing to "Stosh." In the North Country, almost everyone had a nickname. Most eventually faded away, but now, nearly forty years later, grown to his six-foot-five frame, happily married and with a highly successful plumbing supply company, Stosh was still Stosh. And Jimmy was still Jimmy, Stosh's best friend.

"What airport you headin' to?" Stosh asked.

"Dorval."

"Who's pickin' you up?"

"Ray."

"You should get rid of that frickin' jamunk. I'm telling you Jimmy, all he does is sponge off you. I figure he's blowin' more of your money than Clair." To accuse someone of spending more than Jimmy's ex-wife was severe criticism, and while Stosh and Ray had always been fire and ice, Stosh's concern for Jimmy was genuine.

"I'm just telling you, Jimmy, you should clear that wad out of your way. I'm trying to tell you where the frickin' crap is so you don't step in it with your bare feet."

Jimmy looked at Stosh with a wide grin. "How do you really feel?" he said.

"He's a mother frickin' scumbag," Stosh said.

Jimmy chuckled. Stosh was a recovering "swearaholic" who'd always had trouble putting a sentence together without packing in as many outlaw words as he could. The habit cost him in his business and annoyed his wife to no end. Eventually, she confronted him. As a compromise, he acquired a whole new vocabulary of surrogate cuss-words and over the fifteen-plus years of his recovery, he invented or found many intriguing terms that surfaced with a vengeance when he became excited.

"Ray takes care of Camp. He does all the work around the place and makes sure it's always ready for me. He's all right, Stosh. He's not the most motivated, but he's smart, and he's a good guy. He does everything I need him to. I've never understood why you—the most big-hearted man I've ever known—hate him like you do."

"The frickin' guy never worked a day in his life, spent all his time hugging trees and running from anythin' that looked like work. Then the frickin' leech latches on to you. You give him the run of the place, feed the little turdlet, pay him, let him use your pickup, Christos, Jimmy, that blood sucking little fricker is costing you a fortune."

"I can afford it," Jimmy responded in a calm but firm tone ending the discussion.

The traffic funneled onto the Howard Frankland Bridge. Jimmy casually watched the cars. "Best keep in the right lane," he said. Having learned over the years that—except with women—Jimmy's instincts were almost always correct, Stosh automatically complied. As Stosh moved up the right lane, more and more cars jockeyed trying to force their way in front of him. Ahead in the center lane putted along an old rusted truck with a homemade plywood box leaning about thirty degrees to the right. Overfilled with sand with the rear half open it peppered a yellow Corvette convertible driven by a made-up blonde in a light, low-cut summer dress. She wept and brushed grit from her hair and chest while surrounding cars blasted their horns and kept her boxed in. A long-handled shovel carelessly stuck into the pile began to wiggle. As the sand blew, more and more of its flat blade uncovered. Finally, it lost hold and flew off. Jimmy and Stosh jerked back against their head rests as the shovel whipped end-over-end directly at them. Stosh yanked onto the shoulder spinning gravel on the car behind. Jimmy and Stosh braced for impact, but the shovel missed the windshield by a fraction of an inch. Stosh gritted his teeth and swerved back into the lane barely missing the back car's front bumper.

Jimmy shook it off, but Stosh was furious and pulled along-side the dilapidated sand wagon. A slightly built, worn-looking man was clutching the steering wheel with both hands and staring straight forward. He wore an old, skintight, baby-blue Disney tank shirt with Doc the Dwarf on the front, a faded pair of madras shorts, and dark red sunglasses. An enormous gold cross slapped his chest in rhythm with the bouncing from his demolished suspension. Between missing chunks of padded vinyl, the dash displayed dozens of religious icons, saints of every kind dominated by a frantically nodding bobblehead doll of a Tampa Bay Buccaneer reverently placed in the center. A small, faintly pink, blanket covered the shredded bench seat on the driver's side. The radio blasted ear-ripping oldies music from a tinny A.M. station. "Get off the frickin' road!" Stosh yelled. "You mother tapping stick stroker. You almost killed us, you blind bone, can't you see what you're doin'!?"

The driver continued on in his trance oblivious to Stosh and the havoc in his wake. Jimmy took another sip from his beer. "Easy Stosh, he's only doing his job and living the dream." Jimmy looked out the window "Just like us," he whispered. Stosh worked on a rebuttal as he looked at Jimmy and then slapped the wheel, stomped on the accelerator, and roared beyond the old truck.

"No need to stroke out, Stosh," Jimmy said and grinned.

Stosh exhaled and shook his head. "That was close, Jimmy. We coulda' died back there, and I don't know about you, but I'm thinking it ain't time.

"When is it time, Stosh?"

"Not Now!" Stosh drove on silent a few minutes. "Sorry, Jimmy. Things like that frickin' sandman get under my skin."

Stosh smiled, "A close call like that reminds me of when you saved my life."

"We've talked about this a hundred times, Stosh. I didn't save your life; we all saved each other, and we should have had our heads examined for even being there."

Stosh chuckled, "I knew you'd say that."

The traffic now flowed smoothly across the causeway. Stosh reached over and pushed in a light jazz CD and the surround sound gently filled the truck. Jimmy gazed at the green Florida water and watched a slight breeze make miniature waves. A dolphin leaped. Jimmy looked for others, but no more surfaced. Strange to see just one, he thought. He remembered the many times he and Stosh sailed in the Gulf. The sun would be bright and the air warm, very different from Jimmy's destination. Tomorrow was New Year's Eve, and the North Country was bitterly cold with wind and snow. Lake Champlain would soon freeze.

"What's the temperature in Montreal?" Stosh asked.

"Cold."

"You doin' anythin' for New Year?"

"Yeah, a bunch of the gang will be at Camp, you know, the traditional party."

Stosh nodded. "Hope it don't get out a hand. These open bashes you been throwin' might a run their course, you know."

"No one's died yet."

Stosh shook his head and thought a moment. "Jimmy, I know this year's been tough on you, but '03 will be good. And don't let that lunatic get to you. I don't know what happened to her, but she's been out of her mind for a long time, and all that really matters is the girls, and they're gonna be fine, Jimmy."

Jimmy continued to look out the window and sip his beer. "No, they're not," he said.

"Come on Jimmy, you're a good father, and they're good kids."

"Stop petting me Stosh. I'm a lousy father, and they're perfect little replicas of their mother. They've got all they could want but appreciate nothing. They're a couple of spoiled little shits and Clair's determined to keep them that way. Maybe it would have been better if there were no money." Jimmy popped another beer, took a long sip and settled down.

"I wonder what The Old Man thought of us," Stosh said with affection.

Touché Stosh, Jimmy thought. The Old Man, Jimmy's father, a successful, respected and decent man. He had been gregarious with everyone, but could never warm up to his only son. Jimmy looked at the ring on his hand and rubbed the crest with his thumb. "Yeah, I often wonder about that, too," he said. "Chins up, Stosh," Jimmy toasted and took a sip.

Stosh smiled. "Yeah, 'chins up.' You know, we must a said that a thousand times. The Old Man loved that toast. I always wondered where he got it."

Jimmy shrugged and took another sip. "He never said." He never said a lot of things, he thought. As they continued to cruise down the causeway, Jimmy slyly grinned. "When are you coming up?"

"I can't get away from the company now. This is a busy time."

"Sinks and showers and tubs, oh my," Jimmy chanted.

"Come on Jimmy. You know this business as well as I do."

Yes, I do, Jimmy thought.

"And besides, anytime I can get to Camp you're in the city."

"So come to the city."

"Naw, I don't like New York. I know you do, but it's not my thing—too fast. I just don't feel so comfortable there."

Jimmy thought how Stosh had been to New York only twice in his life, "You don't know what you're missing."

"You said that before."

As they reached the end of the bridge, Stosh continued onto I-275 toward the Tampa airport.

"You gonna see Sal?" Stosh asked.

"Yeah."

"You figure he's connected? I don't know how else he can pull off the crap he does."

"I don't think so, but we'll never know. When was the last time the three of us were together?"

"Lot a years. Too bad, we all used ta be so close."

"We still are."

"You're right. Say hello to him. It's been too long."

"That's what he always says about you. I'll be going back to work soon; I'll stop in on the way. I'm sure he'll have plenty of new adventures to tell me about."

"What about Kate? See her much these days?"

"I talked to her last night. She's getting Camp ready for the party. She told me my cousin Gordon sent me a package. Strangest thing, he's never sent anything before. It can't be for Christmas; we don't do that. I can't figure what it is, and it's driving me nuts."

"Shoot, I haven't seen Gord in twenty years."

"I don't see much of him myself now that he's in Vancouver."

"Why don't you call him?"

"I tried, he's somewhere in the Far East on business. I thought of calling Kate again and asking her to open it. But she wouldn't like that. Yeah, it's got me puzzled."

"I see that. You know, I always hoped you an' Kate would get together—"

"Never going to happen, Stosh."

"Too bad, you two'd be a good match."

Jimmy didn't respond.

"When you comin' back down?"

"As soon as I can, and next time we sail."

"Well if you'd come for more than four frickin' days, maybe we coulda' gone out this time."

"I don't know, Stosh. No matter how long I stay, there always seems to be more toilets than time." Jimmy neatly placed his empty can in the trash bag below the dash.

"Take my word, next trip we sail," Stosh said as he pulled up to the curb in front of Jimmy's terminal.

"Why don't you park this monstrosity, come in and have a beer? The office isn't going anywhere."

"Can't and you know I can't. I've gotta' get going. Maybe next time."

Jimmy stepped out of the truck, grabbed his flight bag and suitcase from the back, and returned to the open door.

"Thanks my friend," he said.

"Give me a call when you get in."

"What are you, my mother? You'll know if I crash. I'll see you soon."

"Not soon enough," Stosh said as they warmly shook hands.

"You finish the beer," Jimmy said.

Stosh nodded. Jimmy closed the door and watched as his friend drove off paying more attention to his cellphone than traffic. He smiled and took a deep breath of warm Florida air.

* * *

The doors opened automatically as Jimmy walked into the crammed airport. He quickly found his way to check-in, walked up to one of the idle first-class handlers, swung his suitcase onto the scale and handed him his ticket and passport. "Has your bag been in your possession at all times, Mr. Eagleson?" the attendant asked.

Yeah, since I was born actually, it came out with the after-birth, Jimmy thought, but he just said, "Yes."

After a couple more questions about guns, knives, and explosives, the attendant returned Jimmy's papers, directed him to his terminal, invited him to use the private lounge, and informed him his flight had been delayed. It would be at least two hours late.

As a veteran flyer, Jimmy was used to schedule changes. He gestured thanks to the attendant and looked at the snail-paced economy line, thankful to be at the top of the rich flyers' caste system. As he turned to take his carry-on he bumped a woman in a white pantsuit standing behind him. Her glistening black hair brushed his face. Tall and slender, with bright, angelic blue eyes, she smiled at Jimmy. Jimmy returned the gesture as he picked up his bag. He apologized and offered to help her with her luggage, but she insisted she could do it and thanked him anyway. He was surprised by her strength as she picked up her large bag. They smiled again, and he left.

The line at security didn't discriminate between first class and coach. Jimmy was relieved that only a few dozen people were ahead of him. Two young servicemen stood with sub-machine guns behind the rope divider between the safe and dangerous zones. One guard looked tired and preoccupied; the other stood on full alert sizing up every passenger. They were both clean and neat.

Jimmy never understood why they wore camouflage in an airport. Maybe they plan to jump behind the larger plants and hide. But he did appreciate that at least the government hadn't issued a new pattern to match the commercial carpet and drapes. He knew well why they were there, but the comfort they initially provided had mostly evaporated now fifteen months since 9/11. Jimmy was relieved the man in front of him had been chosen for a full search. Now Jimmy would likely sail through the check.

Jimmy took the familiar stroll to the private lounge where a sign on the door read CLOSED UNTIL 3:00. He took a deep breath and headed to the terminal service area for a beer. The bar was half-filled with travelers. Most were drinking Bloody Marys with full stalks of celery sticking proudly out of large fluted glasses. The bartenders worked from a sunken service area bringing them face to face with the customers who sat on low, upholstered stools.

Jimmy ordered a beer from a rushed and noticeably irritated server who skipped the standard greetings and attempts to sell specials. She quickly served him and left to deal with an unruly customer. In the corner, a loud, overweight vacationer wearing a NASCAR hat stood with friends. His polo shirt exposed his gut whenever he leaned back to laugh. He had no hips or butt and used a wide, over-tightened belt to strap up his jeans. The leather barely fit through the pants' loops and a large rectangular buckle, sporting the Jack Daniels logo, occasionally nipped his flab. His loud high pitched voice made it impossible to ignore his show. On a roll, he told one old, dirty joke after another with roaring laughter from his friends following each worn out punch-line.

The bartender approached him during a pause in his routine and, after tolerating some mild sexual innuendos, politely asked him to keep the volume down. As she returned to her station, he contorted his face like a naughty grade-schooler behind the teacher's back. But the corner became much quieter.

As he finished his beer, Jimmy looked around and noticed a second bartender. She looked attractive and well-proportioned except for her stomach, which pushed out in a uniform sphere as if she swallowed a volleyball. He noticed her pleasant face, but when she smiled to acknowledge him, a large dark spot appeared on one front tooth making her resemble a Mad Magazine caricature of a fairy princess. Jimmy politely asked for another beer. She smiled and nodded.

As she left, another traveler claimed the seat to Jimmy's right. The new arrival looked irritated as he carefully placed his polished leather briefcase in front of his shins. His three-piece wool suit, designer tie, and alligator shoes set him apart.

The bartender returned, quickly left Jimmy's drink, and rushed to a waiting customer.

"Hey, I'm here too you know." the new guy barked.

"I'll be right there, sir," the server politely replied.

He shook his head and took a wad of bills from his pocket. When she returned, he demanded a single malt scotch.

"I'm sorry, Sir, we are out of single malt. Is Dewar's all right?"

"If that's all you've got," he growled.

As she quickly poured his drink, he turned to Jimmy.

Jimmy turned away without responding. When his scotch arrived, he peeled a one-hundred-dollar bill from his stack. Seeing a twenty behind it the bartender asked, "Is there any chance you have anything smaller, sir? I'm very light on change right now."

"No, this is all I've got," he said with a smirk. "Why's the first class lounge closed?"

"I don't know sir, but some of the lounges are being painted. Maybe—"

"Why can't they paint at night?"

The bartender knew she's said enough, shrugged her shoulders and smiled.

"You probably don't know what a first-class ticket costs," he said to Jimmy. "I expect a lounge for that kind of money." He took a sip of his drink, "Well it's just another great start to another great flight," he declared for everyone's benefit.

Again, Jimmy just looked. He had summed up the new arrival quickly. He dealt with the species frequently in New York, guys who were perfectly dressed and groomed—all for show. There had been a contingent of them in Miami when he and Sal were students there. And now he worked with a master member of this club, Barry Gyges. But the trip had already been sufficiently bad; this was no time to start thinking about Gyges. That would all be necessary soon enough.

For a moment, Jimmy felt a rush of concern. What if this guy ends up next to me on the plane? He decided it was worth a question.

"Where you headed?" Jimmy asked.

The man took a long, dramatic sip. "I'm headed for

Indianapolis. The idiots in my office don't seem to be able to find the paper clips, so I got called back from the first decent golf I've had in months to cover their asses." Jimmy was relieved until he heard, "But first I've got to go to goddamned Montreal. It's not bad enough to be pulled out of here; I get to spend three days in the tundra."

The new guy slammed down the rest of his scotch and signaled for another. As the bartender approached with a refill, he asked, "When you due?"

"What?" she said.

"The baby? When are you going to have the baby? You're pregnant aren't you?"

While Jimmy wondered himself, he looked up shocked anyone could be obtuse enough to actually ask. The bartender's eyes glared at the man. Then, while his head turned, she looked at Jimmy and mouthed, "Asshole." Jimmy raised his eyebrows in agreement. Somehow she now looked much more attractive.

"Business sucks," the man continued, "It's the frickin' Arabs. They almost wiped me out. I figured on retiring before I was forty-five. Now, who knows? You know my whole company is filled with morons. There's no reason why I shouldn't be able to get away for a few weeks without shit from the office."

Jimmy was wondering what this guy did when he said, "My boss is going to get his ass chewed for this one. I'm the best damn salesman they've got. I can go anywhere. You know, it's time. I'm going to start looking." Now all of the pieces were in place.

As Jimmy ordered another beer, the salesman signaled him to turn his head for a secret message. Jimmy curiously leaned closer. An East Indian couple strolled by, he in casual Western clothes and a Yankees cap, she with a colorful, long kurta shirt over jeans and a red Hindu bindi on her forehead. With a nod, the salesman directed Jimmy's eyes in the couple's direction and whispered, "They'll get us, you know, one way or another they're going to do it. They've already got us completely mind-fucked. I mean; don't you get nervous when you just see one on a plane? Mark my words, I know what I'm talking about—they're everywhere. Shit man, they say they sent thousands of them over here years ago to try and look like us, fit in, you know? They're just waiting. Then they're going to take us all out." He belched into his fist, and Jimmy realized this bar had not been his first stop. "I'm telling you, Dude, I know what I'm talking about."

Wondering how could anyone be that stupid, Jimmy didn't know how to respond. He thought of pointing out they were not Arabs. Then he cracked a little smile and signaled to whisper in the salesman's ear. "You know what gets me sometimes?" he said.

"No Dude, what?"

"The food. If I'm not careful, the really spicy stuff can give me heartburn, and I'll be up all night. I'm particularly sensitive to the curry and saffron. You know what I mean?"

The salesman, now tipsy and blind to Jimmy's mockery, sucked down the rest of his scotch and nodded. "Food's going to be a big one; it's an easy way to kill a lot of us and never get caught."

Jimmy's eyes widened, and his head cocked as the salesman stood and picked up his briefcase. "I've gotta squirt," he announced. "Hold my seat, we'll talk about that when I get back."

Jimmy considered leaving but figured he'd finish his beer. As he returned to the entertainment in the corner, he felt a light touch on his arm and turned to see the woman he'd bumped at check-in sitting next to him.

"Hi," she said.

"Hello," Jimmy responded politely.

The bartender quickly cleared the salesman's mess. "What can I get you?" she asked.

"A bourbon and a beer please."

"Would you like the large beer for two dollars more?"

"Yes, that would be wonderful." Jimmy was impressed. This girl meant business. "My name is Susan Fort. And yours?"

"Jimmy Eagleson."

"Well, Jimmy Eagleson, here's to good flights," she said as she drank the bourbon and followed with a third of her beer.

"Another bourbon please, the beer is good for now," she said to the surprised bartender.

"I hate flying, so some liquid courage is definitely in order. Where are you going on this fine day, Jimmy Eagleson?"

"Montreal," Jimmy said.

"I've never been there. Actually, I've never been anywhere on the East Coast north of here. I must say I'm not impressed with this area. I like the West Coast much better. But Canada might be different." She was now sipping and seemed calm and remarkably sober. "I came here for a family thing, you know, a sort of funeral reunion combination? It was good to see a few of the people. And what brings you to sunny Florida, Jimmy Eagleson?"

"An ex-wife, two daughters, and a best friend."

"That's quite a list. I'll assume each for different reasons?"

"Yes, for very different reasons," Jimmy laughed. He was usually nervous around smart, beautiful women. But Susan had him immediately at ease.

Susan looked at Jimmy's hand. "That's a very attractive ring. I don't usually like jewelry on men, but that is handsome. May I look at it?" Jimmy offered Susan his hand. "Solid sterling silver," she said. "I like that, not gaudy like the fat gold rings some men wear." Susan carefully examined the crest. "This is beautifully carved. I understand the significance of the wings, Jimmy Eagleson, what's the meaning of the rose?"

"I don't know. I inherited it—an only son thing. The Old Man never said."

"'The Old Man?' not your father or your dad, just 'The Old Man?'"

"The Old Man works fine."

Susan nodded, "And where did The Old Man acquire such a tasteful piece."

"He brought it back from the war, this ring and a cigarette lighter with the same crest. He never said where he got them or what they meant. I guess that was his secret."

"And your mom, did she know?"

"If she did, she never said either; she died a year before him."

"Well, maybe you'll find out someday. My guess is it means something very important."

"As I said, The Old Man never said. If it was important, he took it to his grave."

"Well, Jimmy Eagleson, I know what my ring means." Susan held up her left hand to show off her ornately carved wedding band and smiled. "And that's no secret."

Jimmy smiled and thought of Clair. Fidelity was a concept she somehow never got, ring or no ring. He felt a hand slap his shoulder and looked up to see the salesman standing behind Susan.

"Nice job Buddy," the salesman said.

"And who is this?" Susan asked Jimmy.

"I don't know his name."

"George, Babe," the salesman said.

"Well, George Babe, like your seat back?"

"Nope, it looks far better under a fine looking lady like you."

Susan turned to Jimmy and shook her head.

"Where you headed beautiful," the salesman continued. "And I don't think I caught your name?"

"I'm headed to San Francisco, and you don't need to know my name."

"What's in Frisco, Sweetheart?"

"It's San Francisco, I'm not your sweetheart, and while it's none of your business, I'm returning from a funeral."

"Traveling alone?"

"My significant other and son didn't make the trip." The salesman saw her wedding ring and continued to hit.

"Your husband's a lucky man. He's taking a big chance letting a fox like you out by yourself."

"You mean 'she's' taking a big chance."

The salesman smirked, rolled his eyes, and took a swig of his newly arrived scotch.

"Yeah, sure, I get it."

"Get what? You don't believe I'm a lesbian?"

"Not the way you look, darling," he said as he touched her hair. "You're really gorgeous." He started lightly rubbing her shoulder and looked down into her loose blouse.

Jimmy had seen enough and began to stand. Susan put her hand on his arm and whispered, "Let me." She removed the unwelcomed hand and swiveled her stool to face the salesman. "All right, Curious George, you're making me uncomfortable. I would like you to find another spot, away from me."

"You don't mean that, Honey." He tried to touch her arm.

Susan slapped his hand. "OK, let's try this, if you touch me one more time I'm going to stand and ram my knee into your little balls so hard that after you find a way to walk again you'll need to call your airline and be sure they can carry the ice you'll need."

The salesman picked up his briefcase. "I'm outta' here. I don't need this shit," he said. He gulped down his drink, moved back from the bar, mumbled, "Fucking bitch" and started walking away. Susan quickly stood and announced, "YES I AM!" to his retreating back. He walked on without responding as a group from the bar, including the fat guy in the corner and the bartender, laughed and applauded. One man brought his fingers up to whistle, but his wife slapped him on the arm. Susan turned back to the bar, curtseyed, and sat back down next to Jimmy.

"Thanks," Susan said.

"For what?" Jimmy asked.

"You were going to fix that for me. You were going to be my Galahad. Would you have hit him?"

"I don't think that would have been necessary."

"But if it was, would you have hit him?"

"What do you think?"

"I think you might have broken his jaw. You've got the look."

"What look is that?"

"I told you, you're a white knight, Jimmy Eagleson."

"That's a new one. I think that was a compliment."

"Oh, it was." Susan ordered fresh beers for both of them.

"Let me get those," Jimmy protested.

"See what I mean? I'll get them, Sir James."

Jimmy was full of questions he knew not to ask. But Susan wasn't going to leave him guessing.

"It's true."

"What?"

"What I said. My partner's name is Beth. My son's is Kevin. That's my family."

"Is your son adopted?" Jimmy dared ask.

"That's very good, Jimmy Eagleson."

"I didn't mean to offend you."

"You didn't, you asked a question you thought might not be your business. That's good, keep it up, I'm not bothered. No, I'm his mother. Oh, my door used to open both ways. I was married for a while, to a pretty good guy overall. But I preferred women, and that made sex with him difficult. Then I met Beth and we knew right away we had to be together. She's the most kind and sensitive person I've ever known. I kept it from him; I didn't think he'd understand. You know what's funny? He ended the marriage. He had an affair and fell in love. He didn't have a clue about what I was doing. To this day, he doesn't know I was already with Beth. Well, he's remarried, and as far as I'm concerned, so am I."

"And your son?"

"You're doing well, Jimmy Eagleson. My husband gave me custody. He travels for work, and now he's moved. When Beth and I went public, he was surprised but not mad. I think he felt guilty for breaking up the family. Oh, he gave me a few warnings about this and that, but he sees his son when he wants, and he's a great kid. It's all good."

"How about your relatives?"

"Well, to some I'm an honest liberated woman. A few others call me the family dyke."

Jimmy grimaced.

"It's OK, Jimmy Eagleson; we know what the simple say. My dad took it hard. We were close. I did a lot with him when I was a kid. But we made peace before he died. My mom's been gone for a while, and I think she was OK."

"When did your dad die?"

"Last week. That's why I'm here. It's new, being an orphan."

"I'm sorry. I should have asked."

"But you'd know about that, being an orphan yourself. I take it you and The Old Man had issues?"

"I guess. I don't know how to answer. We were OK. No regrets."

Susan took a long sip from her beer. "I don't think I'm buying."

"Buying what?"

"No regrets. You don't talk much, Jimmy Eagleson, and I'm not going to probe, but I'd bet you've got things to fix." Susan sipped her beer. "You know, I think you've got quite the story, Jimmy Eagleson."

Jimmy smiled. "You'd be bored."

"Oh, I doubt that."

The discussion changed direction and continued for more than an hour. Susan did most of the talking. Jimmy enjoyed listening. She talked about her work in San Francisco. He explained his job in New York. He was surprised she read *The New York Times*. She wasn't surprised he read little from the West Coast.

"It's almost 1:30," she said. "Time for me to go."

They stood, and she gave him a long hug and a kiss on the cheek.

"Maybe we'll meet again," Jimmy said.

"No, let's not end with bullshit. We won't. But I've enjoyed our time. I like you, Jimmy Eagleson, and I think it will brighten up for you."

"You do?"

"Yes, my sixth sense. Farewell, Jimmy Eagleson. I wish you the best."

"I like you too, Susan Fort. And I wish you the best."

Susan picked up her carry-on, looked at him and smiled. She turned and headed to her gate. "Have a wonderful flight, Jimmy Eagleson!" she said loudly without looking back.

Jimmy sat back down feeling alone. He was glad to have met Susan, and he envied her for her contentment. He thought of the last two weeks. After a few days near Clair and the kids, he couldn't wait to leave. It got so bad he cut the stay in Miami short and visited Stosh for a few days. But, even that hadn't helped much. Now he just wanted to go back north to Camp, where he could decompress and put things back together. He stayed at the bar a little longer. He hoped to avoid the salesman at the gate, and a little solitude would be good. The bartender brought another beer and smiled. Jimmy smiled back.

* * *

At the gate, Jimmy waited for the call for disabled and first-class passengers, then quickly cleared the checkpoint and moved down the concourse to the plane. He received the standard welcome, was led to his seat and offered a drink. He quickly accepted, placed his carry-on in the overhead compartment and settled into the large leather lounger with a window view. He looked for the salesman but didn't see him.

A preppy-looking college student scanned the numbers below the overhead compartment, opened one, shoved in his jacket and backpack, and took the seat next to Jimmy. Jimmy nodded, and the two sat without speaking. In a few minutes, the salesman arrived. He avoided eye contact with Jimmy as he took the aisle seat across from the student. He yelled to the flight attendant for single malt and was quickly served. He sighed and continued to complain under his breath about the persecution the world insisted on dishing out to him.

Eventually, the student spoke. "Hi, I'm Stuart." Jimmy

25

introduced himself as Mr. Eagleson. Jimmy had long ago learned to keep his distance from other passengers, particularly younger ones, whenever he had no chance for a gracious exit. He used to fly coach though he could easily afford first class, until one trip when he was pinned between a three-hundred-pound woman and an even more obese man. She was on her way to the funeral of an aunt she had barely known, was weeping, and sought solace throughout the flight. The man was returning to Pittsburgh after attending a college football game and insisted on reliving every bad call that led to his team's 24-to-3 loss. Both had yet to discover the benefits of soap, and the woman would occasionally belch filling the air with the scent of rotting animal, although always with an apology. From then on it was first class where Jimmy could count on more space, more drinks, and less sweat.

Stuart squirmed in his seat, changing positions frequently and fumbling with the magazines from the pocket in front of him. Eventually, he turned to Jimmy and said, "Where you from?"

Jimmy knew a conversation was unavoidable and responded, "I live in New York."

"You must be on the wrong plane; we're heading for Montreal."

"I know," Jimmy said.

"You know you're on the wrong plane or you know we're headed for Montreal?"

"Both." Most of Jimmy's limited ability to suffer fools had been spent on the salesman, and he had quickly assessed the student and he had little to talk about. But Stuart kept going.

"My father owns the best restaurants in Montreal, in Canada in fact. Maybe you've been to some of them."

"Maybe," Jimmy said as he looked out the window.

"Well, there's—"

"Stuart?" Jimmy interrupted. "You said your name was Stuart didn't you?"

"Yup," Stuart replied.

"That's a classic Scottish name with a rich history. Stuarts are known to be very virile; you know I knew a Stuart in Miami who could drink the rest of us under the table in no time and go on to another party. I'll bet you like a good whiskey. Do you drink scotch or maybe good Canadian rye?"

"You know, the guys in my dorm say I'm the best drinker they've ever seen too. Yeah, I drink whiskey. I prefer Crown Royal. I told you my father owns the best restaurants in Canada; I grew up on the stuff. But I'm nineteen, and they won't serve me in the U.S."

"Well we'll take care of that," Jimmy stated as he called a flight attendant who responded immediately. Jimmy asked for a Molson Canadian and a double Crown straight up. She looked at the student with concern but was satisfied the order was OK when she saw only Jimmy's tray was down. Before the student had a chance to say much more, the flight attendant returned and put both drinks in front of Jimmy.

"Chins up," Jimmy said as he handed Stuart the drink. "Drink it fast for full effect and don't let the authorities see."

Stuart drank the whiskey in three forced swallows, wincing and fighting to look as if he enjoyed it. Jimmy immediately recalled the flight attendant, "That was good; now I need one more Crown to keep the knuckles from turning white." The attendant's face showed her reservations, but she brought another double. Jimmy waited for her to serve a passenger behind him and as he snuck the second drink to Stuart, who was hell-bent on living up to his new-found reputation.

This time, Stuart's face contorted. When the attendant passed by, she was surprised at the empty glass, took it, and offered no more. But, Jimmy's plan was in full gear. Looking across the aisle he said to Stuart, "That guy next to you is one of the best salesmen in Canada. I'd bet he eats at your father's restaurants."

Stuart looked at Jimmy with glazed eyes, turned to the man across the aisle and with some verbal difficulty repeated the same opening line he had used on Jimmy. The attention-loving salesman, nearly as intoxicated as the student, responded enthusiastically. Jimmy sipped on his beer and looked out the window.

At the last call for seating, a young Sikh man with a full black beard, white silk suit, and tight black turban strolled on the plane. The salesman stared a moment and then quietly presented his conspiracy theory to Stuart, who having no opinion of his own swallowed the one his new buddy dished out. The flight attendant led the new passenger to the window seat next to the salesman and politely asked if he would stand to let his new companion sit. The salesman's eyes widened showing near terror as he complied. Jimmy took particular pleasure in the luck of the seating and enjoyed the salesman's anxiety. The flight was full, and no one could change seats. But, Jimmy knew the salesman would have been too afraid to try to move anyway. That could make another scene, and Susan Fort had already kicked the wind out of him. He wouldn't risk another humiliation.

After the routine safety show and tell from the flight attendants, the plane taxied and smoothly reached its assigned altitude. Jimmy took in the sun and blue sky above the clouds realizing he would see little of either once he landed in the monochrome of a northern winter. The bright white blanket of cloud cover gave an illusion of safety and peace as if it invited him to step out for a walk. He never tired of this sight. Soon his mind wandered, and he thought back on his trip.

Since he lost his parents, Jimmy hadn't cared much for the holidays. And now, divorced with two daughters and a nouveau-highbrow ex-wife, the season had become unbearable. His ex, Clair, had calculatedly spoiled both girls to the point where, while he loved them, he didn't like them and found them disturbing to be around. Nicole was ten now, and Simone, eight. Clair insisted on coordinating their dress with the finest of young fashion and ensuring each received extensive princess training. They had been taught to gobble up everything in their path like a pair of little Ms. Pac-Men. Christmas morning had been the most gluttonous demonstration Jimmy had ever seen. Each of the girls voraciously tore the wrapping off scores of gifts. Most received a quick look and were tossed onto a pile. Eventually, what seemed like an inexhaustible supply came to an end. With a look of extreme disappointment, Simone asked her father, "Is this all?" Jimmy knew it was time to go.

He recalled first meeting Clair at the University. He had

returned to attend law school after a few years working for The Old Man. She was different then, a real college student who loved to have fun, and their ten-year age difference didn't matter to her. She was Scandinavian with long blonde hair. Her enchanting smile drew him to her. They would frequently take off for the Keys and be together for days without a trace of incompatibility. Things were good for several years. She took care of him, comforted him, and he couldn't imagine being with another woman. She was an upbeat, kind person with many friends. A few years after they married something happened. He never knew exactly what. Overnight, she became critical of everything he did. More gradually she developed an obsession with money. She created a fantasy, turning her middle-class childhood into memories of poverty and hardship. Her daughters weren't going to do without as she had, she would say. She acted entitled and started to mock people without wealth.

Jimmy split with her shortly after Simone was born, not knowing Clair had secretly moved on already. After the initial anguish from learning the truth about her numerous lovers, he felt some peace having at least an explanation for being rejected and a good reason to accept their end. But still—on a rare occasion—that incredible smile would sneak out, and he'd recall how he felt when it was good.

Along with generous support, she kept the property in Coral Gables. Jimmy wanted her to be comfortable and in the divorce settlement gave her what she asked for though he was well aware it was excessive and would never have been legally required. As she increasingly spoiled the girls, he could see he'd gone too far. He kept Camp and the place in New York. She never liked the North Country anyway and was more than content to live the pretense of a South Florida socialite.

While Jimmy often reminded himself of the good days, right now he was too close to the present reality to be anything but repulsed. But he knew he would soon begin mentally panning through the cold, wet dirt to salvage what nuggets of positive memories he could. And he wished for the old Clair to return, if only for her own sake—although with little hope.

Jimmy sipped and looked at the Molson beer can on his tray. He thought of the sand truck that day. Stosh was right; it was close. What Stosh had said about Jimmy saving his life popped into Jimmy's head. His mind flew back to the summer after sixth grade.

Kids loved swimming in the reservoir above the dam on the Saranac River. The water was deep, and many proved their bravery by diving from the high concrete walls. Until a boy drowned, sank and got sucked by the lower current through the floodgate, crushing his body on the rocks below. After, the cops fenced off the access and hung warning signs. For some that only increased the challenge.

It was Sal's idea. He, Jimmy and Stosh trekked along a path in the woods and worked their way through a gap in the fence. With their towels and a cooler painted with the Molson Canadian Beer logo that Sal "borrowed" from his pop, they climbed the ladder from the shoreline to the six-foot-thick top of the dam. They laid out their towels and surveyed the dark water twelve feet below, and the fifty-foot drop to the rocks on the river's side. Sal pulled the cooler open and handed each comrade a Coke. Jimmy remembered how cool it felt to be eleven-years-old and have a beer cooler, even if it only contained soda. Sal said his pop won it as a door prize somewhere and would explode if he knew Sal had taken it.

Stosh was the first to dive. Unlike Jimmy, Stosh wasn't a good swimmer. While The Old Man rarely went near the water, he'd made sure Jimmy swam well almost before he could walk. Jimmy had already won several medals on the swim team, and The Old Man had hired an instructor to teach him lifesaving though Jimmy was too young to earn the badge.

Stosh put his hands over his head and clumsily dove in. He paddled about in the cold water grinning and taunting the others to prove themselves. Sal, a better swimmer than Stosh but far from Jimmy, plunged in landing a foot from Stosh. Sal started splashing his friend's face and laughing. "OK, Eagleson don't be a chicken!" The others yelled. Then Stosh began struggling to stay afloat. He yelled to Sal, who grabbed hold and kept Stosh above water. When Stosh's thrashing hit Sal in the face, he lost his grip.

Jimmy's training took over. "Throw or row before you go" rolled through his head. He dumped the cooler's contents, latched it and threw it to Sal. Sal couldn't get Stosh to grab hold. Knowing Stosh had little strength left, Jimmy dove in, swam to Stosh and waited for Stosh's arms to swing up. Then Jimmy shoved the cooler into Stosh's chest. Instinctively Stosh wrapped his arms around it.

Jimmy saw that Stosh and Sal were exhausted, and they all were drifting farther from the bank. He swam behind Sal and put an arm over his chest. Sal began to struggle, but

Jimmy calmed him, worked his arm over Sal's shoulder and sidestroked both of them toward the shoreline. Stosh had also relaxed, and Jimmy told him to follow.

All seemed OK; they were swimming together and half way in when a sharp pain seized Jimmy's calf. The excruciating cramp made him let go of Sal, wrenched forward, grab his leg and panic. He swallowed water and began to sink. He exhaled a lungful of bubbles and through the blur saw his friends' legs kicking. He thrust his arms up and felt Sal clench his wrist. Sal fought but couldn't pull up Jimmy's dead weight.

Jimmy was completely out of air just as Stosh's soft paw wrapped around Jimmy's other arm. The combined resolve of his two best friends was hoisting him to the surface. Jimmy gasped, grabbed hold of the cooler and spit up. The boys panted and rested while Jimmy's cramp let up, all clinging to their make do life-buoy, then together paddled and kicked to shore.

With their legs covered in muck and scratched from the rocks and brush at the shoreline, the daredevils lay on the bank. Jimmy gazed at the sky a while and then slowly sat up. They all laughed and relived every moment of the near catastrophe. Sal stood and held up the cooler showing off the gouges left by rocks in the shallows. "Oh well," he said. "Pop will just have to win another one. Now, who's up for one more dive?"

Jimmy was thinking of his response to Sal's challenge when the plane jolted from a quick smack of turbulence. He snapped back to the present and watched the little wave and new sparkle in his glass of Molson. He chuckled. He couldn't imagine an event that could bring three guys closer than that day. From then on, the bond was sealed. Those who did not understand, never could.

Stuart let out a deep sigh. He had fallen asleep from the whiskey. Jimmy looked over to see how the salesman was doing with his new friend. The Sikh man had not moved his eyes from his book since he took his seat. The salesman had positioned himself at maximum distance from his companion and was loathsomely staring at the ceiling. All the players had settled in. The flight was slightly ahead of schedule. Jimmy relaxed; he would soon meet Ray and head for Camp.

CHAPTER II

Camp

The plane jostled from the crosswind and hit hard on the icy runway. Most passengers clinched their armrests; Jimmy sat calm, looking out the window. As a seasoned veteran of the North Country, he was used to real winters. He looked forward to meeting Ray at the bar. Ray would bring the Lincoln. Jimmy looked one last time at the agitated salesman who prepared to grab his bag and bolt as soon as the cabin door opened. Stuart continued to snore intermittently, barely waking in time to disembark. The first-class passengers were released well in advance of the others and received the more sincere version of the crew's rehearsed goodbyes.

Jimmy strolled down the connecting concourse through the preliminary customs check and showed his passport. After a few quick questions, he was cleared and allowed to enter Canada for what would be about two hours. The agent directed him to the exit and collection area where his bag would be waiting. He hoisted it off the conveyor, looked for directions to the remaining customs processing, strolled through the "nothing to declare" exit, and headed for the bar to meet Ray.

Jimmy worked his way through the crowd and found a stool. Behind a large horseshoe bar surrounded by dozens of tables, a petite French Canadian bartender stood filling several beers from assorted taps. She nodded at Jimmy, delivered the filled glasses and hurried to him. "Ça va," she said.

"Bien," answered Jimmy. "Une Molson si vous plait."

"D'accord," she said politely.

As the bartender brought the beer, Jimmy scanned the area for Ray. It wasn't uncommon for Ray to be late or to be waiting at the wrong place. Jimmy relaxed and thought back to when they were young. He met Raymond LaFleur in high school. Ray was plastered with cystic acne and had few friends. While others were dating, Ray found his own way. Most girls found him repulsive, so most guys didn't want him around. But Jimmy liked him, and they hung out some, although Ray spent most of his time alone.

Jimmy recalled the first time they met. They were high school sophomores. Ray was standing on a sidewalk in downtown Plattsburgh when two local punks strutted over and shoved him against a brick wall. Trying to get him to fight, they slapped his shoulder, called him "pus boy with your oozing pimples" and "Pizza-faced freak."

Jimmy recognized one of the thugs and darted across the street yelling for both of them to back off. The punks could have easily thrashed Jimmy and Ray, but the one he'd seen before grabbed his buddy and said he saw a cop coming. They threw out a few more insults, slapped Ray's shoulder one more time and swaggered off like champions.

Jimmy knew there was no cop and the bully he'd recognized would know that touching Jimmy Eagleson meant an inevitable faceoff with Sal. Even a dumb shit like that guy wasn't suicidal.

Ray was shaking and embarrassed. He kept his face down and tried to hide his acne with his hands. Making some insulting comments about the punks and laughing, Jimmy relaxed him. Eventually, Ray was chuckling too, and they introduced themselves. Jimmy invited Ray to the soda bar at a nearby drug store, but Ray was reluctant. He finally agreed, and they walked over still talking about their encounter.

They took stools at the counter, and a girl Jimmy knew walked over to flirt—only with Jimmy. Jimmy introduced her to Ray as his "buddy Raymond LaFleur," and the friendship was sealed. She quickly made an excuse and left. Again Jimmy knew the right thing to say, and he and Ray chuckled. Jimmy bought burgers, fries, and Cokes, and they chatted until Ray said he needed to go. Jimmy knew Ray was overloading and nodded. Ray shook Jimmy's hand, thanked him twice and sheepishly walked out taking the least noticeable route.

The acne cleared in Ray's early twenties leaving a rough, masculine look the ladies then found attractive. But Ray had learned the game the hard way and showed no interest in the social or financial things that obsessed most of Jimmy's other friends. He committed to a life without stress, and he spent much of his time reading or mountain climbing. He climbed all of the peaks in the Adirondacks several times but never applied to become an official *Forty-Sixer,* even though the membership was a major badge of respect in the North Country. He told Jimmy he saw no point in obligating himself to an organization that might ask something of him someday.

Ray now looked the part of the recluse—lanky medium height, deep brown eyes and full beard—and was satisfied to work as Jimmy's Camp caretaker and general handyman. Jimmy provided him with a nicely finished guest house over-looking the lake and more than sufficient money. Over the years, Ray proved to be honest and conscientious. It was as much responsibility as he cared for, which drove Stosh crazy. They were two very different men. Jimmy liked and envied both of them for the satisfaction they found in their lives.

"There you are!" Ray yelled to Jimmy from a booth on the other side of the bar where he had been sitting for some time, also sipping beer.

"How are you, Raymond?"

As always, Ray was dressed in jeans and flannel shirt perfectly looking the part of the North Country native. He relocated to a vacated stool next to Jimmy, and they shook hands warmly.

"How was the trip?"

"We can talk later."

"That good huh?"

"Yup," Jimmy said.

They talked about Camp and the weather, then finished the last sip of their beers and headed for the parking area.

As they stepped outside and crossed to the parking garage,

Jimmy took a deep breath of the cold, clean, Canadian air and tried to blow a frost ring. "How cold has it been?"

"Snot freezing."

Ray had parked the Lincoln carefully to avoid any chance of damage. Jimmy could drive any vehicle he wanted, but he chose The Old Man's 1966 Lincoln Continental. He rebuilt it several times but kept its original British racing green and the medium brown leather interior. The immaculately maintained car served as a major comfort zone for him. And, while Jimmy always kept a new four-wheel-drive pickup at Camp, he rarely drove anything but his vintage treasure.

Jimmy took the keys from Ray and climbed in.

"Which way?" Ray asked.

"We'll take the Mercier Bridge."

"Want to hit a bar while we're here?"

"Let's get home and have a couple there."

Ray nodded, disappointed. While Jimmy got out and about regularly, Ray spent most of his time alone. He disliked social environments except with a short list of friends, one of whom was Jimmy. The chance to stay out came rarely. But there would be plenty to drink at Camp, and he would still have Jimmy to himself for a while. Tomorrow night they'd throw the New Year's party. Ray would attend, but for his liking, there would be far too many people, and his friend's attention would be stretched thin.

As they drove by the old Seagram's distillery, Jimmy remembered how as a kid he would lower the window and inhale deeply. He loved the smell of the area though he no longer drank much hard spirits. Now the great Canadian trademark was owned by a French electronics corporation with a kid CEO who dabbled in movies and had a knack for creating bankruptcies. In no time, he turned an important Canadian tradition into just another foreign-owned product. But it was a new game, always more money to be made and the stimulation of another gamble, and no big deal the great Canadian beer maker Labatt had already shown the way by selling out to the Belgians. Jimmy wondered what The Old Man would think; after all, this was also the business Jimmy had chosen—buying and selling companies for big money. And Jimmy was good at it.

As they crossed the bridge, a lone barge chugged up the St. Lawrence on its way to Lake Ontario. The winter had started closing the Seaway down with ice, and the roads were snow covered. But the Lincoln was comfortable. The sand bags Ray packed in the trunk and new snow tires made the ride smooth.

"Do we need to stop for the Brador?" Jimmy asked. The real brew of this high-test Canadian beer was only available in Canada, and Jimmy always made it available at the New Year Bash.

"I picked up a couple of cases on the way up."

"Good." Jimmy wanted to get to Camp, and a stop in Quebec at the Lacolle grocery store always took longer than planned.

The Lincoln turned on to Canada Route 19 and headed for the Champlain border crossing. Jimmy and Ray sat silent for several minutes. Then Jimmy asked, "You seen Kate?"

"Yeah, she's been around checking on the place. She came by yesterday. Said she'll be there early tomorrow night. She took care of things with the caterer, and she put some food or something in one of the refrigerators."

Jimmy chuckled; whenever they threw a party, Kate experimented with a new recipe, though—at Jimmy's insistence—she started letting others do some of the other work.

"Someone told me she's hanging with David from time to time," Ray said. "We talk when she stops by, but I don't ask about shit like that."

Kate had been married for many years. Her husband Steve traveled a lot for his company. The marriage appeared casual, at best, from early on, and each seemed unconcerned about the other's indiscretions. Jimmy figured they stayed together for financial reasons although both of them were relatively well off. David was just one of the guys who darted in and out of the gang, appearing now to be coming back in.

Jimmy, closed his eyes and let his mind wander. Katherine Anne O'Conner, like Stosh, met Jimmy very young. They were always best of friends, and she sometimes seemed to fill the role of the sister he never had. Jimmy played her protector, although she usually proved to be perfectly capable of taking care of herself. With light red hair and bright green eyes, she grew into the figure of a Celtic goddess. And she was smart. Steve recognized the advantages of having her on his arm early on, and they married before either finished college. He went into business, and she earned a master's in psychology. She joined a counseling practice in Plattsburgh. Friends openly wondered why Jimmy and Kate never paired up. Jimmy avoided the subject.

"I know what I was going to tell you," Ray said. "You got a

package from your cousin Gordon. Don't let me forget to give it to you."

"Yeah, Kate told me on the phone. What's in it?"

"I don't know. I don't open your mail—unless it's a bill."

"I wonder what's up."

"Maybe some hot sauce from the West, although it's kind of big for that."

"Big?"

"Not real big. Remind me and I'll give it to you when we get back."

"You've got no idea what's in it? Gord has never sent anything before."

"Stay in your skin; we'll be back in less than a half-hour. Jesus, this has you tweaked."

"Yeah, I guess. I can't imagine what it is, and Gord wouldn't send something that wasn't important."

"You'll be back in no time, and then you'll know."

The lights of the Champlain border crossing shined on the horizon, and Jimmy prepared to stop and face the new interrogation procedures required to let a citizen back into the United States. While approaching the stop-point, Jimmy couldn't help notice once again the effects of 9/11. The need for the National Guard had made the "welcome feeling" disappear. He rolled down the window.

"Identification?" the border guard asked. Though passports weren't required yet, both Jimmy and Ray could see the writing on the wall and already carried them on any trip to Canada. They handed both over. The officer moved his glasses onto his forehead. One by one he held the passports close to his eyes, taking his time as he reviewed them. He moved each into the light and compared the photos to the men, lowering and raising his glasses as needed.

"Where were you born?"

Jimmy and Ray both responded, "Plattsburgh, New York."

"One at a time." the guard snapped. They restated the same answer separately, and the guard looked satisfied that he'd established his authority.

"How long have you been outside of the United States?"

"A couple of hours," Jimmy replied. "I flew into Montreal from Tampa, and my friend came to pick me up."

"Bringing anything back?"

"Just two cases of beer," Jimmy said. Before 9/11 Jimmy wouldn't have bothered to mention beer, but now any deviation from the letter of the law could result in problems. The guard handed the passports back. "Drive through and have a nice evening," he stated in routine fashion.

Jimmy and Ray continued south on U.S. Interstate 87. A large green sign reading FERRY TO VERMONT led them to their exit where they picked up the road that circled for several miles around Cumberland Head.

"Want to stop for a dog?" Jimmy asked.

"Can't, they're closed."

"Why?"

"It's winter Jimmy, remember? Everything shuts down early."

Jimmy shook his head; he craved North Country grub. They passed the state park and drove another couple of miles before turning off the road onto a lighted private drive leading to the

Lake. In a few seconds, a large Adirondack lodge appeared from behind the trees. Camp.

Jimmy activated the door opener for the last bay of his four-car garage. He pulled in carefully, and the two thirsty travelers headed to the bar.

There had been an Eagleson residence on the property since well before Jimmy was born. After The Old Man died, Jimmy tore down the first house and built the place that had always been envisioned. The center was a large great room of about 2,000 square feet. At one end stood a classic Adirondack fireplace made of fieldstone, with a roughly finished oak mantle. At the other, a wall-sized window gave a full view of Lake Champlain looking toward North Hero, Vermont, and the Green Mountains. On a calm, clear day Mount Mansfield stood out in the background, and the Sister Islands—while three miles from the shore—seemed only a few hundred yards away. At other times, with a rough lake and dark skies, the opposite side was impossible to see, and the lake looked endless, like the ocean.

Comfortable furniture was arranged in several strategic seating areas, each with its own ambiance. Kate had taken charge of the interior design, which was manly but inviting and homey, even with the high cathedral ceiling. A twenty-five-foot bar stocked to be the envy of any fine night club, reached along one side in front of a partially hidden commercial-grade kitchen. Ray turned on the bar lights, and hundreds of bottles appeared. When Jimmy was in residence, the bar stools were often filled. But when he was in New York, the room seemed like an abandoned resort.

Just beyond the bar's end was the entrance to Jimmy's suite with a large bedroom with an extravagant bath on one side of the hall and Jimmy's study on the other. This was personal space only a few entered, only to clean or for Ray to borrow a book. On the other side of the great room was an extensive wing with four well-appointed bedrooms, each with its own full bath. Friends frequently stayed here after a night of partying.

Ray came out from behind the bar with two frosted mugs full of fresh Molson draught. The friends chose their usual stools and settled in. The comfortable lighting and lake view with a random pattern of lights from the Vermont side put Jimmy at ease, and he sat back. The warm space was like a gigantic cocoon with a picture window.

Ray lifted his glass. "Chins up."

"Chins up," Jimmy said as they toasted.

"I think of The Old Man whenever we do that," Ray said. "I still wonder where he got it."

Jimmy chuckled, remembering Stosh saying the same thing just that morning. He turned and gazed at the fireplace. Above the mantel hung a black wrought-iron American eagle with a six-foot wingspan. Below sat a small oak, leaded-glass case displaying The Old Man's lighter. Like Jimmy's ring, it was solid sterling, and it bore the same crest— although three times the size. Sal used to joke that The Old Man wanted it recognizable from across a room. Jimmy kept it filled with fluid and would flick it on sometimes just to be sure it still flamed. Jimmy looked at his ring and rubbed *its* crest with his thumb.

"So I gather this one sucked."

Jimmy's thoughts snapped back. "Yeah ... I guess I have to go down there from time to time though I can't say for the sake of the family. But it gets to me ... and it seems worse every trip."

"Well, at least she can't get to you here."

Jimmy took a long sip. "Oh, she gets to me here, there, and any other place, and now it's not only her, it's also her miniature clones. The whole thing is insane. She has become someone I wouldn't have anything to do with if I weren't her ex. And now she's completely brainwashed my girls. We think differently, live differently; I don't see anything I can identify with down there. No one seems to do anything for any reason other than to collect more shit." Jimmy took another sip and thought a moment. "But when I start criticizing them I end up questioning myself. What did I ever do for all the shit I've got?" Jimmy looked around. "The Old Man did all the work; it just fell into my lap."

Ray didn't respond. He'd heard this from Jimmy before, following sessions with Clair, and he knew no answer was expected. The conversation changed to the weather, repairs for Camp, how friends were doing, and plans for the party. They drank their second and third beers. Eventually, they both yawned and decided to call it a night. Tomorrow would be a long one.

* * *

Jimmy awakened about 8:00 to a bright, clear winter day. He slept well and felt relieved from the anxiety his trip had piled on. He showered, dressed, crossed the hall and entered his study—his inner sanctuary. The room was arranged with more of the comfortable furniture Kate had a knack for finding and a large desk. Several marked books waited for Jimmy to return to them. They were part of his extensive library filling wall-to-wall bookcases. Dust showed their neglect. When Jimmy went off to college, The Old Man told him to study anything he wanted for four years; then he was to work in the family business. He chose philosophy, and as a good student was able to party and ace his classes without problems. Sal decided to accompany him but chose the hard sciences. He, too, had little trouble.

Jimmy sat in a large oak rocker and looked at the volumes surrounding him; even when on their shelves these books seemed to be saying something. He fought the temptation to let the atmosphere lead him to thoughts of his time in Miami. He didn't want to revisit the previous day's obsession. Loud banging disturbed his quiet. He got up and headed for the kitchen. He chuckled and watched Kate on her hands and knees rummaging through a lower cupboard.

"Nice ass," Jimmy said.

"As nice as you'll ever see," Kate snapped back.

"How was your trip?"

This was the last question Jimmy wanted to address right then though he knew it would come many more times.

"It's done."

"Well, welcome home," Kate offered in a comforting tone as she turned to look up at him. She rose, and they hugged briefly. "If I can find the frickin' thing, I'll make omelets." Jimmy opened an upper cupboard and pulled out an old iron fry pan.

"Why the hell did you move it there?"

"Easier to reach," Jimmy said with a smile, "and I don't have to flash my ass to get it."

"Very funny, Eagleson. OK, let's get this show on the road."

Kate was a good cook and enjoyed feeding Jimmy. As her husband was seldom home and indifferent to her domestic interests, she focused her nurturing instincts on the needs of Camp. She called Ray and prepared three large breakfasts. The trio sat at the bar and chatted.

"I'm telling you I found the perfect view," Ray said. "It's got everything, the lake, the mountains, Jimmy, it's fantastic. You can see everything."

"You've said that before," Jimmy said. The search for the ultimate eastern view from the mountains had been one of Ray's few goals for many years.

"All right, this time you come and see for yourself before it gets overrun. First chance we get this spring, we go." Ray had no official status with anyone, but his knowledge of the nooks and crannies of the Adirondacks was well known. Once he announced a new find, it was usually ruined by the large numbers who heard through the grapevine.

"Where is it?" Kate asked.

"That's just it; it's off one of the trails around Poke-O-Moonshine. I cut off to get away from a bunch of college kids not far from a place I've snuck into a couple of times before. It's about a half-mile in, and the walk's not bad. I mean it's right there." "Right there" for Ray could be in the middle of woods that no one had been in since before Champlain discovered the lake and was off limits to hikers.

"If you guys are doing it, so am I," Kate said.

"If I can get up here in the spring, I'll go," Jimmy promised. Ray knew the likelihood was remote.

After more catching up, Ray returned to his cottage and Kate went to the supermarket to pick up the remaining supplies for the party. Jimmy put on his boots, coat, scarf, and a toque. A door on the lake side of the great room led to a large, insulated, wraparound porch filled with Adirondack furniture. Jimmy stepped out and looked southward towards Ray's cottage. An elderly couple had lived there until the husband died and the wife decided to sell. The Old Man paid more than it was worth to insure Camp's privacy. Now, a thick hedge of thirty-foot cedar trees on the far side blocked all view of the southern residences beyond it. Jimmy had the place refurbished to match the new Camp. Now with three bedrooms and two baths, Ray had much more room than he needed.

Jimmy walked through to the north entrance and gazed. Beyond the lawn, four acres of undeveloped woods extended for six-hundred feet of lakefront and back to the road. Jimmy had been offered millions for it. But he didn't need the money and wouldn't have sold it anyway. He tramped out the door, felt the cold bite of the wind off Lake Champlain, adjusted his scarf, and started down the stone path and stairs to the lake. He stepped carefully on the glazed walkway covered with ice and the residue of snowfall, but his foot glided out from under him, and he grabbed the railing. He stopped and chuckled as he looked over Champlain. The bay had a thin layer of ice, but the main lake remained open for the time being. Jimmy remembered driving over the thick February ice in a Volkswagen race to Burlington one year when he was young and stupid.

He reached the shore and stepped onto Turtle Rock. At over seven feet in diameter, several people could sit on Turtle Rock. It had four nearly uniform protrusions that resembled legs, and when Jimmy was young, a separate smaller stone was lodged against the body creating a perfect head. But one spring, ice dragged it out of place. From then on, it looked like a botched decapitation. The low profile lake-view from the turtle's back was spectacular. Jimmy came here often to think.

He sat in his favorite spot and surveyed the familiar scene. Looking at Vermont, he remembered how, when he was twelve, he talked Stosh into following him in The Old Man's boat as he swam across the lake. Stosh wasn't as afraid for Jimmy's safety as he was for his own. The Old Man's boat was one of the few things strictly off limits to the boys. Jimmy made it over and wanted to swim back, but a storm was forming, and they returned to the New York shore as fast as the increasing chop would let them. When they reached Camp, The Old Man was standing above on the bank staring at them. Both Jimmy and Stosh had hollow stomachs expecting to be in real trouble as they carefully maneuvered the twenty-one-foot Lyman back on the hoist, covered it, and raised it well out of the water. The Old Man must have felt his stare said enough. He just flicked his silver lighter, lit a cigarette and returned to his office.

The Old Man was a classic success story. Born and raised in Ottawa, he grew up poor but proud and determined. In 1939 when the war hit, he—along with most young Canadian men—joined immediately. The Army trained him as a combat engineer, but he never left England. An early accident shattered a lower leg, and it was too dangerous to put him near the action. But he was good at his job, was made a trainer, and was promoted several times.

The Old Man didn't like talking about the war. Jimmy remembered when an old friend of his uncle in Ottawa took Jimmy and his cousin Gordon to a Royal Canadian Legion hall. The boys came back with many questions. With a piercing silent stare, The Old Man made it clear the subject was off limits. And he was a pacifist. Jimmy was never allowed to have a gun, even a toy one. The Old Man said he didn't like what they stood for, and fishing was better than shooting.

After the war, he returned to his job in a machinery maintenance business in Ontario and then on a gamble went into commercial and residential plumbing, heating and air conditioning supplies. The venture almost failed. But after three years of struggling, one big contract turned the corner. In the early '50s, he opened branches in Quebec and upstate New York.

The Eaglesons owned the property on Lake Champlain since the late '40s. It had always been The Old Man's dream to live there, so he sold most of the Canadian operation and focused on the States. The American business grew rapidly and eventually had five locations in New York and seven in Florida where construction was booming.

A shrieking gull interrupted Jimmy's thoughts. Returning to his trance, he remembered often hearing the story of how The Old Man met Jimmy's mother in Ottawa. They were high school sweethearts, and she was a kind and dedicated wife. The Old Man showed her a special affection not available to others, including Jimmy. They both wanted a large family, but after several years of trying they gave up on pregnancy. Then Jimmy was conceived. He was their miracle baby and would reap the benefits of growing up when they had plenty of resources. He paid for it now; they both died within a year of each other when Jimmy was in his twenties.

Jimmy worked in the supply business from early high school but never liked it. He was far from lazy. He needed a different venue. Stosh loved it. The Old Man hired him to work with Jimmy, and they were, thanks to Stosh's interest, a good team. When Jimmy went to college, Stosh stayed and kept working. When Jimmy graduated, at The Old Man's insistence, Jimmy took over management. He moved Stosh up whenever he could. Two years after his parents died, Jimmy sold the operation to Stosh at a price good for both of them.

A slamming storm door interrupted Jimmy's solitude. Kate was back and coming down the steps to Turtle Rock.

"Hey," she shouted from halfway down.

"Hey."

Carefully managing the ice, Kate stepped up onto the rock and took her place next to Jimmy.

"It's damned cold down here," she said.

"It's damned cold up there too, but the view's better down here."

Kate grinned; with all the care Jimmy had taken to strategically design Camp for spectacular views, he still preferred Turtle Rock.

"So the trip wasn't so good?"

"They never are," Jimmy said as he looked at her.

"I know it's none of my business ... " With almost anyone else this particular opening would lead to something sarcastic from Jimmy. But Kate's thoughts were always welcome, and Jimmy smiled. "... and I've never asked you this before. I thought if you wanted, you'd bring it up, and I know the deal—I don't analyze if you don't ask."

"What, Kate?"

"What happened?"

"You want the whole trip?"

"I mean with you and Clair. At first, you were great together. Then you guys pulled a sudden one-eighty. I've always wondered what happened."

Jimmy had been mulling this question for years. He looked down and then back up. "That, I can summarize very quickly. One fart in your sleep."

Kate hesitated. "Not sure I'm with you."

"You never know when you're going to do it, but at some point, there's that one fatal fart, and instantly passion turns to repulsion, lust to disgust. You know right then and there that whatever you had isn't coming back."

Kate was silent. She always loved Jimmy's wit but was

trying to digest the serious side of his response. Finally, her need to break the mood overcame her.

"Ever try Beano?"

Jimmy smiled, "No. Maybe that's the magic formula."

They both laughed. Kate suggested she should return to prepare for the party. Jimmy volunteered his help, and the two ascended to Camp.

* * *

Ray and Jimmy sat at the bar waiting for the predictable and most welcome early arrivals, the core of the gang. Jimmy surveyed the liquor stock. "How are we on bourbon?" he asked.

"Four bottles behind the bar," Ray answered. "I'll put another on the shelf in a few minutes."

Jimmy looked at the top shelf to check on his prized bottle of Jack Daniels, a limited collector's decanter called "The Belle of Lincoln." The Old Man gave it to him for his college graduation. Jimmy intended to open it on some special occasion, but none of sufficient importance had come along over the nearly thirty years since. Now it was a reserved artifact of the Eagleson bar, a treasure only for the most deserving time. Ray drew two more beers and sat with Jimmy for a few more minutes of pre-party peace.

The open house didn't start until nine but by seven-thirty a few cars arrived. Jimmy had a parking area for about ten plus plenty of room for many more along the sides of the long private drive. The New Year's party had been a tradition for at least a decade, making invitations unnecessary and predicting who would show impossible. The great room was bright with a roaring fire, and the caterer stood by to insure proper presentation of the various hors d'oeuvres and extra colossal shrimp. Kate used to insist on taking care of all the food, but Jimmy eventually talked her into relinquishing her claim to the kitchen and enjoying the party. Almost any conceivable libation was available in quantity, and the early partiers wasted no time in settling down in the familiar surroundings.

Jimmy's friends came from all walks of life. First to arrive were Dick and Cathy. He was a broker for the local insurance agency Jimmy used, and she had a popular gift shop. Dick could put away the bourbon while Cathy sipped wine and was always prepared to drive her to-become intoxicated husband back home. Always good for a new joke, mostly off-color, Dick was gregarious and loud. Jimmy liked him but could only take him in limited doses. Cathy and Kate could gab about antiques for days, and Cathy found many of the pieces Kate placed at Camp.

Next in were Fred and Carroll. Fred became a friend in high school and was still a rough construction worker after thirty-plus years. He had strong callused hands and bulging forearms but suffered from sciatica. Carroll was a cute, petite woman who worked as a secretary in a local office. She smiled more than she talked and everyone liked her. The bantering, small talk, and much laughter made for a festive beginning.

Kate and David arrived at about eight. As always, Kate looked stunning in her carefully selected holiday attire. David wore his usual Dockers and sweater, oddly complementing her elegance. Jimmy had to admit they looked good together. Kate went directly to Jimmy and gave him a kiss. David made the standard greetings expected of one re-entering the fold. Ray kept all glasses filled. The chatter and joviality continued and reverberated in the large room.

As more guests arrived, Jimmy felt pulled from place to place by the obligations of a polite host. Now several dozen people cheerfully occupied the great room, mainly friends, but many later arrivals were not part of the inside gang he enjoyed so much. Most of the ladies had been to the hairdresser, polished their nails and were wearing new semi-formal dresses. Most of the men had put on clean shirts. The music supplemented the festivities with a touch of the old days, as classic rock-and-roll filled the room and a few couples danced.

As the crowd grew, Jimmy saw many more unfamiliar faces arrive. For the first time at an Eagleson party, he became concerned. Small groups of strangers hung together as if at a public event. Ray also looked uncomfortable as he wandered around keeping an eye on everything.

"Jesus Jimmy," Ray said. "There must be a hundred people here, and I've never seen half of them." Jimmy nodded. Ray smelled smoke and made his way past several clusters of partiers to the fireplace where a stranger stood with a lit cigarette, talking with his friends.

"Hey," Ray said. "Sorry, there is no smoking in here."

"My mistake, I saw the lighter and thought it was OK."

Ray snatched the Old Man's lighter and put it back in its place. "That's not for use," Ray said alarmed at the new guest's boldness. "It's a family heirloom. That's why it's in a case."

"Yeah, well like I said, Dude, my mistake."

Ray prepared to ask the group to leave when he heard a glass smash near the bar and scurried over. Another cluster of strangers stood looking aghast, apologized and helped Ray clean up. When they finished, Ray saw the smoker near the mantel had left. Relieved, he returned to his roaming, keeping his eyes open for more problems.

As the New Year approached, most of the strangers moved on to other parties. The crowd now looked familiar, and Ray prepared the champagne for the midnight toast. Most of the discussion was about hope for 2003. The atmosphere turned positive and friendly until someone yelled, "HEY, Eagleson, how the hell are ya?" Tommy Toro had announced his arrival.

Tommy T. was an occasional friend of a few of the guests. He came late as usual, with Fred Anderson, a nice enough guy who for some reason had a soft spot for Tommy. Already drunk, Tommy announced to Jimmy from across the room, "We had to get our asses out here in time for that expensive champagne you always pound down!"

Jimmy walked quietly over to Tommy, said hello, and strategically manipulated the volume to a reasonable level. Tommy was considered a blowhard by most of the gang, sometimes referred to as the hundred-fifty-pound mouth. Short, with a shaved head, oval face, large nose and ears, and a scrub-brush mustache, he saw himself as a gifted intellectual and was an instant expert on any subject that happened to come up. When drinking, he insisted on dominating all discussions. For Tommy, conversation was a competitive sport, something to be approached in the opponent's face. Still, to Jimmy he was manageable. He had from time to time actually helped with a project at Camp. When not in a crowd where he needed his soapbox, he could be tolerable.

Now that Tommy arrived just in time for the toast, Jimmy led him and Fred to the bar. They picked up a flute of champagne and, although Jimmy would have preferred otherwise, joined the party.

Midnight arrived, and Kate made the toast wishing all a fantastic 2003. After the champagne flutes had been refilled several times, most of the gang retreated to the porch for the annual cigar ritual. Jimmy led the group. Ray followed after checking everyone at the bar and refilling any empties.

Jimmy was not a smoker. In fact, he detested the habit. The Old Man smoked at least two packs a day and died from them. Jimmy never started or even showed interest, but he installed a large air filter on the porch for his friends who couldn't resist, and would enjoy one good cigar once a year. Ray opened the box, cut the ends and used fat wooden matches to light each illegal Cuban individually. The participants took long draws and blew thick smoke above their heads as they commented on the smoothness and broke into new conversations.

"When are you going back?" David asked Jimmy.

"I'm going down to see Sal in a few days, then back to the office from there," Jimmy answered. "I have new acquisitions to work on."

"Maybe we'll come down and visit sometime, if that's cool with you," David said.

Jimmy didn't know how he felt about David visiting. David

wasn't an insider; it could be difficult to find anything to talk with him about.

"Just call and we'll set something up," Jimmy said after taking a long drag from his cigar and slowly exhaling.

The conversations continued as the fine cigars shrank to stogies. It was now almost one-thirty. Jimmy had already said goodbye to many of the guests and watched as more were preparing to go. After a few last draws, Ray decided he was overdue to check the bar.

"WHAT THE FUCK!" Ray shouted as he entered the great room.

Jimmy quickly put down his cigar and rushed in. Tommy T. sat at the bar holding court with Fred and two other thoroughly drunk men Jimmy had never seen before. He was liberally pouring from Jimmy's cherished Belle of Lincoln. The floor around him was littered with ashes and stamped out cigarette butts, ground into the hardwood floor. Tommy, now sloppy drunk and irritated at being interrupted, turned to Ray with a glazed stare and slurred, "Whaaat?"

Jimmy turned and looked out the front window, livid. This was it. To turn Camp into a two-bit saloon, open his treasure, and reduce it to fodder for obnoxious drunks who couldn't tell its taste from piss—this was a new low.

Jimmy took a deep breath and worked to compose himself. By the time he regained control and turned toward the bar, Tommy and his disciples had their coats on. With Tommy mumbling obscenities, they left through the garage door. He looked at the bottle and the burns in the floor and was relieved the situation ended without a fight. "It's a damn good thing Sal isn't here," he whispered. Kate gathered most of the remaining crew and led them back to the porch. Jimmy sat at the bar as Ray began picking up the floor.

"You don't have to do that," Jimmy said.

"No problem, just grabbing the butts. I'll sweep in the morning."

Jimmy looked at the half-finished bottle. "You know, I can remember when The Old Man gave me that. I was surprised. At that moment I thought he was proud of me—though he never said. There weren't many times like that."

Jimmy took the bottle and poured two glasses. "Come on Ray, sit down and have some of this with me." Ray sat.

"To The Old Man—Gerret Eagleson, chins up," Jimmy raised his glass.

"To The Old Man, chins up," Ray repeated.

"Jimmy, this is real good. Look, I know how important this bottle was to you. I don't know what to say. Good thing Sal didn't see this."

Jimmy chuckled. "Yeah. You know, I remember the parties The Old Man threw. Not as big as these, just good friends. You know he never drank anywhere but here or at friends' homes—said it was bad for business. But there were always friends around, always sipping. The porch on the first house was the favorite spot."

"My dad was the same. You'd never know he drank unless you lived with him—except, he did visit the V.F.W. a lot. But to him, that was like home."

Jimmy took a sip and looked at his glass. "Yeah, I guess we come by this honestly."

"Yup, apples fallen near the tree," Ray added. They smiled at each other, nodded and toasted.

Jimmy stood and peeked through the window to the porch. Only members of the real gang were left, mostly overnighters. Things looked comfortable with lots of smiling and laughter, as in the old days. He grabbed the special bottle and several glasses. "Come on Ray," he said. "Let's join the party."

Jimmy poured each of his remaining friends a glass from The Belle and pronounced this would be the last open invitation blast at Camp. All toasted to his proclamation with sighs of relief. They all felt a coming-of-age too long avoided. All knew the true friends would still converge on Camp, regularly. The special bottle was demarking an important occasion after all. Jimmy raised his glass. "To all of you, my friends, may you each have an excellent new year and many, many more."

"Chins up!" Kate yelled.

"Chins up!" the gang shouted back.

Jimmy looked at Ray and asked, "Got any more of those cigars?"

* * *

Morning came all too soon. Jimmy was awake by eight, but the others were still dead to the world. He showered and dressed and thought about spending time in the den. But he decided too many people were in the house for that, so he went to the great room. Along with all the guest rooms, two of the more remote couches were occupied. Jimmy quietly entered the kitchen, checked the refrigerator for orange juice, and sat on a stool behind the bar. He looked at the controversial bottle and smiled. Though he was still decompressing from the loss, it had provided the event that finally proved the need for a more limited level of entertaining. He heard activity from the wing and realized his presence was a social alarm clock. Maybe he should have gone to his den after all.

Kate came from the nearest bathroom in her bathrobe, barefoot and fresh from a shower. Feeling an unusual attraction, Jimmy smiled at her as she came across the room. Then David emerged from the same bathroom also in a bathrobe and fresh from a shower. Jimmy felt mild jealousy and fought the temptation to fantasize about their morning. He never understood why these feelings about Kate came from time to time. His relationship with her was clearly platonic. It was good these sensations left him quickly.

Jimmy got up to go to the refrigerator, but Kate ordered him to sit. "Let me do that. You want your Nutter Butters?"

Jimmy nodded and returned to his stool. She brought out a container of orange juice and a package of Nutter Butters and looked for a bottle of cheap champagne.

"I don't think there's anything but the champagne from last night," Jimmy said as he munched on his cookie, "unless there are a couple of bottles of Dom."

Kate stared at Jimmy in disbelief. "I'm not going to use Dom for mimosas, Jimmy. Even the sixty-dollar stuff is a little much, don't you think?"

Kate reluctantly gave up the fruitless search, opened a

bottle of the good champagne and prepared a large pitcher of mimosas.

"You still love those things don't you?" Kate said as Jimmy crunched on another Nutter Butter.

"Decide when you're going back?" David asked Jimmy.

"First thing tomorrow." Jimmy had been toying with staying a few days but decided right there and then it was time to go. "I'll stop for a couple of nights in Lake George and see Sal. Then, back to the city."

Kate looked disappointed but nodded. As she bent to place a large plate of Danish on the bar, her robe momentarily opened exposing her left breast. Again Jimmy was stimulated. Trying to lighten the situation he said, "Always have to flash me don't you?"

"Yeah, she's a great flasher," David quickly interjected.

Jimmy successfully hid his lack of appreciation for David's unwelcome invasion into private banter, and Kate decided to dress before the others came out. David joined her, and again Jimmy was sitting alone, at least for the moment.

As the remaining guests joined the morning festivities, Jimmy was quiet. He listened to the cheerful chatter and one by one said goodbyes until only Kate and David remained.

David disappeared through the garage to warm the car. Kate cleaned up and tried to organize the leftover pastry.

"What do you want to do with all of this?" she asked Jimmy.

"I don't know, give it to Ray; you take some, chuck it, whatever you think."

Kate looked at the excess and shook her head. "When will we see you again?"

"I'll be back here in the spring. Come down whenever you want, only give me some notice so the place is ready."

"How about Saint Patrick's Day?" Kate suggested.

"Yeah, that sounds good, but anytime is good."

David reappeared with Kate's coat. Kate gave Jimmy a long hug. "OK, Eagleson, Saint Patrick's Day it is—and I'll see you tonight."

Jimmy returned to his study and settled into his rocker. He bought the chair in Miami when he was an undergraduate and kept it in his private space ever since. As he scanned his bookcases, he noticed an aging paperback of an obscure dialogue by Plato, *Philebus*, Plato's thoughts on leisure and the good life. Who reads *Philebus*? he wondered. His favorite professor recommended it to him when asked what Plato would have thought of the then new generation. He carefully worked through the book to ferret out exactly what was being said. He wanted to dazzle the academic world with his insight, a typical goal for scholars his age. Now he looked at it on the shelf, trying to remember Socrates' point. He smiled and thought again, who reads *Philebus*? Who reads Plato?

Jimmy looked at another bookcase. In bold letters, the spine of a thick text read *The Logic of Aristotle*. Jimmy snickered, logic—that's what's important. It was four semesters of formal empirical analysis that sailed him through law school, not Plato's idealistic bullshit. The Old Man had talked almost nothing but fact all his life—in the logical world, you don't have to feel, only calculate. Jimmy looked out the window. He knew well that as hard as he tried to follow The Old

Man's example, Plato still found ways to sneak in and disturb his numbness.

His attention turned to his most valued possession, a stick displayed proudly in a specially built rack. He found it near the fort when he and Sal slept there one night. It was shaped almost exactly like a Civil War musket, complete with a hammer and a thick twig where the trigger should be. The bark was long gone by the time Jimmy came upon it, and it looked polished. Sal had lots of guns, but Jimmy had the stick, and Sal would have traded his whole arsenal for it. Sal still made offers.

The fort was their secret place, nestled in a grove of trees next to a stone hedgerow that gave cover as they picked off the attacking enemy. He and Sal camped there whenever they could, using an old canvas tarp as a tent and cooking hot dogs over an open fire. He often remembered how good it was then, and he sometimes wondered who could ever want more, especially when they were warm in their sleeping bags as their makeshift shelter shed off a cold downpour. He couldn't remember ever being happier. In high school, they'd bring a six-pack. Stosh was always invited but seldom came. He had two part-time jobs and a paper route and never seemed to have free time. So Sal and Jimmy had to sip the beer and solve the problems of the world by themselves. After all, none of the other guys was trusted enough, and no girls were allowed.

When they came home from their freshman year of college, it was gone. A small-time developer had bulldozed it and put up a baby blue pole barn. Jimmy felt betrayed but learned a lesson about the inevitability of change, especially for the best

things. He sat for a few more minutes thinking and reminiscing when he heard Ray in the great room and joined him.

Ray was sitting at his usual place at the bar sipping a freshly
drawn beer. Jimmy filled a mug and joined him.

"Leaving tomorrow?" Ray asked.

"Yup, Kate tell you?"

"No, I figured you'd go after last night. Try to forget that
shit. It was a great party."

"It's forgotten, and it was a great party."

The two chatted through a couple of beers, making plans
for maintenance at Camp, including a small renovation and
fixing the new cigarette burns on the floor. Then Ray had a
memory flash and yelled out, "The Package From Gordon!"

"Oh yeah. I still wonder what the hell he would send."

Gordon was one of Jimmy's favorite people. They spent
a lot of time together as kids both at Camp and in Ottawa.
Gord's dad, Uncle Fred, was The Old Man's only sibling; he
died in the late '60s. He was never healthy, born with a club
foot and many other problems. Uncle Fred always felt guilty
about not serving in the war, but The Old Man said it was
a blessing. Jimmy remembered his uncle as a good guy who
liked doing things with the boys. Gordon's mom and Jimmy
were close, and when she died the previous summer, he took
it hard. She was the last of her generation. After her death,
Jimmy intended to connect more with Gord, but life had them
both too occupied.

Jimmy was pleased to be hearing from Gordon. Ray
returned and handed over the package. Looking perplexed,

Jimmy opened it and found one letter and several overstuffed manila envelopes. He read a short message on the sealed letter.

Jimmy, please read this when you have time to think. I believe you will find it most important and will want to be in the right frame of mind. Pardon the mystery, but I know how you may react. I hope you had a wonderful holiday and hope to see you soon, Gord.

Jimmy smirked at the "wonderful holiday" part but was mystified about the contents. He and Gordon knew each other well. Each being an only child with no other cousins made them more like brothers. Jimmy respected Gordon's advice, and right now might not be the time to wander into something this important. Besides, the material in these envelopes might take days to go through. But, maybe he should just read the letter. Jimmy sipped his beer. Ray saw him processing and kept quiet.

The ice broke when Jimmy announced, "This is for another time. Right now the agenda calls for more Molson."

As Jimmy and Ray laughed and chatted, Jimmy faced the mantel to toast The Old Man one more time. "What the fuck now," he said. "Look!"

With its small door ajar, the display case sat empty. The Old Man's lighter was gone. Jimmy and Ray leaped up, found nothing on the mantel, and searched the floor, furniture, and tables. After a frantic ten minutes, Jimmy sat. "Come on over Ray, let's think."

Ray thought a moment. "Shit, Jimmy, I caught a guy using

it last night. I put it back in the case. That asshole must have stolen it. He had a real attitude, Jimmy. Shit. This is my fault. I should have known the son-of-a-bitch would take it. I should have put it in my pocket."

"Nothing's your fault, Ray. Who was the guy?"

"I'd never seen him before. I don't remember what he looked like—there were so many strangers, Jimmy. Well, maybe it's still around. I'll hunt for it until it's found, Jimmy."

"I've got a feeling it's gone, Ray. Maybe that guy stole it, maybe someone else, who knows? I don't think we're going to find it."

Jimmy exhaled, took a sip of beer, and shook his head. He looked at his ring and rubbed the crest with his thumb.

"I've still got you, and you don't cause lung cancer," he said. "Let's have a few more and relax, Ray. If it shows up, great—but I won't count on it. And, Ray, this is not your fault."

"Maybe Kate saw something or picked it up or—"

"Ray, she would have said something, and let's keep her out of it anyway. She'd be very upset and probably—like you—want to take the blame. We need to let it go. It is what it is."

Jimmy smiled and patted Ray's shoulder. After sipping and chatting another hour, Ray rose. "I've got a few things to do; I'll see you tonight." He clinked Jimmy's mug, "Chins up to 2003 my friend."

"Chins up," Jimmy said.

"And Jimmy if I ever catch the guy—"

"Let it go, Ray. We'll drive ourselves crazy obsessing on it. Let it go."

Ray nodded, stood and slowly walked to the porch scouring the room with his eyes. At the door, he sighed and left.

Jimmy walked to the porch. Ray had already cleaned everything from the night before. He strolled to the north door and looked out at the woods. If it were summer, he would take the path to the clearing overlooking Champlain and sit awhile. That spot reminded him of the fort, and he sometimes thought it would be great to camp there. But it wouldn't be any fun alone, and he figured Sal had outgrown it.

He thought of the lighter. What was the big deal anyway? He'd barely been allowed to touch the thing until a few months before The Old Man died. He remembered a rare night when The Old Man wanted to talk and almost told him about the crests. He started, but his eyes welled, his face turned solemn, and he went silent. He never tried again.

Jimmy exhaled. Losing it *was* a big deal and whatever he'd told Ray, he'd have a hard time getting over it.

Jimmy returned to the bar, filled his mug and looked at the package from Gordon and thought again of reading the letter. But he'd had enough surprises for one morning and moved to a large rocking swivel lounger in front of the picture window. He took a long sip. Tonight he would go to dinner with his friends at a little Italian place hidden on the second story above a downtown business. A place they all loved. He wouldn't let The Old Man's lighter ruin it. Right now, he would sit and think about it, and The Old Man, as he stared out the window at Lake Champlain.

CHAPTER III

Sal

Jimmy looked out at a clear, cold morning with a bright piercing sun. He loved driving through the Adirondacks on days like this. After breakfast and a talk with Ray, he warmed the Lincoln and prepared to leave. The lake sparkled, and he sat by the picture window a few moments to say goodbye to his favorite place. Standing, he took in one last visual before picking up his briefcase and heading for the garage. He looked forward to seeing Sal, and he knew it was time to get back to work.

Settling into the car's large leather seat, Jimmy adjusted the stereo, pulled out of the garage and turned up the drive to the road. As he motored around Cumberland Head, he admired the different views of Champlain. A morning like this helped erase the dark thoughts of the past days. The bright sunlight forced frequent readjustments of the visor's height and angle.

On Route 87, the sun sat low in the sky to his left and slightly behind his field of vision. He began listening to a collection of light classical pieces he found in an airport somewhere. He took in the scenery as he drove through the Champlain Valley into the Adirondack Park's 9,375 square miles of wilderness. He thought it unusual to be the only car on the road. It looked like this journey would be private. He glanced at a frozen pond with a near perfect beaver dam covered by a dusting of fresh white snow. His mind wandered as the rustic views passed by one by one. He thought about Sal.

Salvatore Esposito was the third of a trinity formed with Jimmy and Stosh in grade school. He was all about attitude and was the only person Jimmy knew who was truly not intimidated by anything. With a history of failed relationships, he had a cynical attitude toward women. But, with his Casanova Italian looks, he kept getting involved. Sal was cut like a body builder and stood six foot four. In high school, he earned a reputation for being tough. It was said he had "shoulders like Detroit," although no one could remember where this portrayal came from. Many kids thought something happened in middle school, and he'd become mean and moody. Jimmy and Stosh couldn't see it. Sal was just more selective about whom he liked.

Jimmy thought of an incident when Sal was a freshman. For no known reason, a junior from the football team started picking on him. Jimmy could still hear the taunting, "Sal, is that your name? Are you Sally, little Sally? Did Mommy buy you a pretty new dress little Sally?" They met on the athletic field. Dozens of kids were waiting when Sal arrived and immediately went to work. Thirty seconds later, the bully was lying in the dirt bleeding from a broken nose and crying.

Sal was also brilliant. He sailed through college and medical school and was near the end of his clinical internship when he quit. One evening when a senior doctor at the medical center was screaming out ridiculous orders, he hit the end. Jimmy always thought there must have been more to the story. The next year he enrolled in law school, finding it much more to his liking. Though he never formally practiced, he found this education more useful to his real interest, money.

Sal had the knack. He knew how to turn a buck under the worst conditions, at the worst times, and had made himself rich, his way. No one but Sal understood his way, but no one could question its effectiveness. He settled near Saratoga Springs after his folks moved there. It was a better location for his business and close to the horse track.

Jimmy looked forward to seeing Sal and knew their chemistry would recharge him.

An odd sensation in the steering wheel snapped Jimmy from his trance and he instinctively pressed his brakes. The Lincoln went into a slide and began to drive itself. Black ice. The car headed toward a deep incline at the opposite shoulder. Jimmy fought for control but couldn't avoid a 180-degree spin and an abrupt stop that slammed him into his seatbelt.

The sun and snow ganged up and blinded him. He was completely disoriented, even the visor was no help. But he knew he had to move quickly. He cautiously inched the car toward the right to get his bearings when the dopplering scream from a tractor trailer's horn froze him in terror. The truck barreled by slapping the driver's side mirror and temporally blocking the sun long enough for Jimmy to see he was backward on the left lane shoulder.

Silence returned. Jimmy was again blinded but knew which way to go. He was well aware his last maneuver could have taken him into a deep ditch between the road and the median. Now he needed to cross back to the right lane by turning left. Attempting to hear any other on-coming vehicles, he lowered the windows filling the Lincoln with freezing winter air. Still unable to see, he took a deep breath and made the move. The car responded well at first, but then his wheels spun leaving him stuck half-way across. He pumped the accelerator in a panic, and as the new tires finally grabbed, he swung into position on the right-lane shoulder. He sat a minute, adrenaline rushing through him, still scared but now exhilarated. No other vehicles passed.

Jimmy drove on at snail's pace. Gradually, he dared to go faster. After a few miles, he stopped a minute to regroup. As he sat, he gazed into the wooded median between the north and south lanes. A buck emerged from the trees and stared at him. With its rack half gone from winter shedding, its head looked unbalanced and uncomfortable. How the hell did he get there, Jimmy wondered. He watched the buck survey the area until he leaped back into his mini-reserve. Still shaken, Jimmy put the Lincoln in gear and continued his journey. After twenty miles, he regained the confidence to resume normal speed.

Jimmy remembered a greasy spoon from years ago, took an exit, took a back road about a mile and pulled into the familiar parking lot. He slowly stepped out, closed the car door and stood staring at the three-inch gouge in his mirror. He sighed. This was a close one.

Standing by the restaurant's front door a chainsaw-sculpted

bear held a welcome sign. The bear was new, but the rest of the place was identical to its earlier days. Jimmy and The Old Man use to stop here before cutting through the lower Adirondacks on their way to one of their Western New York stores. Filled with old mounted animal heads and fish, and assorted pictures of the mountains, the place still kept its old charm. The old counter was covered with its original light green laminate, worn and faded to nearly white near its edges. Random repairs using a variety of colored plastic tapes gave each of the vinyl covered stools its own, unique design. Behind the counter stood a rotund, bearded man, in a black and red checked flannel shirt. The man approached with skeptical friendliness. "Coffee?"

"Yes please," Jimmy said.

Jimmy glanced over at the only other patrons. Both sat at the end of the counter drinking their morning Budweiser, talking and laughing quietly about a recent out-of-season hunting trip.

Plenty of white ceramic diner mugs were in plain sight, but Jimmy's coffee came in a take-out container with plastic lid. "Figer'd yuze was on da road," the server said.

"I am," Jimmy replied.

"Anythin' else?"

"Give me a minute if you don't mind." Jimmy was still a little shaky.

"Take alls the time yuze wants, Deys ain't breakin' down da doors to get in dis time a day," the server said with a chuckle.

Jimmy smiled. He was always fascinated by North Country speech. Almost-English combined with French syntax, a few unique words and unusual pronunciation that left visitors wondering what country they were in. But to locals, it was the King's finest.

A delivery man walked in and diverted the server. "Where's yuze want dis?" he asked.

"Auh, stick der in da baack der—naw, put it down cellar."

"Dem roads is baad out der. I shit you not. I prit-neer craashed a couple-two-three times."

"Where's da va'ka?"

"I ain't seen't it."

"I telled ya I need it."

"Well, I ain't heard ya."

"Shit."

"Easy, You. I kin pro'ly get it lader ta-day."

"I'm tellin' ya, ya frickin' better, you." The server returned to Jimmy. "Where's yuze from?" he asked.

"Plattsburgh. Used to stop here frequently years ago. Had a little time and decided to come by."

The server walked to the Bunn coffeemaker, filled a ceramic mug and put it in front of Jimmy. "Dis's on me, take alls da time yuze wants. Daat yer Lincoln?"

"Yea, it used to be parked out there quite a bit, years ago."

"How long yuze had it?"

"Long time, The Old Man bought it new."

"Daat ain't no winner rat," the server said surprised to see a classic on the road in January. "Well, gotta get ta da baack and cook," he said and left.

Jimmy nodded and looked around recognizing familiar features. He remembered many of the creatures on the wall— he'd even given a couple of them nicknames. And he recalled business conversations with The Old Man as they sat in one of the worn booths, and how important they seemed at the time. He thought of how The Old Man would half fill an ashtray in the hour they'd stay, lighting one cigarette after another with his silver lighter. He shrugged and smiled. He was glad the place hadn't changed.

As Jimmy drank his coffee, he toyed with the idea of joining the hunters for a beer, but others began coming in, and he felt more and more out of place. He left money on the counter for the increasingly busy waiter. They smiled and waved at each other as Jimmy exited. Several more cars arrived as he pulled out. Stopping had been a good idea—a nice visit to the past. Now it was time to join Sal in the present.

Jimmy returned to the interstate and headed for Lake George. The skies were beginning to cloud. He was still thinking about the old café, a far cry from the resort where he would be staying. A steady stream of traffic formed, mostly bearing Quebec plates. Jimmy would only be with them a short while longer.

Exiting at Bolton Landing, Jimmy followed the familiar route to the hotel. The few cars parked near the reception area proudly displayed ski racks loaded with expensive equipment. Jimmy parked near them and entered the large open lobby. His check-in went routinely, and he moved the Lincoln to its spot in front of his lodge suite.

As he unloaded his bags from the back seat, Jimmy was pleased to see a small cooler. No doubt Ray left it there, and no doubt it was filled with Canadian beer. He thought how it, too, had been shaken in the near crash.

After a quick load-in to the apartment size suite, Jimmy transferred the bottles to the refrigerator, opening the last one after tapping the cap several times. He took a long gulp. He'd had better trips, but this one was among the most memorable. He continued to sip as he turned on the gas fireplace, opened the drapes, and walked out onto the balcony overlooking Lake George. The air was nearly as brisk as at Camp and the view picturesque, but it wasn't Champlain. The lake seemed barren without the overload of boats and Jetskis brought in by summer visitors.

He looked at the new flat-screen TV. The Old Man would have loved one of those, he thought. The Old Man used to love watching sports. Baseball was his favorite. He said it all happened in real-time. You never knew how it would end. He didn't care for much else. If a romance or a war story were on, he'd leave the room. And anything sexual made him cringe. Jimmy didn't own a TV. He took a book from his bag. He would sip beer and read, then nap, and later meet up with Sal.

* * *

Jimmy followed the host to a table by the window. Sal called to say he would be a little late, but Jimmy was getting restless and decided to sit in the exclusive dining room and observe. From the window, the rustic grounds were perfectly man-icured even in winter. The clientele was primarily affluent New Yorkers dressed to fit the North Country cliché they'd learned in the city. Jimmy knew the reality of both places. He watched a well-fed male cardinal a few inches from the glass hopping from spot to spot as if trained to entertain the guests. A family with two obnoxious grade-schoolers sat close by. They were finishing so Jimmy didn't request another table. One boy complained about the nicks and scratches on his new skis while his brother laughed and taunted about how his slope-side pranks put them there. Both ignored their parents' patient attempts to quiet them. Only the promise of new gear for both brats led to some calm. Jimmy thought of his girls and took solace in knowing he wasn't alone. As they left, he was relieved but sorry they hadn't stayed to experience how Sal would have dealt with them.

In Salvatore Esposito strolled. Wearing a dark brown leather bomber jacket, tailored slacks, and a new fedora he looked as if he had come from the set of a 1950's war movie. Sal had "arrived" and everyone paid attention. He greeted Jimmy from halfway across the large dining room, and the few disturbed patrons immediately returned to their own business clearly seeing he was not to be fooled with. Jimmy stood and aggressively shook Sal's hand. The host, who had been left in Sal's dust, caught up and asked, "May I get either of you gentlemen a drink?"

Jimmy and Sal looked at each other and laughed. "A double Crown neat, a Molson, and whatever this gentleman would like, please," Sal replied. He looked at Jimmy and continued. "Now there's one for you Mr. Philosopher, where did this term 'gentleman' come from?"

Sal was always wired, and being with him was like being shot from a cannon.

"So how the hell are you Eagleson? How was your trip?"

With all the action at Camp, Jimmy had put his Florida problem in the back of his mind. Now, between the two little "ski urchins" and Sal's reminder, it all rushed back to the front. "I'm OK," he snickered.

"Just OK?"

"Sometimes OK is enough."

Sal nodded. Jimmy seldom bared his heart on his sleeve; the short exchange said everything Sal needed to know.

"I can tell your Southern excursion was a 'success.'"

"Yeah, a real winner."

"Marriage, what a deal," Sal proclaimed. "Everything is fine, then you get married and overnight everything changes. Any sex that's left comes from some fucked up sense of obligation, or it's a favor or maybe a bargaining chip. Eventually, you don't want anything to do with it. And the part of their brain that remembers anything good you've ever done is regularly erased. Not the part that holds on to any of the things they figure you've ever in your entire life fucked up, that's all permanent. But anything good—that's wiped out. Oh, and the chirping and cackling. All you're there to do is absorb the cost of their existence. Once they're settled into their lifestyle, they only want one more thing— you gone. Yeah, it's a great fucking deal."

Sal's failed marriages had demolished his faith in the idea. Jimmy wasn't quite as jaded but did get a kick out of Sal's diatribe. Jimmy took a sip of beer and replied. "Yeah, it's a great deal. But somehow we keep going back. They must be smarter than we are; they keep winning." Jimmy paused for a drink of beer and changed the subject.

"What have you been up to, Sal?"

"Oh, I got into a little deal building shacks and shanties near Phoenix. Had a partner who tried to fuck me over, but I got him. Man, I love that shit, the confrontation, running around behind the backs, then pouncing and demolishing the opposition. That's what makes business worthwhile. Yeah, that's the best part."

Jimmy knew Sal was serious; that was the part Sal loved.

"How's Stosh?" Sal asked.

"Still selling toilets."

"The ultimate team player—always was. Remember in school? The sports we played? I always thought they showed us how we'd play later. Stosh, the football hero, playing the line and holding back the opposition. You with your swimming, on the team but winning all the medals yourself. Yeah, Eagleson did it all, and everyone else would share the glory. You swam like a fucking fish. And a good thing for Stosh and me— remember the dam?" Jimmy tried to speak, but Sal cut him off. "I used to call you Fins, remember? You liked that. And I played hockey. You know why? Because I loved to get hit. Still do. I mean I *loved* to get hit. Taking a slamming check was even better than giving one. When the gloves came off, I couldn't lose because I love taking the shots. It's next to impossible to fuck over a guy who loves taking the shots."

Sal let out a laugh, and Jimmy cracked a broad smile. The waiter returned to take their orders. "How are you this evening Mr. Esposito? What would you gentlemen like?"

JEFF DELBEL

Again the two chuckled.

"First another round, then we'll talk," Sal said.

"Certainly Mr. Esposito."

"I'll assume you brought the Lincoln?" Sal continued.

"What else?"

"Well, one of these days you'll come into the twenty-first century. The garage is set. Anything you need done to it?"

"Yeah, I almost bought it on the way down. I spun out on the Northway and a truck gouged the mirror."

"A truck?"

"Yeah, a tractor trailer."

"Close call, Brother." Sal was quiet a moment. "And it's not time. Be a shame to check out when it's not time—and fantastic to go at just the right moment."

"And when is that, Sal, 'Just the right moment?'"

"When you're on top—no place higher to go—reached the absolute apex. Oh, I know some guys like the stroll down the other side of the hill—the easy shit after the hike. But for me, that's when there's nothing to look forward to. Casually descending and knowing you're never going back up. Fuck that. The time to go is on top looking down at other side screaming out 'Fuck You!' I'll tell you, Jimmy, if there's anything like a real blessing, going out on top is it."

Jimmy laughed and nodded. "We should be so lucky."

"Here's to our luck. Chins up, Eagleson."

"Chins up," Jimmy repeated as the friends tapped their glasses together.

"How did the party go?" Sal saw Jimmy's face sour. "What happened?"

"Some asshole stole The Old Man's lighter."

Sal eyes and mouth opened wide. "What? Who?"

"I don't know—there were a lot of strangers. Ray thinks it's one of them, but there's no telling. It's just gone."

"Fuck. Well, maybe it will show up. You never know; it may find its way back home."

"I'm not counting on it."

"Shit, you've had a run of 'good fortune.'" Sal looked at Jimmy's hand. "You've still got the ring. That's what's most important."

"Yeah, why is it important?"

Sal smirked "You know why. It's your fetish. The thing you keep so you won't forget."

"Forget what?"

"Don't fuck with me, Eagleson, you know what. What you need to remember. Unfinished business, things left to be reckoned with. And don't feel alone. I've got one of my own. It goes everywhere with me too."

"You, Salvatore Esposito, carry a fetish? What is it?"

Sal smirked and took a long sip of whiskey. "That, my friend, is another story for another time." Sal quickly changed the conversation. "Well, I'll have one of my guys take care of the Lincoln. It'll be done when you need it."

Jimmy nodded and smiled. Since he started working in New York, Sal had been arranging repairs and storing the Lincoln. Jimmy found keeping a car in the city more trouble than it was worth and he preferred cabs anyway.

"Thanks, Sal. As always."

"How long will you be in the city?"

"Well, a couple of months anyway I've got a lot of contracts to review."

"Ah, speaking of which, I've got a little deal I'd like you to look over for me if you've got the time."

"Sure, but you went to the same law school I did."

"And a second pair of eyes is always good. Besides, you're less impetuous and more objective than I am. You know what I got from law school? How to get information. That's the most valuable damn thing. I can find out anything I want. There's a knack to it, and law school helped." As Jimmy laughed, two girls the same age as his daughters paraded by with their mother, all three dolled up to the max. His face became reflective. Sal saw and understood. "Look, you're down. Your Florida visits always do this to you. Maybe you should stop going."

"I've got to go. They're my kids."

"You sure?" Sal winked. Jimmy chuckled. At one point, he'd wondered too and quietly checked it out. The medical evidence confirmed his paternity, even if he wasn't much of a father. He'd kept the results to himself. "You're not yourself when you come back from one of these." Sal continued. "Let it all go. You didn't do anything."

"That's part of the problem." Jimmy was reluctant to continue, but he felt a need to confess. "I don't know—Clair and the girls are so greedy and lazy they leave me feeling like a gutted trout. But how can I criticize them? I inherited The Old Man's fortune without doing shit. I didn't earn a cent of it."

"You can cut the sappy bullshit right now, Brother. Let me

tell you something. You need to get the Eagleson edge back starting immediately, now, and at this instant. Let all of this fucking Catholic guilt you're storing in your gut escape, right out through your asshole. Let me tell you something else. There's no earning it anymore, there's just getting it. That's the way it is."

Jimmy smiled and exhaled. Sal's counsel was why Jimmy had come, and he knew he needed to hear what Sal said.

The waiter returned with a fresh round and took the orders. Sal switched the tone of the conversation asking Jimmy about the gang and interjecting little jabs. He was particularly amused by Kate's new affair. As they ate, they turned the talk toward a few legal issues, funny stories about recent incidents, and a few new jokes. Jimmy told Sal about Gordon's package. Sal was also curious and asked to be kept in the loop if it turned out to be anything. The waiter knew to keep the rounds fresh. Jimmy felt elevated.

"How long you staying?" Sal asked.

"Not long, but let me see this thing you want me to look at."

"I was hoping you would say that. It's in my car."

"Perfect," Jimmy responded with new energy.

"Now tomorrow night, it's *Nasty's*," Sal said giving Jimmy a definitive nod and a broad smile that left no room for argument. *Nasty's* was a dive from way back that still seemed to fascinate Sal. Jimmy wasn't crazy about the place but knew they were going.

As they finished their drinks, Sal insisted the waiter give him the bill. Paying was a form of competition between the two friends and this time Jimmy would lose. Sal raised what was left of his drink, looked at Jimmy with another broad smile and loudly toasted. "Welcome back Eagleson, and chins up."

Jimmy clicked Sal's glass. "Chins up," he said.

* * *

Jimmy neatly rearranged the documents he'd been working on, placing them back in order, adding recommendations and slipping them in the leather folder Sal had provided. As he opened a beer, he noticed the time on the clock near the bed. Sal would be there soon. He was ready, although he had reservations about paying a visit to *Nasty's*. He and Sal'd had confrontations there, and he knew Sal did love being hit. But they hadn't been there in a long time, and they would probably just observe, take in the ambiance of a true dump, and find another bar to finish the night. Not likely much of a crowd would be there at this time of year anyway. Jimmy sank into an overstuffed chair and watched the fire. He knew seeing Sal would be therapeutic. He wasn't disappointed.

Sal arrived in jeans and a solid red flannel shirt. A worn peacoat and a toque finished off his local woodchuck disguise. Jimmy hadn't planned for an excursion like this. He dressed down as much as his road wardrobe would allow, but he would stand out.

"Nice shirt," Jimmy said as he greeted Sal at the door.

"It won't show the blood," Sal said and grinned.

"Come in, let's have a drink," Jimmy said, now really

wondering if this plan was a good idea. He handed Sal a Crown and a beer and opened another for himself.

"Your contracts are done. Suggestions are at the end. There are a few marks where you might change the wording. It would make the conditions a bit vague, all to your advantage. The phrasing isn't likely to be detected unless you're dealing with an ace. I also suggested a couple of additional clauses just for a little added protection. All in all, the thing looks good and tight to me."

Sal nodded as he took a sip of whiskey. "The only ace I deal with is you. Thanks for the help, especially so fast. Whatever you've suggested will be done." He had always admired Jimmy's ability to analyze legal situations like a chess master, preparing for a long series of strategic moves on both sides.

"I've got to tell you one thing," Jimmy said. "I'm not sure why you want this deal."

"I don't right now. Timing is everything in one of these things, and I figure sometime in the spring there'll be a fire sale on this property. I'll need to move in fast with a deal in hand. Then I'll make some real cash. You know the key to this shit is being there. I mean you've got to be 'right there.' You can't pull it off from a distance because you can't feel it. But a few weeks in New Mexico will be worth it."

As the two finished their drinks, Sal said, "*Nasty's* here we come."

Jimmy stood and clicked off the fire. His face showed his reservation. Sal chuckled, and the two exited to the parking lot. Sal had picked a black Escalade for the evening, the least conspicuous of his fleet. They hopped in and were off on their mini-adventure. The drive through the woods would take at least a half-hour.

"Why don't you reach into the cooler behind you and get us both a beer?" Sal said.

As Jimmy was complying Sal asked, "why Clair?"

"Where the hell did that come from?"

"No, I mean you knew a lot of girls. There were options. Then you meet Clair and all of a sudden she's the one. I know she was gorgeous, but so were some of the others. Why do you figure it was her?"

Jimmy popped open the beers and handed one to Sal while he prepared his response.

"Well, what first attracted me was her smile."

"I remember that smile."

"Yeah, hard to forget. But that wasn't it. This might seem strange, but I think it was her smell. I don't mean a perfume; I mean her natural scent. Maybe it was a pheromone thing— you're the doctor, you'd know more about that than me—but I loved the way she smelled. What brought this on anyway?"

"I was thinking about my two. I'm still trying to figure out why I got married, especially the second time after the first disaster. Smell, maybe you're onto something, although I can't remember ever being with a woman who didn't smell good."

"It's not only smelling good. There was something soothing, calming. Early on, I used to sniff her neck to relax. Later I wanted to choke it, but in the beginning, it was good." Jimmy sipped. "I don't know if she still has that scent or if it worked the same on her gigolos, but I think that's what got me."

"Smell?" Sal nodded and pondered.

The sparsely occupied parking lot at *Nasty's* was roughly plowed and poorly lit. Sal took a spot near one of the few working lights, next to a rusted old Ford pickup. The comrades gulped down what was left of their beer and headed into the ratty building. Furnished in early attic décor, the bar room sported several partially lit beer signs and a deer head wearing a New York Giants helmet. A pool table dominated the area near the entrance. Two patrons had strung out a handful of quarters establishing it as their turf for the evening. The room smelled from the pungent odor of an improperly vented wood stove. The bar area was dark and dirty, and the backs of three of the fifteen or so stools had been broken off. In the corner, an old jukebox with a cracked glass front played country songs. Behind the bar hung an old painting of naked trolls under a bridge having an orgy. Below the artwork a homemade sign read "*NASTY*." The bartender, dressed in typical woodsman's attire, had a baby face and looked like a big kid rather than the one in charge.

"Where's Johnny?" Sal asked.

"Sold da place two years baack." the kid responded looking the two strangers over. "Moved ta Floorda. Yuze guys want drinks?"

There it was again, the "North Country Twang," like at the diner the day before.

"Yeah," Sal said. "A double Crown and two Molson."

"No Molson, and what's a Crown?"

"What do you have?" Sal asked.

"It's all der," the kid said as he pointed to a shelf with a row of bottles and a short string of empty cans.

"All right give me a double Seagram's 7 and two Buds."

The kid left without comment.

"You sure you want to stay?" Jimmy asked.

"You bet—where else can we get all of this for the same price of admission?"

The kid returned and handed Sal a disposable plastic cup of whiskey and two unopened cans of Budweiser. Sal and Jimmy took two stools—with backs—at the far end of the bar, and turned to absorb the ambiance.

A handful of drinkers was scattered throughout the bar. One pair sprawled out at a table near the door with their feet extended as far into the room as their anatomy would allow. They both slurred their already challenged speech as they loudly told tales and laughed. A few others sat at the bar. Each threw occasional stares at the two intruders, sometimes shaking their heads or commenting and snickering.

The pool players provided the main attraction. One was a large muscular man with five days of stubble who would have resembled a well-built lumberjack if not for his beer-belly. The other was skinny, mouthy and had the face of a large rodent. He wore a jean jacket without sleeves over a black t-shirt showing off the carnival-quality tattoos on his arms. On the back of his homemade colors was a badly embroidered face of a wolf with the name Cricker stitched below. On his left arm, a barely recognizable rendition of Yosemite Sam pointed two purple six-shooters. On the right, the cartoon demon Hot Stuff held a pitchfork and stared with goggled eyes.

The pool players had left a long string of empty beer cans on a nearby table and were beyond their best game. As the underweight Cricker continued to drink, his play got worse and his mouth bigger. The larger competitor controlled the show, although Cricker snapped back from time to time with smart comments insufficient to start a fight, but near the line. The big man bent over the table to shoot, exposing ample plumber's crack and yellowed month-old underwear.

"Shit!" The lumberjack yelled after missing his shot. Cricker snickered, unveiling his six remaining teeth. "You shut yuze fuckin' mouth, you, if yuze don't want dis stick up daat scrawny, cheewee ass." Cricker, still smirking, took the pool cue and prepared to take his shot.

As the game continued, a few new arrivals added to the woodsy crew, and the drunks near the door left.

"You having fun yet?" Jimmy asked.

"Oh this is going to be good," Sal said. "We have all the elements for a real event right here in front of us."

"That's what I'm afraid of."

"Tell you what. If this opportunity doesn't reach its potential by the time we finish another round, we're out of here."

Screeching and fishtailing from the old pickup Sal had parked next to interrupted the conversation.

"How can you be in such a hurry to leave a show like this?" Sal said.

Jimmy grimaced and nodded.

Jimmy ventured to the other end of the bar, politely fetched another round, and returned to his box seat. As he sat, a new couple made a dramatic entrance. He was of medium build, wearing a Carhartt jacket. A thick mustache, glazed eyes and a long, deep scar on the left side of his face added up to suggest a genuine tough guy. The woman was an overly made-up bottle blonde wearing a tasseled Western-style leather coat. A tattoo of a snake twisted around her thigh. The head was suggestively hidden high on the inside under the hem of her short jean skirt. As she shed her jacket, she proudly displayed her large breasts, nearly spilling out of a tight tank top.

The lumberjack had been struggling to focus on a shot and only caught a glimpse of the arrivals. Once he turned, his eyes fixed on the woman's chest. Her escort seemed used to the attention she drew but was still agitated by the big man, who continuing to ogle, had yet to recognize she was not alone. Almost instinctively and with typical woodsman's charm the lumberjack loudly declared, "Look Da Tits On Daat!"

"That's my wife, dickhead!" The new guy said.

"Too baad, daat's too hot ta be givin' it ta a little fucknut like yuze."

Sal sat forward watching with a big grin, rapidly tapping his foot. He turned to Jimmy. "Here we go, Molly bar the door."

The kid bartender yelled at the impending combatants. "Yuze knock daat shit off. I don't want no trouble from yuze two!"

The men ignored him and squared off. The kid grabbed the phone, and the jukebox started playing "The Boot Scootin' Boogie." The newcomer took a defensive posture while the lumberjack turned the pool cue fat-end-up and grinned. The crowd moved away. A few cautiously left the building. The pool player stood still as if waiting for his opponent to concede. Sal looked at Jimmy. "This is perfect."

"Swing the fucking thing you fat fuck," his challenger

demanded without a hint of fear. The big man became enraged and swung; his target strategically turned, grabbed the cue and slammed it into his adversary's back driving him onto the pool table.

As the lumberjack stood, turned and tried to seize his assailant, the blonde jumped on his back, slapping his head and yelling, "Leave Him Alone you fuckin', fuck-faced, fucker!"

Her attempt to help neutralized her husband's advantage and a wild punch from the big man caught him firmly in the shoulder. As she rode, the lumberjack swung her around, twisting her in a half-circle. Now back to back, one cup of her overstuffed bra worked out of her shirt and her legs opened wide fully exposing her tiny thong and ending any mystery about the snake's destination.

Finally shaken off, she lay on the floor as her husband regained his edge, maneuvered the cue between the lumberjack's legs, slammed upward into his groin and brought him to his knees screaming in pain. Watching from the other side of the table, Cricker started to move toward the action.

"Sit down and leave it alone," Sal said.

"Who da fuck yuze think yuze is talkin' to?"

"A stupid little fuck with cartoons on his arms."

Cricker came at Sal taking a wild swing. Sal spun him, placed his foot on his rear and sent him into the pool table.

"Yuze knock daat shit off—da cops is comin', and dis is all yuze's fault," shouted the bartender as he pointed at Sal and Jimmy.

Cricker turned from the table, stared at Sal, and pulled a hunting knife from a concealed sheath sewn into his jacket.

Jimmy stayed in his seat, this is what Sal had come for, and he knew not to interfere. As Sal took a stance, Cricker ran toward him swinging and stabbing into the air. Sal seized a chance to grab Cricker's hand, squeezed like a vice and the knife dropped to the floor.

Two state police cars rushed into the parking lot with sirens screeching and lights flashing. Sal, now raging, turned the little pool player and landed a powerful punch to his rat-like face. Again Cricker was sent to the pool table. He lay still a moment as blood from his split lip added to the felt's stain collection, then struggled to raise his head, opened his mouth to grab a breath and revealed his tooth count was down to five.

A sergeant and three troopers rushed into the bar. The blonde and her husband managed to slip out when the fight changed opponents, but one trooper quickly moved to retain the lumberjack sitting in a chair holding his testicles and moaning. Two others headed for the bar area. The sergeant was questioning the bartender when one of his men tried to move Cricker from the pool table, causing another wild swing and another trip to the felt. As Cricker was being cuffed, the third officer approached Sal, who sipped the last of his whiskey.

"Not him!" the sergeant yelled. The bartender shook his head in protest as the sergeant calmly explained. Once finished, the sergeant left the still peeved kid and walked to the other end of the bar.

"Are you all right, Mr. Esposito?"

"I'm fine, Sergeant," Sal answered.

"I'm surprised to see you here."

"I'm not here often."

The sergeant nodded. "Whose knife?"

"Shit for brains here." Sal gestured toward Cricker.

"Well, it's probably a good idea to leave," the sergeant suggested.

"Yeah—no problem."

Jimmy and Sal put their coats on and took one last look around as they strolled out. Sal reached into his pocket and held out two small Cuban cigars.

"Smoke?"

"Yeah," Jimmy said, thinking three in less than a week might be a new record. "The knife was a nice touch."

"Yeah—I didn't see that coming." Sal lit Jimmy's cigar.

"What's the story with the cop?"

"You remember Jake Flanagan?"

"Sure." Jimmy remembered Jake from several outings years ago and knew he still worked for Sal from time to time.

"That's his son. I made a few calls and helped him get into the academy years ago."

Jimmy chuckled. Never underestimate the magic of Salvatore Esposito.

Approaching the Escalade, Jimmy noticed something on the rear door. "What's on the car?" he asked. Scratched into the paint was a message reading FUCK YOU FROM SANTA.

"You want me to get one of the cops, Sal?"

"No, fuck it, I'll take care of it tomorrow, it's chicken shit."

After taking a long drag on his cigar, Sal smiled at Jimmy. "Say, shouldn't that holiday greeting be on *your* car?"

As the two laughed and smoked, two officers came from the bar escorting Cricker to the caged back seat of their cruiser.

"Fuck yuze two cocksuckers!" Cricker yelled.

"Shut up Cricker," one trooper said as he stuffed Cricker into the car. "You've got no idea who you're messing with, and you're already in enough trouble with us."

"Everyone is full of cheer tonight," Sal said as he and Jimmy threw their cigar butts into the snow and hopped into Sal's festively graffitied SUV.

The road was abandoned, and the tall evergreens blocked what little light the moon could push through the clouds. Still, Sal plowed along at a good clip.

"Enjoy the show?" Jimmy asked.

"Yeah—it was pretty good, somewhere short of perfect, but good."

"What could have been better?" Jimmy asked surprised.

"I could have been hit."

Jimmy grinned and shook his head. "How's your hand?"

"OK—the bones feel sprained, but it's OK."

"Well, at least that's something."

"Yeah, good point Eagleson, at least that's something. You going down tomorrow?"

"Yeah, I've got an early afternoon train."

"I'll send a driver."

"I can hire a ride."

"I'll send a driver," Sal repeated.

"When are you coming down?"

"Don't know. Got to go back to Phoenix next week and I don't know for how long. But, I'll see you the next time you're in the area or if I wind up in the city for some reason."

"I'm looking forward to it," Jimmy said.

"OK, now on to a less entertaining establishment. This time, you choose." Jimmy picked a small place near the hotel with a full selection of booze and good bar food.

"Excellent choice," Sal said.

The two drove without speaking awhile. Sal broke the silence. "Smell."

"Yeah, smell," Jimmy confirmed.

Sal nodded. "Smell—I'll have to think about that."

* * *

Tommy Toro staggered to the bar, plopped down on a stool, and ordered a beer. He stared with glazed eyes at the stranger standing next to him looking around the room and jotting in a notebook. "What's up?" Tommy asked.

"Remodeling," the stranger said.

"Shit, I like this old joint the way it is. Why they gotta dick around with it?"

"New owner. He wants a new look to bring in the college crowd. Too bad, the place has done OK just like it is for a lot of years. Trendy changes like he's planning almost always backfire. But I'll give him what he wants and move on."

"You some kind of designer?"

"Yeah, I'll make some sketches and drawings then, send them back here to a contractor and in a few days you won't recognize this place."

"Shit," Tommy took out a pack of cigarettes, slapped the

open end against his hand until one poked out and wrapped his lips around its filter.

"Won't be doing that much longer."

"What?"

"Smoking inside. New law goes into effect in New York City in the spring. Just a matter of time before the whole state follows."

"Shit. You from The City?"

"No, Jersey, but I do a lot of work there."

Tommy reached into his pocket, pulled out a silver lighter with a large crest, and lit his cigarette. He snickered as held The Old Man's lighter in front of his face. "Fuck you, Eagleson, treat me like a hunk of shit," he mumbled.

"Nice piece," the stranger said. "May I take a look?" Tommy handed him the lighter. "Yeah, solid sterling with a custom crest—looks like World War Two vintage."

The stranger put on his glasses and looked more carefully. "Oh yes, definitely World War Two and beautiful workman-ship. Interesting design, definitely one-of-a-kind. They used to make them this way to commemorate something important and to identify the owner. Where did you get it?"

Tommy snatched it back. "Off a guy I know. You seem to know a lot about this kind of shit."

"Oh, that one's not shit. But yeah, my father was a jeweler. He made things like that for special events. The crests are like signatures, each one's unique. I'm surprised your friend gave it up."

"Didn't say he was a friend and he didn't give up shit. He owed me. Probably found it in some junk shop anyway."

The stranger's brows lowered and he smiled. "Maybe, but, as I said, it's one-of-a-kind and whoever owned it would always know it was theirs if they saw it." The stranger returned to his business while Tommy nervously hid the lighter and thought a moment.

"How much you think it's worth?" Tommy asked.

"Is it hot?"

"Fuck no, I told you. The guy owed me."

"Well as someone's personal lighter it's probably worth a lot. But if, as you say, it came from 'some junk shop' maybe thirty or forty bucks. Solely for the silver content mind you."

"Want to buy it?"

The stranger smirked and looked up. "How much?"

"A hundred bucks."

The stranger shook his head. "You're dreaming."

"OK seventy-five, it's gotta be worth that."

The stranger looked into Tommy's glassy eyes. "I'll give you fifty. I leave for New York in the morning. You never know who might recognize something like that in a small town like Plattsburgh. But in The City ... In Jersey ...?" The stranger smiled and shrugged. Tommy nodded, and the stranger took fifty dollars from his wallet. Tommy held The Old Man's lighter in front of his face, flicked it several times, and handed it over. He took the cash, smiled, and looked into his beer. "Yeah, fuck you, Eagleson," he said.

CHAPTER IV

A Walk in the Park

Late in the morning, a black Lexus arrived at Jimmy's suite. Two large young men introduced themselves, being sure to address Jimmy as Mr. Eagleson. Then one loaded Jimmy's bags into the trunk while the other helped Jimmy clear a few things from the Lincoln's back seat. The ride to the station went quickly, and the train was on schedule. Jimmy had little time to wait. Once boarded and settled into his first-class seat, he ordered a beer. He usually enjoyed this trip because of the view. Today was foggy and grim. But there were few passengers, and the train would at least be quiet.

He felt energized from his visit with Sal and the anticipation of New York City and looked forward to seeing his New York buddies. For the rest of the weekend, he would settle in at his place, relax, listen to music, go for drinks with friends, maybe even go for a swim at his health club, and then ready himself to return to the office. He enjoyed his work—once he re-acclimated—and liked many of his colleagues. Except for one, Gyges, Barry Gyges. Gyges was the "king of the show" and made the salesman in the Tampa airport look like a rank amateur. Gyges could get under Jimmy's skin in a way no one else ever had. He was slick and advanced his private agenda with every move. He had grown beyond the typical loud, intimidating technique, learning a quiet, covert approach worked better. He'd developed the ability to charm the wits from a man and the pants from a lady—for a while at least. He carefully chose his every maneuver to maximize his own gain while making others, whom he cared less about, feel they were the center of his universe. He was a complete narcissist, and dangerous.

For Jimmy, the real topper was that Gyges was no good at anything else. He was all façade. In several business deals, he had developed plans that looked reasonable on the surface but then revealed sloppy preparation and critical mistakes. Still, Mike, the boss, had a soft spot for him, and Gyges continued to advance.

Jimmy recalled an instance when Gyges handled researching the sale of a series of convenience stores in northern Pennsylvania. His conclusions included a selling price that would net the company more than three million dollars for a relatively simple transaction. Mike asked Jimmy to review the plan. Through a "non-conventional investigation" Jimmy discovered the owner's wife was romantically involved with her husband's largest competitor, the only other bidder. The two had arranged to submit a phony offer that drove the final price up by more than twenty million. When the dust settled, potential legal actions forced the withdrawal of their bid. The business was acquired for much less than it was worth, and Jimmy's company's profit tripled. In the aftermath, the devoted wife still left her husband responsible for plenty of alimony. Jimmy saw the case as another great American love story, although he thought it might have been a fitting end for a couple that built their fortune selling cigarettes to kids and lottery tickets to basket cases. Still, in the end, Gyges was able to divert all criticism of his work and got the lion's share of the credit. As infuriating as he could be, Jimmy also had to snicker. Gyges was what he was, and aware or not he was paying for that every day of his life.

While Jimmy didn't have to work, he enjoyed some of the projects his New York company became involved in. It wasn't a traditional firm like in Miami. He'd done well in Florida and made partner in record time, but when he split with Clair, he wanted out of Florida. When he met Mike at a conference, Mike extended an offer that Jimmy decided to take. In New York, he worked side by side with CPAs, MBAs, and others at all levels. He wasn't surrounded only by tireless, high testosterone attorneys.

Jimmy respected and liked Mike. As the first African American in the company, Mike felt a need to prove his worth beyond others and had succeeded. And he understood Jimmy, always giving him extraordinary flexibility both in time and work style. Besides, he liked New York and had a core of friends there too, although not as close as those in the North Country.

After nearly an hour of traveling, Jimmy decided to use the time and quiet to get a jump on his preparations for Monday. Having several contracts to review he placed his briefcase on the empty seat beside him and popped it opened, expecting to see his always methodically ordered documents. His eyes widened. On top of his work sat the package from Gordon. Jimmy had nearly blocked the mystery from his mind on the short excursion with Sal. Now there it was and almost as much a surprise as before. His curiosity raced back. Jimmy re-read the message on the letter and with a couple of hours to kill decided it was a good time to begin his investigation. He carefully slit the top of the smaller envelope and removed the letter inside, and started reading.

Dear Jimmy,

I hope this letter finds you in good health. Let me jump right into what I have to tell you. When my mum died and I came back east to take care of the arrangements, I took a couple of weeks to go through her things and get the property ready for sale. In an old trunk, I found the letters I've sent. I'm quite sure they were never meant for either of us to see. Mum once told me how your dad would write to mine during the war and tell him things that couldn't be said to anyone else. I had assumed she had destroyed the letters, as she said your dad had requested. I always knew how close our fathers were. But, I didn't really know much about your dad until I read these. I must admit I fought with the idea of destroying them myself. But with some guilt, I read them anyway.

I know you remember how much I took to your dad

when we were kids. But I don't think you know all he did for us. After my pop passed, we had very little money and your dad became our guardian angel. I'm sure you never knew he paid for my college and supported me so I wouldn't have to work while I was studying. University wasn't easy for me, and without his help I don't think I would have finished. Once I got the job here in B.C., I was able to take over for the family. But I know that even after, he continued to send money to Mum, despite her protests. When I read his letters, I began to understand what it took to make such a great guy.

It's hard for me to explain how looking into the past affected me. It wasn't all good. In fact, at first it was disturbing. But after it settled in, I was glad for the insight. I struggled with the idea of sending these to you. I often felt there was distance between you and your dad and wondered if I should just let things be. But now I think you should have them. I can't tell you if you should read them or not, but I can say I am glad I did. If you do, I would suggest it be at a time and place where you won't be disturbed. I think you will find some of this hard to deal with.

I'm sorry to be so remiss in visiting. I miss you and the lake very much. Things here are quite good despite the fallout from 9/11, and I have been very busy. I was promoted again last year and have built a new house for Meg and the kids. As you know, I could live in a shoebox, but I must admit I enjoy making the family comfortable and happy. I pledge I will be visiting soon. I believe I can take time this spring and will contact you when I have specifics. Maybe we could fish if you still enjoy it. But whatever we do it will be great to be with you again, drinking plenty of good beer. My one concern right now is I may be placing an undue burden on you. I hope that's not the case, but if so, I know you will understand my intentions. You're the closest I ever had to a brother and you know my true concern and respect for you. Until the spring, take care of yourself.

With sincerest affection,

Gord

Jimmy sat back. He always knew about The Old Man's generosity, but what Gordon said was news. He often wondered why there had been such a lack of openness. Jimmy realized The Old Man had in his own way had tried to show love. But they seldom talked about anything personal. Jimmy remembered one time in high school when a friend's father died suddenly. His buddy was devastated that he had never told his dad he loved him. Jimmy made sure this didn't happen to him. At what he felt was an appropriate moment he awkwardly blurted it out. The Old Man turned, gave him a forlorn stare and said, "Jimmy, I don't go for that stuff."

Now, here were letters he'd been told to prepare himself for. Letters whose effect on Jimmy worried his cousin. Letters that warranted a warning. This was a whole new dimension.

It didn't seem possible the stoic and distant Gerret Eagleson could be the source of such drama.

Jimmy thought more about his relationship with The Old Man. He remembered a time when he came home and found him on the porch drinking beer with Stosh. Jimmy felt jealous. After all, The Old Man had never done such a thing with his own son. Jimmy wrote it off as a fluke. But at other times with other friends, he remembered the same feeling of being on the outside of something. Jimmy had written them all off in due order. He felt he had come to a passable understanding of The Old Man's nature and had processed his death relatively well. Now, here was something new, complete with a disclaimer. He took a sip from his beer, looked at his ring and rubbed the crest with his thumb. One thing he knew for sure; now was not the time to start reading this.

* * *

The train arrived on time at Penn Station. Jimmy gathered his bags and made his way to Seventh Avenue. Once outside the station, he could feel the concrete vibrate with the energy of New York. It was getting dark, and the lights were beginning to pop on, signaling the start of evening action. Jimmy had experienced many cities, but there was nothing like the instant electricity and excitement of Manhattan. He flagged a taxi, gave the cabbie instructions to his place in SoHo and thought back. Jimmy had just started high school when The Old Man bought the property in the sixties. Much of the area was slated for demolition. A preservationist movement led to massive reconstruction, and he made a lot of money as the HVAC supplier for many buildings. When the unit became available, he quickly invested. He always liked New York, saying it reminded him of London, and Jimmy's mother enjoyed Broadway a great deal.

They frequently visited when they first got the place, then less often, and then so infrequently they rented it and used hotels for their visits. Jimmy moved in when he accepted the job in New York. It wasn't Camp, but it felt like a home and had plenty of space. Twenty-five-hundred square feet with three bedrooms and baths in New York was a mansion.

Jimmy hopped out at his street, took a deep breath, paid the driver and made his way up the stairs. Inside he detected the smell of recent cleaning. Everything was in order and prepared for his return. The large living room was adjacent to an open kitchen separated only by a granite-topped bar. Jimmy opened the refrigerator to find the small list of groceries and beer, always freshly stocked before he returned. He looked on the counter. A jumbo sized package of Nutter Butters lay there with a note that read "Welcome back."

He opened a beer and looked around. Kate's influence was pronounced. Jimmy asked her to set things up, and she managed to create a decor modern enough for New York and rustic enough for Jimmy. It had leather sofas, bookcases, plenty of tables, rocking chairs and recliners. Large Adirondack paintings and photographs substituted for the picture windows at Camp. A small but efficient study was isolated in one corner with an oversized desk equipped with a computer monitor and keyboard that waited patiently to be reconnected to his laptop. The desk was accompanied by low, matching file cabinets with extended tops that provided two hundred and seventy degrees of functional work surface. Above the desk hung a message board. The space was neat and orderly as it had been left, with a few papers arranged on the surface to the desk's right.

At the living area's far end, a hallway led to the bedrooms, baths, and a large storage closet. A half bath was tucked into a corner near the kitchen area. The front room had four large, tall windows with full drapes and beautiful exterior encasement that proudly displayed the neo-classical architecture of their day.

Jimmy took his bag to his room, carefully unpacked, and then moved to his study to relocate some papers from his briefcase. He unlocked his files and opened the case. On top lay the letters from Gordon. He thought of reading a few, but this still wasn't the time. Once put away he also knew the danger of ignoring, avoiding or even forgetting about them. He took an index card from the drawer, wrote a note to himself, pinned it on the board and placed the package in the file immediately to his right. Jimmy looked at his watch and saw he still had time to catch the guys at *Doc's Pub*, the establishment preferred by most of his friends. He grabbed his coat, took a look around to see if he'd forgotten anything and left to get a cab.

* * *

Doc's was a classic New York tavern with a long bar supplemented with high top tables covering every available inch. The room was authorized for one hundred and five occupants but would house twice that several nights a week. Jimmy spotted two of his buddies at the end of the bar. The pub was in between its early and late crowds with a mixture of weekending businessmen and young singles looking to hook up.

Jimmy made his way to his friends who grabbed a barstool for him. Tony and Art were regulars, and Jimmy liked them both. Tony was a hardcore conservative Republican, who supported Bush like a Nazi supporting Hitler. Art was his opposite: a liberal Democrat, who criticized everything the administration did. Their political differences had provided many entertaining battles in the past few years. And yet the two were inseparable best friends.

"Hey Jimmy, welcome back," Tony said.

"Thanks, Tony. It's good to be back. Hi Art," Jimmy said as he shook hands with each comrade. "Anything going on?"

"Not much, just coming out of the holidays and getting back to the routine," Art answered. He and Tony both worked near Jimmy's office for a firm specializing in medical litigation. Thanks to national advertising, most of their cases were straightforward, matter-of-course deals that bored both of them. But it was lucrative.

"Where's the tan?" Tony asked. "You're not supposed to come back from Florida without a tan."

"Yeah, I left it at the airport you know, new regulations. You can't take one on a plane anymore."

Tony's face contorted a little, as Jimmy expected. "Now let's not try to get us going," Tony said with a smile. "It's been a nice quiet night."

Jimmy took the stool reserved in his honor, ordered a beer and a round of drinks for his friends, and nodded a greeting to the very busy bartender, Gail. She winked back as she scrambled to fill the order, then flew over to Jimmy and hurriedly placed the drinks on bar napkins while injecting, "Welcome back, Darling." By the time Jimmy could respond, she was at the other end of the bar taking a large order from a second-waver.

Gail had a romantic connection with Jimmy a few years before. It faded quickly and simultaneously for each of them, leaving the two as good friends. She was still protective of him and would need to learn the details of his trip when she had time to talk.

In the seconds he'd turned away from his companions, a flying political spark had ignited a floor show. Jimmy turned to listen to Art and Tony arguing.

"He's an idiot. He doesn't know his left nut from a kumquat. Cheney is pulling the strings, and you know full well it's all about oil."

"He's our commander-in-chief, Art. He was tossed into a shitty situation by a bunch of fanatical religious lunatics, and he's done an excellent job with it. Come on, the fucking guy is a Yale grad, like you, and you act like he's a moron."

"He is a moron! And I haven't sent my distinguished alma mater a cent since I found out they sold Bush number one a degree for his baby boy, number two; and I do mean number two. And let me tell you something else: Afghanistan isn't all; he's going to try to finish up for his old man in Iraq. We'll be in a full-fledged shooting war with Saddam before we know it. We're headed right back to Vietnam. And the bonehead has already spent every cent of the surplus Clinton left. The first time in forever this country had a surplus, and it's gone in less than three years. Hell, even my wife can't spend that fast."

Jimmy had to chuckle. Obviously, Art had never met Clair.

"Tax incentives and rebates, that's where the money was spent, and it worked, or have you forgotten the shape this economy was in. And, what do you think would have happened if your tree hugging buddy Gore had been elected. He'd have spent it all on seals and birds."

"HE WAS ELECTED! Have you forgotten how your boy and his brother rigged Florida? And, he'd have done a hell of a lot better than the shithead you voted for. Let's face it, Tony; you guys elected Alfred E. Newman president. He's the biggest embarrassment this country has ever had."

"Embarrassment my ass; he's an excellent president and he's on the right track. The economy is coming back, and we finally have accountability."

"His administration is about as accountable as a fart in a mitten. Accountability? That's the biggest joke yet. You know that dumbass—"

Jimmy hated to leave the discussion just when it was picking up steam, but he needed to visit the men's room. He walked through the noisy bar to the opposite side. As he closed the outer door, the sound level decreased to nearly quiet. He took a stall for a private piss as two young members of the late crowd came in bantering about their hopes for the evening.

"I think I've got a good shot at Kerry tonight. She's been rubbing on my shoulder."

"She's definitely on my 'to do' list. Go for it. Jack says she's great."

"Yeah, guess it's time to find out."

As they moved to the sinks, Jimmy couldn't help continuing to eavesdrop, finding the young performers of the never-ending ritual amusing.

"Aren't you going to wash your hands?"

"What are you, my mother? I'll get to it although I don't understand why we bother. I mean what did I just do? I took a leak, right? Now either I got piss on my hands, or I didn't, right? Now if I did, piss is sterile, isn't it? And if I didn't, then I'm washing my hands because I just touched what I hope will be in Kerry's mouth later tonight."

The two broke into laughter, and Jimmy had to snicker too, more at the would-be player's rank bravado than their wit. And after all, these guys were part of the next wave of America's leaders. Jimmy shook his head at the thought of them being in charge. But, then again, how much worse could they do?

Jimmy returned to the bar to find the conversation had changed to next year's Giants team, a topic Tony and Art totally agreed on. In a matter of minutes, their demeanor had changed from contentious to agreeable, but Jimmy had seen this before and wasn't surprised. The three chatted as they consumed a couple more rounds. Then they decided it was time to concede the premises to the young invaders. For Jimmy, it was time to get some rest. Tomorrow was Sunday in New York.

* * *

Jimmy opened the drapes and filled the large living space with the bright natural light of early morning. *The Times* had been delivered, and the coffee was ready. He would read awhile in his favorite New York rocker and then make breakfast. He didn't cook much, except on Sunday mornings. Today he thought he'd like an omelet, but not until he was really hungry.

After sailing through the paper, he fried his breakfast and slowly savored his personally prepared dish. Then he cleaned up and was ready to take on the city. Most Sunday mornings he'd visit his health club and swim, but not today. Jimmy loved to walk in New York, and the apartment was close enough to work, and *Doc's*, that he could hoof it when he wanted to, and today, he wanted to. He left his apartment and felt the wind blowing between the buildings. A city winter couldn't compare to the North Country, but it still had a bite that could make a walker shiver. He headed to Battery Park.

As he walked south on Broadway, he watched the other Sunday morningers. The New Yorkers clearly stood out as some jogged, some lingered about, and some purposefully made their way about. All had the same confidence and mastery of the streets that set them apart from the sightseers who walked with their heads toward the sky, read maps, and blocked the unofficial egresses known to all residents. The sky was still clear as he marched by City Hall Park. He had entered the zone. No matter how many times he walked this way since 9/11, the aura always set in. He wouldn't fight it this time and diverted down Vesey Street to the site.

The demolition area was partially populated by hawkers, disrespectful adolescents, and curious tourists. An occasional panhandler and a few possible pickpockets rounded out the unavoidable negatives a popular location drew. Still, there were always plenty of sincere mourners and patriots with respect for the site's profound meaning. After a brief stop at ground level, he moved up to the observation deck.

Jimmy gazed at Ground Zero. Crews were still removing the rubble twenty-four-seven. Even with the sounds of heavy machinery and chatter from other spectators, he experienced the same somberness that came with every visit. Jimmy lost many friends that morning. Most people in New York who worked in his business had been housed here. At one point, his company had plans to relocate into the north tower. But Mike put a stop to it, arguing a move for the sake of appearances would be a mistake. How right he had been. He thought of Julie, a girl he had met a few weeks before the attack. They had planned their first real date for the evening of 9/13. He'd had high hopes for their relationship and was haunted for some time by thoughts of how she had jumped from a window like so many others.

He thought of Bush's swift retribution. But, unlike Desert

Storm, the surgical precision of modern warfare wasn't well suited to Afghanistan. The often indiscriminate bombing bothered a few; others were ambivalent, and many cheered. The media found it impossible to present the conflict as more than an abstraction. They tried to focus on real people, on actual soldiers, civilians, and enemy insurgents. But to the public, their coverage seemed like an ongoing action adventure. Rumsfeld contributed to the confusion by dropping tons of bombs immediately followed by planeloads of "TV dinners" for the innocent bystanders who were "too stupid" to get out of the way. "Bomb and feed"— what a concept. Twenty-nine obsessed religious fanatics had pulled off a criminal and cowardly act of such magnitude they destroyed a confidence in America's security enjoyed for nearly two centuries. The Fourth Amendment would never be the same.

Jimmy remembered how people treated each other right after the attack. The disaster pulled them together in a common cause. Thousands who had never owned an American flag before proudly flew one. Even with the arguments that followed, an overwhelming sense of patriotism permeated the country. For a short while, it looked like the business world was entering a somber period of re-evaluation. But, soon everyone went back to selling each other lunch, trinkets, and stocks for things that don't exist. American capitalism was recovering, with new and better ways to rebuild the *caveat emptor* foundation for a system based on big profits for a select few. But then, Jimmy knew all of this well. This was his profession, and he was damned good at it.

He looked with concern at five men and three women in

impeccable military uniforms. Unlike in airports, they were real to him here, and he feared for their safety. Jimmy had never served, missing the Vietnam War with a favorable draft number. But he had always appreciated and respected those who did. Some of these kids might die, and in most people's minds "that would be that." He redirected his view, and after a few more moments of staring blankly at the ongoing demolition, he looked up. It was time to leave the contemplation to others and finish his walk to the park.

Lower Manhattan was bright and chilly with few visitors, and Jimmy relished the privacy as he walked along the park's paths. He always enjoyed this area. Even in winter, it had a sense of order and space. He sat on a bench looking out toward Ellis Island. He thought about how many immigrants came here with nothing and managed to make decent lives, and wondered how it could be done now, with corporate America exporting most entry-level jobs. But, many still came and found a way.

He left the park, walked through the financial district, then up past a now bustling Chinatown and Little Italy. The ethnic neighborhoods were common Sunday destinations for visitors, and Jimmy liked watching them adventurously explore. He walked a bit farther and then checked his watch. It was well past noon, and *Doc's* would be open. Jimmy smiled; with a mere change of direction, he would be headed to his favorite New York retreat.

The bar was nearly empty at this time of day, and the thick cigarette smoke of a busy night was noticeably absent. Jimmy was pleased to see Gail behind the bar. She often worked through the weekend, preferring to keep a few weekdays in a row for herself. She'd moved to New York ten years before, from Chicago, and had never picked up the city's accent. This gave her a kind of exotic appeal to the natives and transplants as well, and she was very popular. She rarely dated a patron and never without getting to know him first. She had enjoyed the time with Jimmy and still liked to be the woman on his arm for the right occasion. But they both felt far more platonic than amorous now. She smiled broadly when she saw Jimmy. He strategically chose a stool to minimize her distance from the other customers.

"How are things?" he asked as he sat.

"Just ducky, and with you?" Gail answered as she instinctively fetched a Molson from a nearby cooler.

"Good. Back to work in the morning."

"You vacationed out?" she asked with a pinch of sarcasm as she poured the beer into a short, cold glass.

"Yeah, you could say that. How were the holidays?"

"Good, twice as good as last year. Looks like things are coming back; people were out a lot and tipping well. Good thing, last year was a little rough. But the juice is flowing again now, best I can tell." Gail read the world from the eyes of a New York bartender. No more accurate report was available as far as Jimmy was concerned.

"How's the bitch?" she said.

"Same."

Gail knew to let that subject go and changed direction.

"I'm glad you're back. Your posse isn't the same without their leader. You back a while or has Mike got you traveling?"

"I'll be right here, as far as I know."

"Good. I went by your place on Wednesday; put some eggs and the other stuff in your fridge. I hope they're OK. Everything looked good to me; that service you use is good."

"Thanks, I had eggs this morning. They were fine. I appreciate your taking care of that."

"Say, how's your friend Kate?"

"She's fine. She might be coming down in the spring."

"Good. I like her; I think she's one of the good ones. You know you two should—"

"Coming down with her boyfriend," Jimmy said.

Gail smiled and nodded. "Well, I hope you will all be spending plenty of time here when they're in town. I like talking with her."

Gail's sharp eye detected an almost empty drink nearby; she nodded to Jimmy and attended to the refill.

Doc's was set up with a rear service area offering a limited pub menu, only before eight, and only from one designated counter. Jimmy went back to order fish and chips. When he returned, a fresh beer was waiting, and Gail was ready to continue their talk.

Jimmy liked to hang with Gail here when it wasn't crowded and decided to plant himself for a few hours. Gail picked at his fries as she brought him up to speed on his friends' recent activities. The TV was tuned to a football game, and the other patrons were relaxed and content. Except an occasional outburst to a play, it was quiet. It would be a pleasant afternoon. Jimmy was pleased. Later he would return to his place and focus on the next day's tasks. For now, *Doc's* was perfect.

* * *

Jimmy rose at seven, ready to take on the day. He cleaned up, made coffee, and quickly scanned the morning papers. The weather was reasonable so he walked to one of his favorite breakfast places.

Monday morning in New York is the opposite of Sunday. The streets are crowded with business people rushing about without concern for courtesy on their way to their cubicles. At this time of day, everyone in New York is the most important person in New York.

After a hurried breakfast, Jimmy skillfully negotiated his way to his building. The guard in the vestibule welcomed him back and cleared his passage to the elevator. The company occupied much of the complex with offices on several floors; Jimmy's group was on the top. As he entered, he was pelted with greetings from all areas of the busy open workspace. He acknowledged everyone and entered his territory, a corner office with a view. On his desk sat two new folders, each bulging with papers and stamped urgent. His contracts in process would have to wait. A note from Mike asked him to call as soon as he was in. Jimmy decided to get coffee before beginning the new games.

He felt a hand on his back as he poured a cup. He turned to see Annie Young. Short and stocky, she had been with the company longer than Jimmy but was skittish and much less aggressive. She frequently fretted about possible disasters from legal loopholes she might overlook and be blamed for. This made her sheepish for someone in this kind of work. Although she was marginal, Jimmy liked her. After 9/11, the company had to downsize and let her go. Jimmy pulled in a chit from Mike, and she was reinstated. She knew Jimmy had gone to bat for her but not how difficult the argument had been. She convinced herself he had merely pointed out she was invaluable, and her release would be disastrous.

"Good to see you—talk to Mike yet?" Annie asked in a squeaky, nasal voice.

"As soon as I have a little more coffee."

"Well, he was asking for you earlier. You know how he can be."

Jimmy grinned. Mike's bulldog approach on her and most others didn't apply to him.

As he turned, Jimmy was confronted with his unavoidable irritation. Fresh from the cover of *GQ*, Barry Gyges sauntered in. At medium height but with handsome features, Gyges looked like a Ken doll, groomed to perfection in the finest, fitted clothes. For many, his appearance masked his minimal ability. But for Jimmy, Gyges's number was clear.

Gyges gave Jimmy the smirk, a smile and sneer combination that simultaneously conveyed caution and contempt. This was Gyges's special face, for Jimmy alone. Gyges was smart enough to realize he hadn't the wit for verbal jousts with Jimmy. He was also far too afraid to risk direct confrontations. But, he knew how much the smirk got under Jimmy's skin and used it whenever he could. Only to mask his irritation, Jimmy returned a smile. It didn't work, and Gyges victoriously strutted off. Jimmy shook his head, took a sip, returned to his office and called Mike.

Mike energetically entered Jimmy's office smiling broadly. He was Jimmy's boss, but they had become good friends and were genuinely glad to see each other. Mike was a tall, serious, heavyset man. He had a lighter side, hidden at work except from Jimmy. They exchanged small talk and then got down to business.

"I need you to focus on these," Mike said picking up the contracts on Jimmy's desk. "These are tender and need the eagle's eye. They got here after the first of the year. Listen, the timeline is really short here. There's no wiggle room. If we miss the deadline, the deal's gone. It's that simple. I've told Victor that anything you need is top priority, so he's at your disposal. Sorry to spring these on you like this."

Mike gave Jimmy a calm but serious look. Jimmy nodded. This was his specialty, and he was more than ready to dive in. He also knew the real task was likely to be long and boring.

"What about—"

Mike interrupted. "I've already reassigned your other work to Barry." Jimmy's face contorted. He hated turning over anything of his to Gyges, especially when the hard work had already been done. "Now don't get a twist in your shorts. I knew you'd be pissed, but these are much more important. The others are routine anyway. They don't need you. Turn what you've completed over to Barry this afternoon. I need you on this, Jimmy."

"Mike, they're ninety percent finished. They'll be done in one or two more days."

Mike stared back a clear no.

"So what's the timeline?" Jimmy asked.

"No later than one week from Friday." Mike was apologetic. "You can skip the staff meeting this week, but be there next Wednesday."

Jimmy nodded. On several occasions, he had worked with minimal sleep on deadlines. Turning his work over to Gyges still angered him, but he knew he'd get past that quickly if only for Mike.

"Victor's coming in a few minutes. Listen, when this is finished, let's get together and catch up."

"Mike, one other thing—"

"No, no one has seen any of this but me."

As usual, Mike had anticipated Jimmy's concern. Jimmy nodded. Mike's cell chimed, he stood, shook Jimmy's hand, and hurriedly left.

As quickly as Mike was out, Victor was in. Victor was a well-built Hispanic, originally from Cuba and still with a pronounced accent. He combined the skills of a gifted statistician with an impeccable work ethic. Victor tended to be naïve, but Jimmy respected him greatly. Jimmy also found him fun to work with. Victor managed to combine his serious Catholic upbringing with a Buddhist interpretation of forgiveness and non-judgment. This shotgun wedding between dogma and karma resulted in an absolute commitment to uninhibited kindness and gave Jimmy a fertile field for poking fun.

"I guess we have our work cut out for us," Jimmy said. He explained what little he knew about the project. The two agreed to meet late that afternoon after Jimmy had had a chance to review the mission.

"I'm pleased to be working with you again, James," Victor said with a smile as he left.

By mid-afternoon, Jimmy had devised a preliminary plan of attack. When Victor arrived, Jimmy had prepared a list of data needed to start. The two discussed strategy. They knew they were in for a long and tedious week and a half. As Victor readied to leave, Jimmy reached reluctantly for the contracts to pass to Gyges. "Would you mind dropping these off for me?"

"Certainly, James, it will be my pleasure. Who do they go to?"

"Shit-for-brains." Jimmy chuckled, knowing this would tweak Victor.

"James, I know you don't care much for Barry, but I believe him to be a good person and an asset to our company. He's quite valuable, you know. He's not without vision."

Jimmy knew Victor had fallen for Gyges's P.R. and expected this kind of response. "You're right; he does have vision. The same vision as anyone who has his nose lodged up his ass. He sees everything backward and upside down. He's pure shit from top to bottom."

"I know he appears to be hard, but I believe he has a soft center and is a good man."

"You know, Victor, maybe we're not that far apart. I believe he has a hard outside too—of dense, dried turd. And I agree he has a soft inner core—of warm, loose diarrhea. He's total shit."

Victor realized he had been pulled into one of Jimmy's amusements. He smiled and shook his head. "If I believed in such a place as hell, I would also have to believe you might be going to join its population."

Both laughed, and Victor left to do his delivery.

The next days indeed were long and tedious. Jimmy worked eighteen-hour stretches straight through the weekend and stayed overnight at the office twice. Early in the second week, he could see light through the tunnel.

When he entered the conference room filled with members of the elite group for the Wednesday senior staff meeting, he was noticeably exhausted. Mike arrived last, took the seat at the table's head, called the meeting to order and began receiving reports and information. He reached Gyges about an hour in. Mike offered compliments for the way the contracts Jimmy surrendered had been prepared and delivered. Jimmy was already irritated when Gyges announced, "I have to give credit to Dr. Eagleson, who did some of the work."

Jimmy was now as angry as he was tired. Gyges had worked in a dual dig, referring to Jimmy's ninety percent as "some of the work" and calling him "Dr. Eagleson." To the staff, it would appear he was complimenting Jimmy for his competence. But Jimmy knew the real meaning. He'd once told Victor he had always regretted not pursuing a doctorate in philosophy, a secret Victor innocently revealed to Gyges. Victor had also told Gyges about Jimmy's ring. Gyges didn't know the ring's significance but saw Jimmy ritualistically rub its crest at times and knew how important Jimmy felt it was. Gyges stored that information for future ammunition.

Gyges finished his report, turned toward Jimmy and gave him the smirk. Jimmy was tempted to raise his middle finger. Instead, he worked on shedding his irritation in time for his own presentation.

Mike saved Jimmy for last. He explained the importance of Jimmy's contracts. "These may be the biggest deals we will make all year. They're extremely complicated but potentially very lucrative. I gave the assignment to James last week and must admit I underestimated the technical preparation that will be necessary after he is finished. Now, I can't tell you what I would give for one more day. Everything has to be in the hands of all parties by Monday morning. So as things stand, it looks like the support people will have to work through the weekend, and we'll have to hope they can pull it off."

Mike turned the meeting over to Jimmy, who detailed the intricacies. His report took a half-hour and held everyone's full attention. Except for Gyges, whose attention span was insufficient and interest was less.

"Any questions?" Jimmy asked and saw none. "And Mike, I don't know what you would give for another day either, but I'm wondering what can I get for two? I finished my work just before this meeting and asked Victor to start the rest of the process."

Mike looked at Jimmy with wide eyes and an enormous smile and shook his head.

"Let's hear it for Dr. Eagleson, people!" As the group applauded, Jimmy enjoyed watching Gyges force himself to look like a team player. Jimmy felt good; he not only had the limelight, he had a triple trump on Gyges. His "Dr." was now established as a real compliment, removing one weapon from Gyges's left-handed arsenal. Jimmy's work was noted as far more significant. And Gyges himself had led the group to think he needed Jimmy's help to do his own assignments.

As the staff filed out, Mike took Jimmy aside and thanked him again. With new breathing space, they agreed to meet for dinner that night and catch up.

* * *

Jimmy was waiting at the bar when Mike arrived. They'd chosen a steakhouse Mike liked. After several days of sandwiches and Chinese, Jimmy was looking forward to good red meat. He was still exhausted, and the beer tasted especially good after many days without. Mike took a long slow sip from a bourbon. Both were feeling the relief of completing an unusually tricky project.

"Thanks again," Mike said. "You did a fantastic job."

"My pleasure. Keeps me off the street."

"You're the only one we have who could have brought that in on time. There's no one else with your analytical skills in the company. Sometimes I worry we only have one of you."

"What about Gyges?" Jimmy said sarcastically.

"You had to get that in, didn't you?" Mike was smiling. "Everyone plays a role. Barry is young and hungry. He never had money, and he wants it bad. So he's always looking. New ways of financing, different profit angles, properties we overlook. He finds that kind of thing. His logistical abilities are limited, but he's got a new perspective. I've been in this a long time, and I'm getting to be conservative. Sometimes I need to hear his slant."

"He's come up with some crazy ideas."

"That's why I'm there. A guy like me keeps a guy like him in perspective and under control. And, you know, I had a professor once who used to say 'the cream rises to the top.'"

"So does shit."

Mike snickered. "Yes, it often does."

"Mike, there's not much underneath this 'new approach' that's finding its way around. I don't understand how these things could possibly stand up over any reasonable period of time. It assumes there's unlimited wealth. Best I can tell, that has to come from overvaluing assets. And it seems to be spreading like a virus. Look at the real estate market in many parts of the country. No way those properties are worth their appraisals. No way. Things will have to equalize at some point. Investors will take a plunge." Mike listened as he sipped.

"Well," Mike shrugged, "we've always assumed something was worth whatever someone would pay for it. In my years at this, there were times when I wondered the same thing. But things always seem to at least maintain. None of us knows if it will ever crash, but we can't operate under that assumption. I'm glad you see it the way you do though. As aggressive as you are, you always bring sobriety to the table. Keeps us all," Mike smiled, "under control. But I'll tell you one thing, people have been doing this for a long time, and they'll be doing it long after we're gone. Let's just hope it doesn't crash first." They both laughed as the bartender delivered two more drinks.

"Now Jimmy, before I forget, what you get for bringing that monstrosity in early is the time you saved us. I want you to take the next two days off. Don't come in until Monday."

"Mike I can—"

"Don't come in until Monday. Find something to do for yourself; get your mind off work and come in fresh. Come on, it's bad for morale when someone pulls off the kind of thing you just did and isn't recognized."

Jimmy nodded. As they turned the discussion to small talk, Mike noticed a dessert tray on its way and smiled broadly.

"Tonight I do dessert," Mike said. "They're always on me about cholesterol and triglycerides and weight. Not tonight. I had a good friend who used to commute from Binghamton. Twice a week, he'd stop at a diner on Route 17 for lunch. I used to join him when I was in that area. That place had the best homemade pie you've ever tasted. But his wife was always on his case about his weight, and he rarely snuck a piece. The last time I ate there with him, he was a good boy and declined. A few hours later a delivery truck hit him head on. I've often wished he'd had the pie. Yup, tonight I do dessert."

* * *

Jimmy woke at eleven o'clock, still logy. Strong coffee would cure that. A free Thursday and Friday were rare, and they were not expected. He had no plans. After cleaning up, he hit the streets to get breakfast. As he strolled along without a clear destination, he realized he didn't know what to do with himself. A cup of espresso made him wide awake but offered no ideas. After a few blocks of aimless walking, he returned home to devise a plan. He put on music and rocked in his chair. This didn't relax him much, and his restlessness was becoming uncomfortable. He considered going into work despite Mike's directions but decided it wasn't a good idea. He would at least check his e-mail in the remote hope he had been summoned. As he sat in his workspace and turned toward his computer, he was drawn to a lone note card, pinned to the message board in front of him, READ THE LETTERS. The blunt reminder called back his mood from the holidays. He wondered if this was the time to face The Old Man's secrets. The week's work had given him purpose and goals. Now he was withdrawing from his sense of conquest. Should he risk returning to the frame of mind he was in before, the venerable Jimmy without his edge? He sat thinking a few more minutes and then pulled open the drawer.

Inside the package were five large envelopes packed with letters. He removed the contents and saw it was chronological. Groups of letters were clipped together with paper fasteners and marked on the front with dates and a number. Aunt Lucy's careful arrangement told him their order was important, and he needed to read them in sequence. He took the first batch and returned to his chair. Carefully, he separated the aged letters and started reading.

> Dear Frank,
> My apologies for not writing earlier, things here have been quite busy since we arrived. It's hard to

believe we've already been here for six weeks. The trip over was uneventful although the conditions on the ship were bloody shit, to say the least. It took two weeks just to get the smell out of my nose. We were crammed in and slept in hammocks so close to each other it made you afraid if the guy below you got a hard on it would pop up into your ass. We have been training daily, mostly on the rifle range. I've been made a marksman. The asshole who promised me engineering was full of shit. But, they still keep promising and I'm still waiting. In the meantime, I'm becoming a very good shot. I just wish I had the chance to kill Germans instead of sitting around and watching the coast near our base.

The beer here stinks. It's warm and bitter and mostly flat. It tastes like piss mixed with a few hops. What I'd give for some cold Canadian stuff. And the Brits aren't very happy with us, except for a few of the women. We spend much of our off time in the pubs where they fish around for some Canadian meat and a few bucks. I must admit I've obliged once or twice. I hope not to catch anything as they tend to circulate at will. And the Tommys aren't much sport in a row. All they need to see is a Canadian badge and they want to fight. Most of them end up limping back to their bunks. I think we're doing more damage to them than the Germans. Some guys just never learned when to keep their fucking mouths shut. A drunken corporal gave Jimmy and me a rasher of shit just last week. I waffle-stomped the bastard so hard he'll probably have a Canadian boot print on his face for the rest of his life. I hope so at least.

I hope all is well with you. I can't say I miss being home, but I definitely don't like it here. And I do miss you and Lil. I've written her often, but I can't tell her the things I can say to you. Jimmy gives his regards. I'm glad at least the two of us are together. We're in the same barracks now. You'd think being overseas with your best friend would be fun, but we're both bored. And the food they give us is the worst shit you've ever seen. It's always some kind of mush with a real rancid flavor. I know there's a war on but how can they expect us to fight if we're always puking? Well, not much more to say. Life goes on, at least for now. Take care and write when you can.

My regards,

Gerret

Jimmy put the letter on his end table and sat back in his rocker. He looked at his ring, swallowed hard, and gazed out the window. The Old Man he knew would never have spoken in such a lewd way, let alone put it in writing. In his entire life, he'd never heard him use foul language; in fact, it was one of the few things Jimmy was punished for growing up. And the brawling and whoring were beyond comprehension. Gerret Eagleson was a disciplined family man, never the sort of person who could write this letter. And who was Jimmy? This new person was obviously important, but he'd never been mentioned at home. Why the secrecy? And what about his marksmanship? The Old Man hated guns.

Jimmy went to the refrigerator for a beer, feeling obsessed with the new Gerret Eagleson. The letter was definitely in his handwriting, and he hadn't used any language Jimmy hadn't heard plenty of. Jimmy himself could shoot off a string of obscenities and insults with the best of them. But this wasn't The Old Man, the rock, the example, the perfect image of respect. This was a smutty Canadian yahoo, far too close to an ordinary asshole for Jimmy's comfort.

Jimmy spent the weekend reading more letters and contemplating. Each revealed more, but the stories were always the same—stuck in England, waiting for a transfer, wanting to fight, and behaving badly. Jimmy visited *Doc's* a few times but didn't mention any of it. Who'd understand? Gail commented he seemed out of sorts.

On Sunday, he read a letter where The Old Man described a woman's naked body and the things they'd done. He felt sick. Reading on seemed futile. His feelings toward The Old Man grew worse. He wondered what Gord had been thinking. Why all this had been sent and what possible value it could have at this point in his life.

Jimmy carefully placed the letters back in their drawer and walked to the athletic club. All the way, he obsessed over the letters.

He snapped his locker open, hurriedly pulled on his swim suit, grabbed a towel, and marched to the pool. The echoing of swimmer's hands slapping the water and the strong smell of chlorine pulled a long submerged memory to the surface.

His mind traveled back to a Saturday swim meet when he was eleven.

Jimmy had just moved into a new age bracket. The coach placed him in the fifty-meter freestyle, mostly to fill the slot and knowing Jimmy had little chance of winning. When Jimmy stepped onto the platform, he surveyed his competition, all taller and more developed. He wondered why he was there. He glanced at the bleachers. The Old Man sat in the second row at the end. He'd never attended a meet before. Why now? Jimmy was amazed. He curled his toes over the platform's edge, bent forward with arms raised behind him, and at the sound of the starter's gun, flew off and sliced into the water. He surfaced, and his hands reached farther than ever, perfectly cupped to pull him forward at maximum speed while his feet kicked in sync.

He performed the best flip-turn he'd ever managed. Back on the surface, he saw he was nearly even with the leader and found furious energy. His feet went perfectly flat, and his frantic flutter kick almost raised him from the water. He swam the remaining meters in a trance, and when he felt his hand slap the pool's side, he heard the local crowd cheer. He looked up at the clock and smiled, first place by over a second. He proudly pulled himself from the pool and looked toward the bleachers. But The Old Man had left. His teammates surrounded him patting his back and clapping. He looked down and shook his head. They thought he was being humble—not knowing he was struggling not to cry.

Jimmy waited most of his life for that empty seat to be filled, just once. It was always vacant. He found ways to deal with it, and with Kate's help, came to a satisfactory understanding. Now Jimmy wondered why he'd ever cared. Was the "genuine" Old Man the piggish brute he was learning of? He dove into the water and began a slow, steady breaststroke with a rhythmic frog-kick. As the soothing swash massaged his thoughts, he gradually felt relief—the water always calmed him. Today he'd swim at his own pace and for his own benefit.

As he left the club, he knew he would be processing the new version of The Old Man for a long time. But right now he needed to put all of this aside and regroup. Work would be nothing but a long series of tedious contracts for the foreseeable future, and a good Sunday walk would help put his head back in the business world. After, he'd stop at *Doc's* for a while to see Gail and get himself back in order.

* * *

Gyges held his whiskey glass and rattled the remaining ice cubes at the bartender.

"You could just ask, Barry," the bartender said.

"I just did." The bartender reached for a bottle of single malt scotch, refreshed Gyges's ice, and poured one exact jigger. "When are you going to learn to pour a full drink?" Gyges said.

"When you learn how to tip."

Gyges looked around. A typical crowd for a Sunday: most barstools occupied, a few couples at tables finishing off the weekend, and Gyges. He looked toward the bar's corner and watched a man reviewing a set of drawings rolled out in front of him. "What's he doing?"

"The owner's decided on a new look," The bartender said. "Doesn't think he's getting the business he should. So he's going to redo everything and completely fuck things up. That's the guy in charge. Some kind of 'miracle designer.' By the time he's done, you won't recognize the place."

"Doesn't sound like you're on board."

"Don't have to be; the asshole recommended a change in staff—three bartenders including me. I've been here for five years, and this little fuck looks the place over for a couple of days, says a few words, and I'm gone."

"Welcome to New York."

Gyges noticed a glint as the designer pulled a shining silver lighter from his pocket and lit a cigarette. Gyges squinted to focus on the crest on the lighter's side. He sat back. "It can't be," he said under his breath. He took a cigarette from the pack in front of him, tightened his tie, put on his best professional façade, and walked over.

"Excuse me, could I get a light? My lighter's dead."

"Yeah, sure," the designer said not looking up. He took the lighter from his pocket and placed it on the bar.

Gyges picked the lighter up, examined the crest, and grinned. "This is a beauty. Looks real old. Is this sort of a common crest?"

The designer raised his head and smiled. "No, it's one-of-a-kind. World War Two vintage."

"Jesus, where did you find it?"

"I bought it from a guy in Plattsburgh a few weeks back."

"I'm surprised a guy would sell a one-of-a-kind like this."

"He didn't know what he had. Got it from someone else. Said the guy 'owed him.'"

"I get it; he swiped it."

The designer smiled and shrugged. "Don't know, but he was laughing and cursing out some guy after he sold it to me. I can't remember the name, but I think it might have been his."

"Why?"

"From the crest. You see the wings? Well, the guy had a bird-like last name like Hawkinson or Falconson or something. You seem awful interested."

Gyges smiled, "Not really, just that you see a lot of Bics in a bar like this. This lighter's different."

"Well, hopefully you'll see a more upscale clientele soon."

"You redoing the place?"

"Yeah. Time for the old fern bar to bite the dust."

"You're right about that. I'm not sure why I come here. The place around the corner is much better for a professional guy like me."

"*Doc's*?"

"Yeah."

"You go there often?"

"Often enough," Gyges said.

"If you've got a couple minutes, I'd like to ask you some questions."

"Sure, let me get my drink and I'll join you."

Gyges walked to his stool grinning and shaking his head. How could this guy have stumbled onto Eagleson's lighter? The Gods of war were smiling upon him. Gyges gathered his cigarettes, gloves, and drink, and signaled the bartender over. He bent forward and whispered into the bartender's ear. The bartender thought a moment and asked, "How much?"

"Forty," Gyges said.

The bartender pondered, then nodded. "Fuck yeah," he said.

Gyges relocated to the seat next to the designer. The designer drilled him about *Doc's*; how it was set up, what the bartenders were like, how was the food, and were there any faults Gyges could see in the operation. Gyges had only been to *Doc's* a handful of times in his life but, as always, he acted the expert and threw out several elaborate bullshit opinions. The designer fell for his crap.

Gyges again asked to borrow the lighter. The designer reached into his pocket and handed it over. Gyges lit a second cigarette and laid the lighter on the bar.

He pointed around the bar room and suggested he show the designer some ideas. They wandered around the room for ten minutes as Gyges fabricated one proposal after another. Finally seeing Gyges's limitations, the designer suggested they return to the bar just as a young man in an old leather jacket quickly walked by, stormed out the door and jogged up the street. "Shit!" Gyges yelled, "My gloves!"

"And my lighter!" the designer shouted.

The two scurried to the bar verifying their losses and shaking their heads. The bartender rushed over. "What happened?"

"The asshole that just ran out must have stolen my gloves and this guy's lighter. Where the fuck were you?"

"Hey, it's a busy bar, and I can't watch everything." The

bartender pointed to a sign behind the bar, PLEASE DO NOT LEAVE PERSONAL ITEMS UNATTENDED.

Gyges looked at the designer. "One more suggestion," he said. "Get rid of this guy."

The designer exhaled, rolled up his drawings and packed his notes into his briefcase. "That's it for tonight. I'll finish this shit tomorrow," he said. He looked around one more time, stared silently into the bartender's eyes, and strolled out.

Gyges sat and drank the last sip of his now watery drink. The bartender walked to the door, watched a moment, and returned behind the bar, smiling.

"I'll have another scotch," Gyges said. The bartender poured a double jigger into a fresh glass and put it on the bar, along with The Old Man's lighter. Gyges picked up the lighter, examined the crest, and rubbed it with his sleeve.

"OK, Barry, time to settle up."

"Nice touch, having that guy run out like that."

The bartender nodded. "And that nice touch cost you another ten." Gyges placed thirty dollars on the bar. "You're twenty short," The bartender said.

"I'm light right now, I'll catch up with you later this week." Gyges quickly shoved the lighter in his pocket.

"Fuck that, let's have it," the bartender said.

"Later this week," Gyges repeated as he gulped down his drink and stood to leave. "Where are my gloves?"

"Twenty for the gloves."

Gyges smirked and pulled a twenty from his wallet. The bartender dropped one glove on the bar. "Twenty each," he said.

"You're a real asshole."

"And you still owe me twenty later this week."

Gyges slapped down another twenty, and the bartender dropped the other glove. Gyges reached into his pocket for The Old Man's lighter and gazed again. "It's more than worth it. Now I've got a piece of you, Eagleson. What a score."

CHAPTER V

Peggy

After several tedious weeks of work, Jimmy looked forward to Kate. Even the idea of David staying for a few days didn't bother him. It was nearing Saint Patrick's Day and New York had taken on its traditional early spring lightheartedness. He enjoyed Central Park at this time of year. It was becoming green with new grass and new buds. As he walked, Jimmy watched the workers raking away the winter debris—leaves, branches, and contributions left by the city's canine population. Camp was still snowed in, but here the sun was bright, and the snow was gone. Jimmy took a deep breath of cool air. In the summer, the park was far too crowded, but in the early spring, there were fewer visitors. Those who were there moved slower.

Later that afternoon, Kate and David would be arriving for a week. Jimmy's place was clean and provisioned. The few hours he had to himself now would be his last for a while, and he was savoring his solitude. He sat on a bench and watched mallards on the lake. Not Champlain for sure but still a taste of the wild smack in the center of New York.

For two months he'd worked on reconciling with the "new" Old Man. He felt like a child discovering the flaws in his heroes. Mickey Mantle a drunk, O.J. a murderer, and The Old Man—what exactly was The Old Man? Dealing with this person in the letters hadn't been easy at first. Now it was old news. The Old Man lived much more like Jimmy, and much less like the glorified demigod Jimmy had envisioned. But at least The Old Man's business was honest. For most of the winter, Jimmy processed one deal after another, moving funny money around between banks—some losers, some winners— all on paper. Not so with The Old Man. You buy a toilet, you shit, shit's gone. A good honest bargain.

He left the park to catch a cab and passed through Strawberry Fields. The loud whining from a small gas engine disturbed the usually peaceful area. Jimmy watched for a minute as a power washer blasted the grime from the round stone memorial to John Lennon. Jimmy smiled; even "Imagine" was getting hosed.

Cabs were plentiful on Central Park West, and Jimmy was home soon. The apartment smelled fresh and looked bright and clean. Jimmy inspected the rooms. They all passed; he was ready for house guests. He poured a beer and sat in his rocker to enjoy a few more minutes alone before his regularly structured life turned to accommodating the comforts and wishes of others. He knew Kate would have an itinerary. Shows, museums, shopping, restaurants, clubs, and even the zoo were likely candidates. As much as he was looking forward to seeing her, he hoped he wouldn't be expected to be part of most of it. The role of third wheel never worked for him. He knew his civility toward David might be tested during a week-long visit. But he also knew he could escape back to work if he needed, with apologies in the name of duty. Right now he appreciated his space. It was good.

Their train was on time. Kate and David were delivered to Jimmy's in the late afternoon. David had never seen the New York property and was taken by the neighborhood's old cast iron architecture. Jimmy's place was in a particularly ornate building, carefully restored to its original 19th-century condition. David told Kate he was surprised Jimmy was so comfortable here since the neoclassical style was so different from Camp. He had only been exposed to one side of Jimmy's personality, and superficially at that. The visitors climbed the stairs to the front door and rang. Jimmy quickly swung it open.

"Hey Eagleson," Kate said as she grabbed him in a long, tight hug.

"Welcome," Jimmy said holding on. After a few seconds, the two remembered David and Jimmy made a recovering greeting.

"Hi David, what do you think?"

"I'm impressed. Kate told me to expect old New York, but this is remarkable."

"Thank you. Well, come and I'll show you around the place."

Jimmy gave David the three-minute tour as Kate inspected the kitchen. She checked the fridge and cupboards, carefully assessing the foods Jimmy was keeping. She seemed satisfied; it appeared he was eating properly. The beer fridge was fully stocked, and the liquor cabinet left nothing to be desired.

All appliances, utensils, and plates were in their place. She checked the living room for dust and dirt, paying particular attention to the carpets. Everything was in order. Relieved, she poured herself a drink and sat in a favorite chair she'd chosen for him a few years before.

The boys returned. Jimmy poured David a scotch on the rocks and grabbed himself a beer. As they sat in the living area, Kate reviewed her itinerary. Jimmy was pleased; she wasn't aware Jimmy had taken time off and she'd planned most of the week's activities assuming his absence. After the long weekend, he would be released. That night the three would dine at an Italian place she liked, and then over to *Doc's*. The beginning of a three-day St. Pat's celebration was underway.

* * *

At dinner, Kate and David filled Jimmy in on the latest North Country scuttlebutt, and he found himself relaxed and amused. Ray had been invited to come down but declined. Kate said he hiked in the woods frequently. Otherwise, he just read in his cottage, part of his annual winter recluse mode. Camp was in excellent shape, and the work Jimmy had requested was mostly done. After dinner the three went for gourmet ice cream; then Jimmy flagged a cab and they moved on to *Doc's*.

It was Friday night and busy. Tony and Art were at the usual spot at the bar's end, facing off. As the trio worked their way over, the sounds of confrontation increased.

"I told you that dumb bastard will have us in another war.

Weapons of mass destruction my ass. There are no weapons of mass destruction and those lying sons of bitches know it. It's all a ruse, just bullshit to get us to invade. And we both know it's all about oil, Tony, nothing but oil; Bush, Cheney, oil, DUH."

"Bullshit to you. Those weapons are there, and we'll find them as soon as we get there. Besides it's about Hussein more than anything. He's another Hitler, and if we don't go in while we can it'll be too late. Haven't you paid any attention to what that bastard's been doing?"

"So we go after every dictator we don't like? Are you out of your Rogaine-infected skull?"

Jimmy was amused; the boys were at it full bore. Kate was snickering, having seen the show before. David, unaware of the unique dynamic, prepared to join the discussion. He was irritated when Kate put her hand on his arm in a gesture to stay out, and he tried to jump in anyway. Then Art noticed the new arrivals and tapped Tony on the leg.

"Greetings," Tony said with a welcoming face.

"Yes, it's good to see you again," Art added looking mostly at Kate. "We've met before."

"Yes, last year about this time I think. The discussion wasn't quite the same, but close," Kate said with a smile.

Both Tony and Art chuckled. Art put his arm around his friend and jested, "I'll never get through to this guy."

"All right, you'll see, you'll see; yes, it's good to see all of you," Tony said as he turned to David. "I don't think we've met. I'm Anthony, and this is my distinguished colleague Arthur."

"I'm David, nice to meet both of you."

As hands were shaken, David stood dumbfounded. He had never seen such a confrontation end so quickly and amicably and was now embarrassed he hadn't understood Kate's signal. From behind the bar came the distant greeting of a frantically busy bartender. "Kate, great to see you. Jimmy told me you were coming. I'll be down to that end in a minute."

Gail quickly returned, placed a beer in front of Jimmy and took Kate's and David's orders. She could chat with Kate only intermittently when drawing a beer or mixing a drink, but the two were still able to make plans for the next week. The St. Patrick's Day bash on Monday would be packed, and Gail promised to reserve an area for the Eagleson party.

David began a discussion with Art and Tony about New York sports and was occupied for the rest of the night, leaving Jimmy and Kate to talk and wander about. She recognized a few people from previous visits and wasn't shy about reintroducing herself and jumping into a good gab. Jimmy had always liked that about her. In a few hours the yawns began, signaling time to leave. The trio made their way back to Jimmy's place, had one more drink and called it a night.

* * *

For the first time in months, Jimmy awoke to the sounds of others in his house—a welcome feeling, particularly on a Saturday morning when New York would be theirs for the taking. As he entered the kitchen, he was immediately handed a cup of coffee, prepared exactly as he liked.

"Here you go, Eagleson," Kate said smiling. David was showering. Neither Kate nor Jimmy had cleaned up yet. They looked like a long-married couple who'd just rolled out of bed.

"I don't know how much longer I'll be seeing David," Kate said quietly though the shower insured her privacy. "He's becoming possessive and directive. He even seems jealous once in a while. Well, it was never meant to be a serious thing anyway."

"Does he see it that way?"

"He said he did up front, but now he's moving in too close, too complicated for me. I made the mistake of telling him I might officially split up with Steve. My bad; from then on he's been behaving in ways I don't like."

"You and Steve have a lot of time in. This is the first time I've heard of a split."

"Yeah, a lot of time in and apart. He's had a real girlfriend for quite a while, something new for both of us. And, you know, I like the guy, but the flames have been out for so long I don't have a clue anymore why we'd stay married. For a while, it was about money, but we're both OK now. Continuing the act seems so silly."

"I can't think of a reason why I'd be surprised, but I am. Maybe because it's been so long. So what will you do about David?"

"Oh, he'll give me the right reason to make the break. He already has once or twice; and you know he's kind of a dork too. He's into his architecture, but there isn't much else to talk about. The sex is pretty good though, but, c'est la vie."

Jimmy was ruffled by Kate's candor. "Well, yeah, c'est la

vie," he said in quick recovery. The shower went silent, and the conversation came to a quick close.

"Well, good luck with it all. I'm pretty sure you'll come out of it without a scratch. I don't know how either guy will fare. But then, I don't care about them. I don't dislike them, but neither of them was ever a friend."

"I know," Kate said as the bathroom door opened. They both smiled and took a sip of coffee.

Kate's itinerary began with the Metropolitan Museum, one of Jimmy's favorites and a place where David could also be entertained. The three stood and gazed at a column from The Tomb of Mausolus. Jimmy was thinking of the incredible skill of ancient cultures, Kate about the love and dedication the sister/wife had for her brother/husband, and David was attempting to estimate the circumference to determine load-bearing capability. So went the morning.

Lunch was pleasant: a good New York sandwich and a cold beer all around. David quickly ran out of conversation and was quiet, except when responding to a direct question. Still, Kate was comfortable and happy to be in the city. The afternoon found them working through the crowds at the Museum of Modern Art for a glance at Van Gogh's "Starry Night." Then they returned to the apartment to freshen up before dinner at a French place Kate had heard about. All went well, and they finished the evening with drinks at the apartment.

Jimmy's first day as host was a success. Tomorrow was Sunday, and Kate had only two tickets for a matinee, leaving Jimmy time to himself. Late in the afternoon, they would meet at *Doc's*.

* * *

"Man the smoke is thick in here," David said as they maneuvered through the loud Saint Patrick's Day crowd.

"Not for much longer. In two weeks no more smoking in New York City bars," Jimmy said. As promised, Gail saved the far end of the bar for her regulars. Now that she knew what everyone drank the alcohol flowed automatically. Bush had delivered his ultimatum to Saddam and his sons guaranteeing another war, and Art was gloating over the accuracy of his prediction. But the reality of the impending conflict was lost in the overwhelming cheer of the evening. Kate and David somehow found something to talk about and Jimmy relaxed and enjoyed himself. Much of the stress of the past few months evaporated. He felt peaceful.

Jimmy caught a glimpse of a figure reflecting from a Michelob mirror behind the bar. What the fuck is Gyges doing here? he wondered. He turned to confirm that Barry Gyges stood midway down the bar with a few people from work. Jimmy controlled his repulsion; he felt good tonight, and even Gyges wouldn't disturb that. Their eyes met, and Jimmy nodded. Gyges responded with the predictable smirk: the old, worn out, stupid, smirk. It didn't work. Not tonight, tonight he wasn't playing. Jimmy just smiled. He acknowledged the others with a wave. He didn't see Gyges take The Old Man's lighter from his pocket and hide it in his hand as he waved back.

As Jimmy turned toward the corner, he was drawn to a small group of women, three or four layers behind him. One in particular caught his eye: a medium-height brunette with short, styled hair, a perfect, full figure and unusually large brown eyes. She smiled and laughed like Clair had and was so full of youth and energy, he couldn't look away. His attraction was intense and inexplicable. For the next half-hour, he kept looking back to see if she was still there and still as fetching. Finally, when Gail came near Jimmy signaled to her. "Who's the girl behind me with the short hair in the red?"

Gail glanced. "Margarette Jones. Her friends call her Peggy. She's in once in a while, good kid, I think. Looks like Mr. Eagleson is interested." Gail winked and smiled. "When I get a chance I'll introduce you."

Gail scampered back to her crowd, and Jimmy sat in nervous anticipation. She was so young and beautiful, and it had been a long time since he'd been so attracted to a woman. And that enchanting smile, like Clair in the old days. He felt back in time, like a kid at a high school dance. His palms were sweaty; he fidgeted. He thought about telling Gail to forget it but gathered the courage to let the scene play out. In a few minutes, his new idol approached the bar to order, and Gail pointed him out. Margarette looked, smiled and nodded to Gail.

Gail abandoned her post as she wove Margarette through the swarm.

"Margarette Jones, this is Jimmy Eagleson," she said. "Now I have to get back to work." Jimmy and Margarette both chuckled at Gail's quick exit.

"Hi, my friends call me Peggy."

"And I'm Jimmy. Nice to meet you."

"Nice to meet you too."

"Could I get you a drink?"

"Just got one, thanks." Without taking her eyes off Jimmy, Margarette took a sip of her vodka and cranberry.

"What do you do?" Jimmy asked.

"I'm an administrative assistant. I've been in New York about a year with a company near here. You?"

"I'm an attorney with a company near here."

The two easily made small talk for several minutes. Jimmy noticed Gyges looking their way. Peggy and Gyges briefly shared smiles.

"You know him?" Jimmy asked.

"Not really. Seen him around. Barry or something. He went out with one of my friends awhile. Looks like you two aren't buds."

"That would be correct," Jimmy said with a broad smile.

"Well, like I said, I don't know the guy."

As the two continued to chat, Kate was observing from the corner of her eye with interest.

Eventually, it was time. "Well, I'd better get back to my friends; it was nice to meet you," Margarette said.

In a flash of guts Jimmy blurted out, "Maybe we could get together sometime. You know go out, dinner or whatever you'd like."

Margarette was silent. Jimmy was sure he had blown it. Then she looked at him with a big broad smile and said, "Yeah, I think I'd like that. I'll give you my number."

Jimmy was elated. Margarette handed him a piece of paper. She looked into his eyes again. "I really liked talking to you. Please make sure you call."

"I definitely will; I've enjoyed talking to you too."

The couple parted with a tender handshake.

Kate couldn't wait to get the scoop. "Well, what's that all about, Eagleson?"

"Her name is Margarette. Gail just introduced us. What do you think?"

"Too soon to tell; she's very young, very attractive, seems nice enough from what little I could hear. Could be a man-eat-er, you know."

"I don't think so."

"You going to take her out?"

"I think so."

"Well, good. We were thinking of registering you at the local monastery. It'll be good for you finally to get out. Just be careful. You're a vulnerable one, and women can smell that on a man."

Kate took Jimmy's hand and held it tightly before they returned to the affairs of the corner. Jimmy continued to sneak peeks of his new infatuation until she left with her friends.

As Jimmy exited *Doc's*, his eyes were drawn to a bright near-full moon, a rare sight in the city. A layer of dirty slush covered the streets as the three walked to the corner. Jimmy casually observed the traffic signals and stepped off the curb. In a panic, Kate grabbed his shoulder and yanked him back. A short Cadillac limo running a red light barely missed him. He stood splattered to his knees. The three companions stood for a moment and retrieved their breath.

"That asshole," Kate declared.

"Yeah, that was close," David added.

"I didn't care much for these pants anyway," Jimmy said in an unsuccessful attempt to lighten the mood. Their heart rates soon returned to normal, they laughed, and all shook their heads. Kate hailed a cab, and they returned to Jimmy's.

* * *

With Kate and David off on a walking tour of New York's architecture, Jimmy sat in his rocker and mulled over the night before. He felt nervous about calling Margarette. Was it too soon? Maybe she has a boyfriend and is just being nice? Was the age difference a problem? He fantasized what she was like. Knowing so little allowed him to make her into anything he wished. She became perfection, flawlessness, beauty, understanding, and intelligence. He worried he might not be good enough for her. Surely she could do better. What would she like to do? What places would she like to go? A fear popped into his head: shit, he'd been away from anything even remotely romantic for some time. Would he be able to be intimate, if it ever got to that? Maybe he should leave it alone; she probably didn't want him to call anyway. His speculation continued, off and on, throughout the day. Then he decided to wait. He'd seek Kate's advice later.

Kate and David returned at about five o'clock. David made

a beeline for the bathroom. Kate looked at Jimmy and rolled her eyes. She had had enough of her dork for one day and needed a drink. As Kate sipped, Jimmy opened the subject of Margarette.

"OK, Eagleson, you asked so let's analyze this. First, she's below your station in life."

"What does that—"

"Jimmy please, let me finish. We've talked about your Pygmalion Complex before. Oh, you're a white knight for sure, but you've never been interested in rescuing a princess; you're much more attracted to the peasant girl who you believe will love you for bringing her into a better world. And you know how *well* that's worked." Kate paused and smiled. "But, Margarette could be good for you if you keep your head about it, and it's far too early to think about a long-term relationship anyway. Take it slow and keep your guard up.

"So you think—"

"Just call her, you've got nothing to lose, and she's got everything to gain. Call her."

Jimmy knew Kate would build his confidence, but he still worried how Margarette would react. But he knew a call was the only way to settle the question and went to his room to take the plunge.

"Hello," Margarette answered pleasantly.

"Hello, Margarette, this is Jimmy Eagleson. We met last night at *Doc's*. How are you?"

"I'm good. How are you?"

"I'm fine. I thought I'd call and see if you were still

interested in doing something together." Jimmy heard activity in the background. "Did I call at a bad time?"

"No, I'm just getting ready to leave work. Yeah, getting together sounds good. I can't do anything until the weekend, but that's open."

Jimmy thought he sensed a matter-of-fact attitude but took her at her word. "Well, how about Friday?"

"Sure, that's good."

"What do you like to do?"

"Whatever you like. I'm easy." Margarette's tone was beginning to seem more genuine.

"OK, I'll make reservations somewhere and we can take it from there."

"Great."

"Do you want me to pick you up? I don't know your address."

"How 'bout I meet you at *Doc's*?"

"That will be fine. About seven?"

"Yeah, that's good."

"OK, well, I hope the rest of your week goes well, and I'll see you on Friday."

"Yup, see you Friday. Thanks for calling."

Jimmy immediately began analyzing. The call had its ups and downs; the end seemed awkward. "Thanks for calling" sounded more like a polite way to get rid of a telemarketer than a girl looking forward to a first date. The negatives he'd processed before resurfaced. But the event was on, and he would have to wait until the weekend to see how it played out.

"How did it go?" Kate asked as Jimmy returned to the kitchen and opened a fresh beer.

"OK, I guess. We're on for Friday night."

"You guess?"

"Yeah, she didn't seem as excited as I hoped."

"That's the way we play it, Eagleson. Too much excitement, as you put it, makes us look too eager. What would you think if she jumped all over you like a puppy this early in the dance?"

Jimmy paused. "Well, I've never been good at the dance."

"Yes, I know," Kate said. "Look, it'll all be fine—or maybe not. Either way, remember, you're the prize in this, not her. Don't overthink any of it, and whatever you do, don't put her on a pedestal. You've had enough problems with that approach."

Jimmy knew Kate was right. He was overreacting. Kate had also helped restore his perspective. He'd made a lot of mistakes with women and didn't want to go there again. But he remembered Margarette's smile and thought of early days with Clair. He'd never been happier.

The days passed slowly. Jimmy accompanied his guests to a few events, and they had dinner each night. He wondered if he should call Margarette again, just to talk, but Kate talked him out of it. On Friday, just before leaving for Penn Station, Jimmy gave Kate a long hug. David was noticeably annoyed.

"I see what you mean," Jimmy whispered into Kate's ear.

"Yup. He's *got* to go," Kate whispered back. Then Kate repeated her advice about Margarette. Jimmy was appreciative but still nervous. Kate wouldn't be there after the date for a post-game analysis, and coaching on the phone wasn't the same. He'd be flying solo on this one.

* * *

Jimmy got to *Doc's* at seven and secured seats at the bar. It was quieter than usual. Bush had begun the war with Iraq the day before and the televisions were full of the new drama and over-analysis. Gail had taken the night off, leaving a new bartender in charge. Neither Art nor Tony was there. Jimmy recognized almost no one. *Doc's* felt like a strange place. He ordered a beer and nervously waited.

Margarette walked in looking even better than on St. Patrick's Day. Jimmy felt a rush. Her tight, low-cut dress was on the cusp between sleazy and elegant, ideally chosen to intensify her charge. Her oversized eyes spotted Jimmy; she smiled the familiar smile like the other night and briskly approached him. She extended her hand, he took it, and she squeezed warmly.

"Hi. I'm really glad you called. I wasn't sure you would. Some guys just collect numbers and never follow up."

"I'm glad to see you too; you look great," Jimmy said awkwardly. "Here, have a seat; what would you like to drink?"

"Vodka and cranberry would be good if that's OK."

"Anything you'd like is OK."

Margarette smiled. The new bartender was less attentive than Gail, and Jimmy had no special status, but he eventually flagged him down, and the drinks came. Jimmy was still nervous and desperate to get into relaxed conversation.

"Where are you from, Margarette?" he asked.

"Dayton, and please call me Peggy; all my friends do. Margarette is just for work anymore. I've been in Manhattan, oh, 'bout a year now. I was in the Bronx awhile, but I always wanted to be here, you know? Manhattan's where it's happening. So I got a place together with my friend. It's smaller than we had in the Bronx, but we don't need the subway as much, and like I said, we're here. So it works out pretty good."

Jimmy was pleased. It looked like talking wasn't going to be a problem.

"Now I think you said you were an administrative assistant?"

"Yup. It's a good start. I want to move up, but I figure I have to pay my dues like everybody else. I think the place I work is pretty good. I know moving up won't be easy, but I think I'll make it. Could I get another drink?"

In no time, she had finished her first cocktail and was ready for the next. Jimmy was beginning to feel comfortable.

"Absolutely," Jimmy replied not realizing his pun until Peggy laughed and said, "That's funny."

"You said you're a lawyer?"

"Yeah, I'm in acquisitions contracts. My group buys and sells businesses and properties for major clients."

"Sounds complicated."

"Sometimes, sometimes it's just boring."

"Well at least you're doing something that pays; Manhattan is so expensive. Do you pay a lot in rent? We do. Not much left over at the end of the month when you live on The Island. But it's worth it."

Jimmy was reminded his situation was rare. The day-to-day world Peggy was in was very different.

"No, I have a place of my own."

"On Manhattan?" Peggy blurted out, almost startled.

"Yes, in SoHo. It's a few blocks from here."

"Wow."

"Well, the place has been in the family since the sixties. I actually inherited it. But I do OK."

"Sorry I asked you those questions. I hope you don't think I'm only interested in money and stuff like that. It's just that living here costs so much and even sharing things with a roommate—it almost wipes me out. But I don't want to be anywhere else." Peggy took another sip. "And, I really am glad you called. I know I've barely met you, but I like you. You're not a come-on—like most guys I meet. You seem to have it together. I saw that Wednesday. Glad you asked that bartender to introduce us."

As odd a turn as the conversation had taken, in one quick statement Peggy had relieved Jimmy's anxiety, putting him at ease. Now he was eager to spend the rest of the evening with her.

"I'm glad we've met too. You're easy to talk to. I made reservations for eight-thirty at *Monte's*—I hope that's OK. I wasn't sure what you'd like, so I figured Italian was probably safe."

"I love Italian, and I've never been there. Heard it's great."

"Oh, good," Jimmy said with relief. "Well, we've got time for another drink if you like."

"Sure," Peggy said without hesitation. Jimmy liked this girl more and more.

Jimmy and Peggy arrived at *Monte's* a little late but were

greeted warmly. A quiet table away from main seating had been prepared for them. Jimmy was recognized and addressed by name; Peggy was impressed. They ordered wine and dinner and, again, talked.

"You never told me where you are from," Peggy said.

"Plattsburgh."

"Where's that?"

"It's here in New York, near Montreal, nothing like the city."

"You ever get back there?"

"Yeah, I have a place there on Lake Champlain."

"I don't go back to Dayton much. My mother and I don't really get along, and there's no one else left I know. I never liked it much anyway."

"Well, I love the North Country. I get back when I can."

"Tell me about it."

Jimmy described Camp in some detail, including a brief introduction to his northern friends and life in the Champlain Valley. Peggy's already large eyes widened like a child listening to a fairytale.

"Well, I'm rambling on," Jimmy said.

"No, no, keep going. Your place sounds wonderful. I've never been to a place like that."

Jimmy felt sorry for her. He wondered what her life had been like, if she'd ever been happy. His instinct to protect and provide had been activated. "Well. Maybe we'll go up sometime."

"That would be wonderful. Even when I have the time, I don't go anywhere. I don't have the extra money. But there's always so much to do here that it's OK." Now Jimmy was touched.

Their waiter stepped forward to pour the wine. Jimmy's immediate impulse to fix Peggy's life subsided as the two settled into their dinner. Peggy told Jimmy about the places she liked in the city. They found common ground with the parks and a few bars. She was careful to point out her roommate had been her guide, and she hadn't ventured far on her own. Jimmy went through a list of his favorite places, asking if she had been. In all but one case, the answer was no. Her circles were those of the economically strapped; his were not.

"I'd really like to see *Cats* sometime," Peggy said. "I've heard it's amazing."

Cats wasn't his favorite show, but if he could please her, it sounded good. "Well, maybe we could do that," he offered.

"You mean it?" Peggy asked with adolescent enthusiasm.

"Of course, I'll see what's available."

"Oh thank you! I'm so excited!"

Talk continued through a full Italian dinner. Dessert was offered, and they both ordered, a rare indulgence for Jimmy and an enormous treat for Peggy. When they finished, Jimmy asked Peggy if she wanted another drink at the bar. She nodded, and they relocated.

"This is such a beautiful place; thank you for bringing me here," Peggy said looking directly into Jimmy's eyes.

"You're more than welcome; I haven't had as lovely a night in a very long time."

"Really? A guy like you could get any woman he wants and be out all the time."

"Well, thank you for that. But I can't tell you exactly how

long it's been since I was out on a date. I think we may have had a different president."

Jimmy looked at the clock behind the bar and noticed it was nearly midnight.

"Look at the time. Is it time for you to go home yet?" he asked, hoping not.

"Not unless you want me to; I won't turn into a pumpkin."

Jimmy smiled. "Good, let's go back to *Doc's*; this place will be closing soon."

After a quick cab ride, Jimmy stepped out on the curb and took Peggy's hand to be sure she didn't stumble. Peggy gripped firmly, looked into Jimmy's eyes and smiled her enchanting smile. The crowd at *Doc's* was light for a Friday, so the two had no trouble finding a comfortable place at a small high top. Jimmy fetched drinks, and they settled into more conversation until they realized it was nearly two-thirty. They looked at each other simultaneously and knew it was time to go.

"I had a wonderful time tonight," Peggy said.

"So did I. Let's do it again."

"I'd love to. You say when. You've got my number."

"Tomorrow night?"

"Well, I'm sort of busy tomorrow," Peggy said sheepishly.

"Another date?" Jimmy asked in an understanding tone.

"Sort of. But—I'd much rather go with you. Would you think I was awful if I tried to get out of it? I don't do that kind of thing, but I want to see you."

Jimmy was flattered and encouraged. "No, I would not think you were awful. But I don't want to cause trouble for you."

"No trouble. Let me try to take care of it in the morning. I'll call and let you know for sure. OK?" She looked concerned as she took his hand.

"Great." Jimmy reached in his pocket, wrote down his cell number and looked up to give her the card. Out of nowhere Peggy placed her hand behind his head and gave him a long passionate kiss on and beyond the lips. "Time to go for now," she said. "Thank you again for everything." Still reeling, Jimmy nodded and escorted her to the street. "I'll take you home," he said.

"No, I'll go alone. There's a stop right near my place."

Jimmy was concerned about her using public transportation so late and insisted on hailing a cab. As the taxi pulled to the curb, Peggy gave Jimmy another good-night kiss. The two uncoupled and looked deeply into each other's eyes. Jimmy grinned, helped her into the back seat, prepaid the cabbie, and waved goodbye as she rode off. It had been a good night.

* * *

The morning crept slowly as Jimmy waited for Peggy's call. About noon the phone rang.

"Hello, Jimmy?"

"Yes, Peggy, how are you?"

"Great. Still up for tonight?"

"Yes, definitely."

"Great. I got out of the other thing."

"I'm glad. Hope it wasn't awkward."

"Nope. I just told him I wasn't feeling good."

"Well, I hope we don't run into him."

"Doubt it, New York's a big town. If we do, we do. No big deal."

"Long as you're comfortable."

"I'm very comfortable, and I can't wait to see you. Meet at *Doc's* again?"

"Or I could pick you up."

"Let's meet at *Doc's*, if that's OK."

"Perfect; about seven again?"

"Yup. Can't wait to see you. Hope you have a great day. Bye."

Jimmy felt high and immediately went to work planning the evening. He was flattered Peggy had chosen him. He felt victorious, unusual for Jimmy Eagleson outside work. He made reservations at a restaurant in the Seaport area. Even at this time of year, the lighting made the area majestic. For the rest of the day, he would have to wait.

Like the night before, Jimmy arrived early. Gail was working, and the place was packed. She signaled him to an open stool, and he established turf at the bar. She was too busy to chat but quickly brought him a beer. Peggy arrived looking stunning, spotted Jimmy, hurried through the crowd, embraced him and gave him a long kiss. Gail was impressed. She had introduced them less than a week before, and now they looked inseparable. Go, Jimmy, she thought, although with some concern. Guessing, she made a vodka and cranberry and put it in front of Peggy, giving her a tacit smile, one of those communications between women impossible for men to decode. "You two seem to be doing quite well," she interjected as she was making a drink. "Big plans for tonight?"

"Dinner and maybe back here," Jimmy said as Peggy sipped, looking directly into Gail's eyes with a big smile.

"Well, you kids have fun."

Gail hurried to the other end of the bar.

Jimmy presented Peggy with his plan for the evening, much to her liking. They chatted a few minutes and left for The Seaport. There were plenty of bars there that might be less crowded and loud. The night was clear and the ride quick. Once in the mall, the couple found a quiet little tavern, ordered drinks, and took a breath. Again the talk came easily.

At dinner, they were seated at a table by a window overlooking the water. Just as Jimmy had hoped, the lights highlighted the view. Again, dinner was excellent. They returned to the little bar and again took a quiet corner.

"Tell me about your place," Jimmy said.

"Not much to tell." The question surprised Peggy. "It's small, but my roommate and I like it, mostly because it's close to work. There's only one bedroom, but we make it work OK."

"Who gets the bedroom?"

"We share it. We got a couple of beds in there. There's not much room between them, and we have to share a closet. Cassie—she's my roommate—she's pretty nice. We get along good. But the place is small, too small to have people over or anything."

"That's why you don't want me to pick you up?"

"Yeah. It's usually a mess. Hard to keep clean—not enough room for all of our stuff. Tell me about your place."

"Well, my Old Man designed it in the sixties when they

were redoing SoHo. He was the HVAC supplier for most of the block and got the property as part of a deal."

"HVAC?"

"Heating ventilation and air conditioning equipment. The Old Man sold the stuff and landed the contract, kind of on a fluke. But he did well on the deal and got the place too."

"Were you close to your father?"

"I guess, about as close as anyone in my generation gets." Peggy was going somewhere Jimmy preferred to avoid. He looked at his ring and rubbed the crest with his thumb.

"I like your ring. Was it your father's?" Jimmy nodded. Peggy took a closer look. "I think I've seen this design before."

"I doubt it; it was a custom design. He got it during World War Two."

"Oh, then maybe not. I'm not good at things like that."

"Tell me about your father," Jimmy said.

"Never really knew him. He and my mom didn't get along, and he left when I was a little kid. She married another guy who was nice, but I was kind of left out if you know what I mean; they did their thing, and I did mine. No big deal, most of my friends had the same thing going. Most of us did OK."

Jimmy was again emotionally touched. "But, tell me more about your condo," Peggy asked. How big is it?"

"About twenty-six hundred square feet. It was intended to be two units, but The Old Man combined the space."

"How big is twenty-six hundred?"

"Pretty big for New York."

"More than one bedroom?"

"Yeah, three."

"Three bedrooms is big."

"Most of the space is in the living area, though. There's quite a bit of room there."

"Sounds beautiful. Like to see it sometime."

"Anytime you'd like. I'd love to have you over."

Peggy sipped her wine, smiled her enchanting smile and looked into Jimmy's eyes. Quietly she asked, "how about tonight?"

Jimmy didn't know how to respond. Then he smiled and nodded. "You sure?"

Peggy returned the nod. "Yes."

Little more was said as they finished their drinks. Cabs were plentiful, and they were soon on their way to Jimmy's place.

Peggy's eyes were as wide as Jimmy had seen as she walked into his living room. He pointed out a few features as he made his way to the bar to open and pour another bottle of wine. They toasted and sat beside each other on the couch. Jimmy was beginning to ask a question when Peggy assertively locked with his lips. They were in private now. The little subtlety they had shown in public was no longer necessary. The quickness of her advance took him by surprise but lessened the awkwardness he usually felt before a first romantic encounter. Jimmy settled into the continuous kiss. Peggy encouraged him as his hands began cautiously to explore, skipping several stages Jimmy had learned to expect. They placed their glasses on the coffee table and were quickly horizontal. Peggy was pressing and squeezing as they continued to touch each other.

Then she stopped, sat up, took a sip of wine. "You never showed me the rest of your place. I'd love to see your bedroom."

Still embracing, Jimmy slowly led her down the hall. Peggy plopped on the bed and held out her arms. Jimmy unbuttoned his shirt, and she unzipped her dress. The disrobing ritual continued as the passion accelerated. At one point, sensing Jimmy was uncomfortable, Peggy became submissive. He relaxed; the now complete sexual connection was natural and uninhibited. Peggy had assumed the perfect angle and Jimmy was taken in.

Between periods of embraced sleep, the new lovers repeated their coupling several times. When they awoke in the morning, Peggy sprang out of bed and bounded down the hall to the bathroom. When she returned, she stood before Jimmy, still naked, looked down on him and gave him her smile. Jimmy noticed an unexpected decoration, a small tattoo of Tinker Bell on her right side just below the bikini line. Tattoos on women had always repulsed Jimmy, but this little addition seemed just another element of her perfection.

"Like my tat?" Peggy asked in a bubbly voice.

"Yeah—come back to bed."

"In a minute my love, need to brush my teeth."

"Yeah—I should too. I've got a new toothbrush for you in the guest bathroom—I'll get it."

"That's OK, got mine with me, in my purse."

Jimmy had to grin. Apparently, Peggy had decided on the night's events in advance. Her self-assuredness only made her more attractive. Jimmy put on a robe, got out of bed fully covered and stood next to Peggy in clear contrast to her comfortable nudity. Together they headed for the bathroom. They each freshened up and returned to bed.

At about ten o'clock, the new couple finally emerged from the bedroom. Jimmy was exhausted, Peggy still full of energy. As they entered the living area, Peggy took her first good look around in daylight.

"I love this place," she proclaimed as Jimmy went into the kitchen to make coffee. "So much space here. I just love it."

She investigated as Jimmy puttered. She examined each print, painting, and piece of furniture with admiration.

"How do you like your coffee?" Jimmy asked.

"Regular," Peggy replied. Jimmy placed the cups on the kitchen bar. Peggy pulled herself away from her exploration and joined him.

"Let's go for breakfast," Jimmy suggested.

"I'm sort of a mess," Peggy replied.

"You look fabulous," Jimmy retorted with a smile.

"Well, as long as you think so, OK."

As they slowly finished their coffee, Peggy asked many questions about things in the apartment, and Jimmy enjoyed explaining. When he mentioned Kate's involvement in the décor, Peggy looked at him and frowned.

"The woman with you on St. Patrick's Day?"

"We've been friends since we were kids. She was with her boyfriend, David. The two of them visited for a few days. I was the third wheel that night."

"Never know that the way you guys were talking so much."

"Well, by that time in their trip they were running out of things to talk about. And David may be on the way out."

"She'll be interested in you then?"

Jimmy was having a hard time understanding Peggy's concern. Putting Kate in context was not a simple matter.

"She's a friend. That's all."

"Sort of like a sister?"

Not quite right, Jimmy thought, but it would have to do. "Yeah, sort of like a sister."

The conversation jumped to how much they both enjoyed Sunday in New York. In no time, they had planned another day together. Peggy was willing to wear her clothes from the night before but had to have a shower. They each took a bathroom and revived themselves.

The day began with brunch at a little place off Central Park. Then they wandered. Peggy's shoes limited their walking, but they still covered nearly a mile before Jimmy hailed a cab.

They were lost in each other. The country was in two wars, the towers had been destroyed less than two years ago, and the economy had tanked. But Jimmy and Peggy were oblivious to it all. They visited parks and bars as they buzzed around town for the afternoon. Jimmy suggested they go to a restaurant for dinner, but Peggy felt uncomfortable in her second-day dress. So they settled on *Doc's*.

The bar was quiet. Gail quickly ascertained their last 24 hours. Jimmy ordered food, and the three snacked at the bar while Jimmy and Peggy had a few drinks.

The evening moved toward its inevitable end. The realities of the workday tomorrow set in. Jimmy knew Peggy wouldn't be staying another night, but he asked anyway. She would love to but didn't have what she needed to get ready for work in the morning and had to be there early. But she couldn't wait for their next date. They committed to the next weekend, and Jimmy promised to call as soon as he got home from work the next day to see if they could connect during the week. As they secured a cab, Peggy once again gave Jimmy a deep, passionate, and public kiss.

As she rode away, Jimmy relaxed and realized how tired he was. They had met less than a week ago, and he had been consumed with her since. Their first anxious date was less than forty-eight hours before. And now they had already crossed all the thresholds and become fully committed lovers. Jimmy's entire perspective, his sense of priorities, his concerns and criticisms had all changed. He was smitten.

* * *

Monday dragged on until Jimmy got home and called Peggy. She was giddy on the phone, and they carried on like kids. They could see each other for a few hours during the week but would have to wait for the weekend to really get together. Jimmy's longing was almost painful. He found himself envying Peggy's lingerie for its unlimited access to her. When Friday finally came, Peggy went directly to Jimmy's, and they feverishly released their suppressed desire. This time, she had all she needed for a weekend. They had two full days and nights to play. Jimmy arranged another romantic dinner for Saturday.

"This place is beautiful," Peggy said. "Every place you take me is beautiful."

"I'm glad you're here."

"By the way," Peggy said. "I just found out I have to take vacation in two weeks. I put in for June, but I'm the newbie and got April instead. You'll still be working, but maybe we can hang out some that week if it doesn't get in the way of your stuff. I don't have the money to go anywhere. I'd rather stay here with you anyway. And I should try to catch up with my other friends too."

Jimmy was flattered by Peggy's compliment and offer, but somehow he felt demoted from "her man" down to just one of her friends.

"Let's plan on spending the whole week together. I can usually get time when I want, and I'll see if I can take the week too. It would be great to hang out together like that."

"Really? That would be wonderful. Thank you. Can't wait."

He felt content. Their time would be exclusive.

"Now next Friday, if you're up for it, I got tickets to *Cats*. They're not the best, but they're very good. It's hard to get anything worthwhile for weekend shows, so when these came up, I went ahead and booked them hoping it would be OK with you."

"OK with me? I've wanted to go forever. I'm so excited. Thank you so much!"

Jimmy predicted Peggy's reaction when he bought the tickets. He was getting a rush from finding ways to please her. It seemed she had done so little, and he wanted to show her the world—at least his world. The wheels in his head were turning with ideas for their week together. He would definitely make it special. For now, he had a gourmet dinner to enjoy, a night on Broadway to discuss, and the anticipation of the rest of the evening to savor.

The following week the two talked every day and met for drinks a few times. Mike was fine with Jimmy taking time; he knew Jimmy would give it back several-fold when needed. On Wednesday, Jimmy had a brainstorm. After rolling the idea around a few hours, he called Stosh. It would be short notice, but the long-range forecast looked good, and the Gulf Coast would only be disturbed by a few late spring-breakers. It might be a good time to sail, and if not, there would be plenty of other alternatives in Florida. For Stosh, any time Jimmy wanted to visit was good, and he thought this time of year offered much potential. Even more vigorously than usual, he encouraged him to come. He was looking forward to meeting the new woman in Jimmy's life and knew Deb would agree. Feeling no need to consult with Peggy, Jimmy booked flights and a Gulf-side suite on Indian Shores just a mile from Stosh's.

Jimmy couldn't wait to spring the surprise. Before they knew it, it was Friday. Another full weekend together with more, much-anticipated intimacy. Jimmy would choose his timing carefully. But first, out to dinner and then *Cats*.

Dinner was good, but they found themselves rushing. Knowing how excited Peggy was, Jimmy wanted to be sure they didn't miss a minute of the show. They were quickly directed to their seats, front row, first balcony. From the beginning Peggy was sitting forward, swaying side to side, and occasionally bouncing up. She was so involved and springy the people behind her became noticeably annoyed. Jimmy chuckled. At the intermission, they went for drinks and chatted.

"I love this show," she said. "You see, it's about how animals are really people. But people don't know that. Some of my friends and I always thought so, but this proves it, don't you think? Did you know in France, I think, there are some guys who found out people's souls come back to life after they die and go into cats? I forgot what they call it, but they're all real scientists, so I know it's true. I'll have to call my friend and tell her about this show. She'll flip out. She'll be real excited to know we were right."

Peggy had said the first thing Jimmy found befuddling. While the two had talked for hours on end, they had never covered anything approaching an intellectual topic. Jimmy had assumed Peggy was smart and understood his thoughts. Here was a new side. Jimmy, the new boyfriend, found it cute. But to the philosopher, her attempt to dive deep was a belly flop.

"I like the Siamese. I always loved those cats. It's amazing how that actress can look just like one. I think I'd be a better Persian. Maybe that's where my soul will go next. You know? Into a Persian."

Peggy's elaboration might have seemed comical and been the springboard for a fun discussion. But she seemed serious. Jimmy wanted to explain the fundamentals of reincarnation, but under these circumstances, he didn't know how or where to start. Peggy looked at him with her smile. Jimmy felt comforted. He let it go. Maybe she was joking, and he hadn't caught on.

After the show, they hurried over to *Doc's* for a nightcap. Once they settled in with drinks in front of them, Jimmy decided it was time for the surprise.

"Peggy, I made plans for our week together."

"OK, whatever you want, Babe."

"Well, I thought we'd spend most of it in Florida."

"OK," she said and blinked. "FLORIDA!"

"If that's OK."

"If that's OK—You mean it?"

"Oh yeah. I already arranged everything. We fly out Saturday."

"I can't believe it. Never been to Florida—never been on a plane," Peggy paused. "I'm a little scared."

"I'll be right there with you."

"OK. Florida. I can't believe you. You are wonderful. I'll have to get some new clothes."

"There are several places near the hotel where you can get things."

"OK. Florida."

"One of my best friends lives near our hotel. He and his wife are excited to meet you. He has a sailboat, and if we get good weather, we'll go out for a couple of days."

"Hope they like me."

"I'm sure they will. And you'll like them."

"Never been on a sailboat. How do you go out for two days?"

"You sleep on the boat."

"Like camping?"

"Not on this boat. More like a floating house."

"Wow, you'll have to stay near me. I don't swim so good."

"I will, and you'll be fine."

This would be a trip of firsts for Peggy, a true adventure. He was pleased and found her fear of flying and sailing stimulating. She would need him. The white knight was back.

That night, their intimacy was even more intense. Peggy asked many questions about the trip, and each time Jimmy answered she embraced him tightly. The plan was paying off well in advance. The weekend was filled with Florida talk and looking at maps. Any concerns from Peggy's revelation at *Cats* were forgotten.

CHAPTER VI

Clear Sailing

"Come this way," Jimmy said.

"What? I can't hear you. It's so loud in here."

Jimmy moved near Peggy's ear. "Just follow me."

Jimmy led Peggy past long lines of colorfully dressed people of all shapes and sizes, some standing, some sitting on luggage, waiting to be checked in. A bored little boy whined and boxed his father's thigh. His old man looked away with a stern compressed face, trying not to explode. Others attempted to rest in contorted positions on bags or whatever free floor space there was. Unsupervised children ran everywhere, playing cops and robbers and tag while carelessly plowing into grumpy strangers. The lines were long and disorderly. Travelers waited patiently like well-dressed refugees at a sluggish border crossing.

A lone airline employee stood behind the counter. Between scripted questions about potentially sabotaged luggage and glancing over photo ID cards, she strained to hoist bag after bag of overweight luggage onto a conveyor. Six feet to her right stood two men, each behind a vacant check-in station. A woman with a sleeping infant approached one who politely told her his counter was for first-class passengers and directed her to the end of the winding mass.

Jimmy and Peggy strolled up to the idle agents and were received as dignitaries. Impressed, Peggy looked inquisitively at almost everything. "Where are all of these people going?"

"Disney. This time of year the Orlando flights are murder.

"Are we going to Disney?"

"No, we're going to Tampa, sailing."

"That's why we don't have to wait?"

"No, we're flying first-class."

Peggy smiled. Jimmy had explained the basics of the trip to her, but now it was first-hand. She was beginning to understand and liked what she saw.

They quickly cleared security and found their way to the lounge. This time, it was open and full of well-dressed, professional types, mostly men. Several engaged in aggressive discussions while others sat in comfortable chairs, sipped stiff drinks, and enjoyed a break from the office. Peggy wore her usual knockout attire and was immediately spotted by a few young "executives in training." Some looked curiously at Jimmy—was he a father, a relative, or the real thing? Peggy took his hand and gave him a quick kiss deciding the question. Jimmy walked proudly. The stuffed suits outnumbered him ten to one, but he was clearly the source of their envy.

The happy couple found a remote table, and Jimmy went to the bar to fill their preflight prescriptions. As soon as he left, a parasite zoomed over to Peggy. She was more than pleasant to her admirer. When Jimmy returned, she was explaining the trip. Knowing he wasn't going to score but still enjoying his bit of success, the invader excused himself.

"Well, I guess I should leave you and your friend alone. I hope to see you again sometime." Peggy smiled.

Jimmy was annoyed. Barely acknowledged on his return, he was once again "just a friend." Why didn't she say he was her man, her lover, or at least her boyfriend? Why hadn't she simply cut the guy loose?

Jimmy shook it off; it was probably her inexperience in the woods of corporate wolves. They talked a little about the trip and what to expect on the plane, and were called to their flight.

"I hope I'll be OK. I could have used another drink. Still a little scared."

"Don't worry. I'm right here, and you'll get all the drinks you want on the plane." Jimmy offered a comforting smile.

Onboard, the flight attendant immediately took drink orders. Peggy settled into her seat. She wondered why so many passengers were still waiting at the gate while a few had been seated and served. Another advantage of first class, Jimmy explained. She smiled. She was adjusting to privilege well.

The take-off scared her, but once in the air, she was fine. After all, Jimmy was right there, and the drinks were plentiful. When they landed, she showed no signs of nervousness. Her first flight had been fun.

Jimmy dropped the top of their rented convertible and headed for the causeway. They both reached for their sunglasses as the bright clear sky challenged their eyes. The warmth and smell of Florida spring air flowed into their faces as they motored in style along the long span across the aquamarine saltwater. Peggy looked everywhere, mesmerized. The cold from the rainy, dark morning in New York had chilled them. Now, they felt paradise.

After several miles of fighting traffic past used-car lots, strip malls, and drugstores, they stopped for an open drawbridge.

"I've never seen one before," Peggy said.

"A drawbridge?" Jimmy asked.

"No, one of those." She pointed to a tall palm tree.

On the Key, the salty smell strengthened. Tropical foliage and thick-bladed, dark-green grass surrounded the shops and vacation homes. Peggy could feel the strong warm breeze as they stopped in front of the hotel.

Jimmy left the car and luggage to the valets and led Peggy into a large open lobby looking out onto the beach. She gazed at the Gulf's endless water for the first time. Tanned bodies swam and rolled with the waves. Others stood in knee-deep water throwing frisbees. She watched sunbathers, some in comfortable loungers, some walking gingerly across the hot white sand, and others shuffling their feet in the surf looking for shells. All were wearing the latest bathing fashion. The seaside cabana-style bar was busy serving colorful drinks and oversized beers. In the elevator to their suite, Peggy asked, "Is there a place where I could buy a new bathing suit? I don't think mine will fit in here so good."

"Babe, you'll be the best looking one out there wearing anything. But sure, there are places near here we can walk to. We can stop at a couple bars on the strip too."

The enormous suite had a living area, full bar, hot tub, large balcony, and a bedroom with an oversized king. Peggy stared out at the panoramic sea views and watched the rolling waves as Jimmy came up from behind and put his arms around her. She took a deep breath, turned to him, gave him a long deep kiss, took his hand, and led him to the bedroom.

In the mid-afternoon, they finally dressed and left to shop. Jimmy led them to a boutique a block away specializing in the newest beachwear, bright summery clothes, and semi-formal dresses. Peggy walked aisle to aisle like a sleuth.

"There's so much in here, but I'll just find a suit so we can go. I can see shopping isn't your thing."

Peggy was right; shopping wasn't Jimmy's thing, particularly in a women's shop. But Jimmy wanted her to enjoy herself and not feel broke for a change.

"I'm going to leave a credit card account for you. Get whatever you want and take your time."

"I'll just look at suits, if that's OK."

"Why don't you look at everything? Get a couple of suits and some dresses and whatever else you'd like. This is your vacation. I want you to have the time of your life."

"You sure?" Peggy asked in disbelief.

"I'll be disappointed if you don't come out of here with a pile of things." Peggy gave Jimmy a big hug and went to work.

"I'll be next door at the bar."

Jimmy sat sipping on the large open deck. He fought off flashbacks of his early times with Clair. He was feeling the same excitement, and once again he was the mentor. Both girls were very sexual and turned heads. Both loved to shop. He wondered how to keep this relationship together. It was new, so problems were hard to foresee. As a wounded warrior of romance, though, Jimmy was sensitive to the dangers. And she was so young. In New York, no one batted an eyelash at a couple like them. Here there were already frowns. He knew the young Turks would try to score despite his presence. She'd still be hot well after he was on social security, he thought. What then? He took a swallow of beer and looked out onto the waterway. He relaxed. For now, and for a long time, he would be content with her and all of her loveable idiosyncrasies; any problems would be fixable. All would be good.

Peggy pushed the door open with her rear. She walked through the bar clutching a large, stuffed shopping bag in each hand and found Jimmy outside. "I hope this is all OK. I can take some stuff back," she offered as she took the seat next to Jimmy.

"It's more than OK. I hope you found lots of good things." Jimmy smiled broadly.

"Thank you, Baby; no one's ever treated me like you do." She gave him a hug.

The deck looked out on the Intracoastal pylons, docks, and many species of birds. Pelicans came and went, diving for snacks and then gliding on their broad wings back to their perches, where they threw back their heads, opened their throats and gulped down their catch. Powerboats and cruisers slowly navigated the canal, some stopping to moor at a favorite hang-out. Jimmy ordered shrimp and Peggy giggled as she tossed the tails to a bold begging heron. She looked across at the mansions on the far bank, most with pools, all with extensive manicured landscaping.

"Who lives in those houses?" she asked.

"People with a lot of money."

"More than you?"

"I don't know," Jimmy said, surprised.

"I'm sorry—that just came out—I'm really sorry—I didn't mean anything."

"Don't be—truth is I don't know. I have money, but I don't keep track of it. A friend takes care of all that. I know I have enough to do what I want. Maybe more than I should. I don't really know."

"Well, I know something. I know you're the best guy I've ever met. And you make me feel safe."

"Thank you. To me, that's an incredible compliment."

Peggy took Jimmy's hand and kissed him, lifting brows on the couple at the next table. They sat and sipped awhile until Jimmy said, "We'd better head back and get ready for tonight. Stosh and Deb are meeting us for dinner at eight."

"I hope they like me."

"They will love you."

As they walked toward the hotel, Jimmy noticed a jewelry store across the street.

"Come on, let's cross over and check that place out."

"OK, but why?"

"I feel like really buying you something."

Peggy held up her oversized shopping bags. "You just did."

"Come with me," he insisted as he took one of her bags to lighten her load. Inside the shop, Peggy was awed by everything and stunned by the prices. Jimmy quickly noticed a pair of diamond earrings.

"Like these?" he asked. "I think they were made for your ears."

"But they're so expensive."

"Try them on." A salesgirl carefully removed the earrings from the display case and helped Peggy put them on.

Looking in the mirror, Peggy announced, "They're so beautiful!"

"I agree. We'll take them," Jimmy said as he turned to the salesgirl and nodded.

Peggy looked at him stunned, dropped her bag, and threw her arms around him. "God, Jimmy, why do you treat me like this?" She kissed him.

Back in the room, Peggy pulled Jimmy down on the bed where they worked their way out of their clothes and spent the next half-hour. Then she showed him her new wardrobe and asked his advice on what to wear that evening. He suggested she model the new dresses and—though he was exhausted— he was stimulated as he watched her strip between changes. But for now, there wasn't time. They decided on one just as Stosh called from the front desk and Jimmy and Peggy had to scamper.

As they exited the elevator, Jimmy heard a familiar voice. "Hey, you frickin' son of a loon!" Stosh yelled from across the room.

"Good to see you too, Stosh," Jimmy said as he hurried toward his comrade.

The ladies waited awkwardly to be introduced as the two old friends greeted with a bear hug and a few words. Peggy's dress set her apart. But Deb and Stosh extended a warm welcome. Jimmy's friend was their friend. Stosh looked at his watch, corralled everyone, and led them quickly out to his car. He had chosen a well-known Greek restaurant on the Intracoastal where they could watch boats and drink in peace. Later in the evening, there would be a band. They made small talk as they piled into Deb's Suburban and headed out.

A line stood outside the packed restaurant. But Stosh had reserved a specific table with plenty of space, and they were quickly seated. Every chair offered an excellent view of the water. Stosh watched Peggy as she reached for Jimmy's hand and smiled. It had been a long time since he had seen his friend happy.

"Do you like my new earrings?" Peggy asked Deb.

"They're beautiful," Deb said. "How are things in the Big Apple?"

"Good. Ever since we met, we've been out on the town a lot. He even took me to see *Cats*. It's my favorite play. It was so good. Ever seen it?"

"We haven't, but I heard it was quite a production."

"It was. You'd love the Siamese."

Deb smiled and nodded. Jimmy and Stosh talked about old times while Peggy and Deb continued to chat. Jimmy filled Stosh in on Sal, Kate, and even Ray, although Stosh scowled through that part. They all ordered fresh seafood for dinner, and the drinks flowed. At around nine, a jazz trio began playing. The mellow, rhythmic music perfectly matched the clear Florida night. Peggy convinced Jimmy to dance, which shocked Stosh and Deb.

"There goes Fred Astaire again," Stosh said as Jimmy took the floor the third time.

"More like Forrest Gump," Deb said. They laughed.

"Well, what do you think of Peggy?" Stosh asked.

"The jury's still out. She's very young, doesn't have much to talk about, and I don't see what they have in common. But he's obviously nuts about her, and I definitely see why from a totally physical point of view. She might be good for him awhile. But I don't see anything long term. Notice the earrings?"

"Yup, that's our Jimmy. Well, it's just good to see him so up for a change. Whatever he wants is all right with me."

"He's up for sure. I just hope the laws of gravity don't grab hold of him too hard later on."

As Jimmy and Peggy were returning from the dance floor, a young man approached them and asked if he might dance with her.

"Is it OK?" Peggy asked.

"Of course; I'll be back at the table." Jimmy wasn't concerned about the dancing. But once again he was in no position to intervene without appearing possessive, and that made him uncomfortable. Back at the table, he snuck peeks as they danced and laughed through a couple of numbers. Finally, Peggy broke loose and made her way back to the table.

"He seems like a nice guy," Peggy said as she sat. "He's on a business trip and really misses his wife. I think that's sweet. I had to tell him all about our trip and how wonderful you are."

Once again the lovable, naive Peggy had gone for a harmless

swim with the sharks. This time, she'd come back making Jimmy feel like a king.

"Well, the weather looks good, the boat's ready, so we sail Wednesday," Stosh announced. "Think about where you wanna go. Don't be mad, but we have to be back in by Thursday night. I got business in Daytona early Friday."

"That will be great Stosh," Jimmy said. Having no idea of what to expect, Peggy nodded.

* * *

The sun shined brightly for the next few days, and Peggy took advantage of nearly every minute. She found a favorite spot on the beach and spread out glistening with oil in one of her skimpy new bikinis. She enjoyed the attention she attracted and the men who ambled by to introduce themselves. After a quick flirt, she would always point to Jimmy and remove the hook—catch and release. Jimmy sat next to her at times but more often chose the shade of a cabana bar where he sipped and read. At night, they dined and roamed the strip listening to bands and absorbing margaritas.

On Tuesday evening, they packed a few things for the boat and ordered room service. As they relaxed on the balcony, Jimmy gazed at the full moon. It had been only twenty-eight days since they met, one lunar cycle. It seemed much longer.

* * *

Only a few sailors bustled about the marina when they arrived. Jimmy knew better than to bring provisions, but he did stop for a bottle of Johnnie Walker Blue Label. Stosh liked scotch but, while he'd spend anything on Deb or a friend, he bore in mind his poor and frugal childhood and would never buy the best for himself. They quickly found their way to the slip. Stosh and Deb had been on board for a few hours. Everything was ready.

Stosh's fifty-one-foot Morgan was immaculate. The fore and aft berths provided plenty of privacy. The rest of the interior was appointed like a floating luxury apartment. After a short tour for Peggy's sake, she and Jimmy were led to the large front bedroom where they stowed their things, and then back on deck for the first round. Deb mixed a picnic jug full of Bloody Marys and poured three. Stosh would abstain until they anchored. Peggy had never been on anything larger than a runabout, but she quickly adapted to the opulence. She liked this lifestyle.

Stosh motored the sailboat out from the dock area and into open water where he raised the jib and caught a light wind. Deb and Jimmy took their places and followed each of Stosh's directions. Ropes squeaked through pulleys as they skillfully raised the mainsail. The canvas fluttered for a few seconds, then filled with a loud WOOOMP. The hull plowed into the choppy water spraying the deck and filling nostrils with the smell of brine. In minutes, the craft was moving at nearly eight knots as it cut through the water accompanied by the sounds of captured air and the rush of the wake. The salty spray increased as the boat heeled hard to starboard.

The angle scared Peggy, who was sure they were going to capsize. She clutched a life jacket as the others manned their stations and enjoyed the boat's command of the elements. Soon she was enjoying the ride.

Stosh headed for a quiet cove a few hours away that was part of a natural preserve with no structures or facilities of any kind. Only day visits were allowed, and anything brought on land must by law be removed. The beach was pristine and the wildlife unthreatened. Signs on the island read, *Take Only Pictures and Leave Only Footprints*. Here they could anchor and relax far from all but a few other sailors, each looking for the same peace and quiet.

Stosh slowly entered the calm bay and anchored about a hundred and fifty yards from shore and well away from other craft also just arriving. Jimmy helped set the anchor and secure the gear; then they all became comfortable in the large cockpit.

Jimmy could feel the heat through his light shirt. The air tasted of salt, and the bright blue sky made the perfect background for scores of seabirds. He listened to the waves wash against the hull. Turning his face to the sun, he grinned and exhaled.

"Chins up," Stosh declared as he raised his first drink of the day.

"Chins up," Jimmy and Deb responded.

"Cheers," Peggy added.

Stosh fired up the ship stereo.

"What's that?" Peggy asked.

"Light jazz," Stosh answered.

"I've never heard it; sounds kind of oldish." Stosh looked at Jimmy, surprised. Jimmy shrugged.

Peggy went below to change. She emerged in a red and white checkered bikini that barely held her oversized assets in place. Deb was in her conservative one-piece suit. Jimmy and Stosh wore their ancient, knee-length trunks. South Beach had collided with the retirement center pool.

After lathering up with oil, Peggy spread out a large beach towel near Jimmy and stretched out to work on her already deep bronze tan. She smelled of coconut and banana. Jimmy opened his nostrils and breathed in her liberally applied bouquet. As the old friends chatted about the economy, the two wars, and business, Peggy took her towel and bag and relocated to a spot on the bow where she could listen to her music.

Peggy returned a few times to reload her glass with a new Bloody Mary and then for lunch. Deb had ordered fresh New York deli-style sandwiches. Everyone thought they were delicious and briefly all had something in common. After the feast, Peggy returned to her spot to continue her project, and Deb went below for a nap. For the first time on the trip, the two old friends were alone.

"Well—what do you think of Peggy?" Jimmy asked.

"Nice girl."

"I know she's young, but we've really connected, and she's a lot of fun."

"Whatever you want is good with me," Stosh said reassuringly. Jimmy didn't respond, and Stosh felt a need to expand. "Look, you been through a ton of crap. If this gal makes you happy, that's all I care about. And, you know, it's early. Let it ride out for a while. Play it by ear. There's lots a time. If it works, great; if not, that's gonna be OK too. There's lots a time."

"Is there? I'm not feeling so young anymore. Sometimes it seems like we look sort of temporary and out of place. But she turns me on so much. I don't want to give it up, and if this one crashes, I don't know if I'll ever be able to get another woman like her. Am I making any sense?"

"Look, I been married a long time. I don't know what you're feelin'. But it seems to me you figure you've got your nuts on the line, and I don't see it that way. There'll always be more women if that's what you want. You're smart, good lookin', rich, and a hell of a guy. But, this might work out fine too. Just because she's young don't mean it isn't gonna work out. The older-man-younger-woman thing happens all the time now. Just be careful. You got this knack a over-thinkin' things and not figurin' on what's best for you. I don't know where you got it, not from The Old Man for sure, but you got it."

The Old Man, the subject would have to come up though it hadn't been on Jimmy's mind awhile.

"I got a load of letters from Gord," Jimmy said. "Stuff The Old Man wrote during the war. I didn't know he was such a wild asshole when he was young. I'm still figuring it out. I probably shouldn't even be talking about it, but it looks like my take on him was all wrong."

"Wild A-hole?" Stosh asked. "You sure? Doesn't sound like the guy I knew?"

"Me neither. You wouldn't believe the shit he pulled." Jimmy gave examples of The Old Man's escapades, and they started laughing. Each new story made them laugh harder.

"Wow—well, maybe he was more like us than we figured. But we never went so far as you're sayin' he did." Stosh paused. "Ya know—I was never able to tell you how I felt about the guy. I mean, you and Sal always had the brains and the loot. But I had to work. And I wanted to work."

Stosh took a long sip. "I know you remember my dad. He was a good guy. But he never got a break, and he didn't have much ambition. I think it was the war. He was in the infantry, you know. Probably shot some guys. You just don't know how that could mess you up. He worked odd jobs, and he seemed OK with it. He didn't want any more. To him, it was enough and a lot better than he'd grown up with. But, Jimmy, your Old Man, your Old Man worked his butt off. He put it on the line and made it happen. I know you didn't like the business much, but it was my shot. Your Old Man made sure if I worked hard, I did good. He showed me the ropes. Then when you all but give me the business—"

"Just a second," Jimmy interrupted. "We both did fine in that deal. And you'll still be paying me for a lot of years."

"Yeah, crap. You coulda' sold it for five times what you give it to me for, and if you hadn't figured out the financin', which I still don't understand, it woulda' never happened. You two gave me the shot. I don't think I ever told you, but when you and Sal went off to college, your Old Man wanted to send me too. I didn't want nothin' to do with it. Heck, I barely made it outta' high school. Hated it. The idea a college made me sick. I wanted to work. Working with him taught me more than I was ever gonna get outta more school. And it felt good. I felt I was earning my money, and I had more than I thought I'd ever see.

"What The Old Man really showed me was how good it feels to work hard. And when you came back and ran things, I loved workin' for you too. I knew you wanted to do somethin' else. That gave me the chance to make decisions and learn how the whole thing worked. Now I got more than I know what to do with and I still love to work. To me, it's not the dough so much as how it feels. You know? Earning it, that's what The Old Man taught me. And now that the boys are in the business, it's even better. Oh, they can be a couple a frickin' boneheads, but they're hard workers. Without the Eaglesons, I don't know what me and mine woulda' done."

Jimmy was quiet. How could two people have taken away such different views on life from the same man? And, here was another story of The Old Man's generosity, topped off by the stinging contrast between Stosh's and Jimmy's children. But what hit the hardest was, once again, the idea of earning something. Stosh enjoyed life, making plenty of money with an honest business where lots of people found good jobs. And Stosh felt like he was worth something, like The Old Man. Sometimes, when he let himself think about it, Jimmy felt like a rich failure. But, maybe Sal was right, for Jimmy at least, maybe there was no more earning it.

"Anyway," Stosh continued "if he was more like us than we figured, I guess it's OK with me. Fact, I think I like that."

Stosh looked at his drink. "You know, The Old Man gave me my first beer. I was at the old place. You were gone somewhere. Well—" Stosh laughed, "The Old Man yelled from the porch for me to come join him. He grabbed a beer from that old fridge he had out there—you remember that thing—and he popped it open and handed it to me." Stosh laughed again. "I sat there drinkin' for a half-hour with 'im. Yeah, until you came and we left for somethin' or other. First drink I ever had. My dad woulda' never done nothin' like that."

Neither would The Old Man with me, Jimmy thought.

A loud musical alarm from a cell phone came from the bow. Peggy quickly rummaged through her bag and answered. Phones, beepers, or any other non-essential communication devices on the boat were taboo.

"I'm sorry," Jimmy said. "I didn't know she had one with her. It's not her fault."

"What was that?" Deb asked as she appeared from below. Stosh nodded in Peggy's direction; where she chatted away holding what looked like a business card in her hand.

"Who's she talking to?"

Jimmy and Stosh shrugged in unison as they both took a gulp of beer. Deb shook her head, poured a drink, and rejoined the party in the pit.

After the call, Peggy returned for a fresh cocktail. For the afternoon, Deb had mixed a large batch of margaritas, and Peggy wasn't shy about helping herself.

"It's nice out here—a little quiet, but nice," Peggy said.

"We like the quiet," Deb responded. Peggy glanced at the other three and nodded. The ear-buds she'd left on her blanket cranked out a fast, high-pitched, rhythmic snapping that attacked the tranquil light jazz. Peggy was impervious but soon took care of the problem anyway as she again bored of the conversation, returned to her perch, and stuffed the buds back in her ears.

In the late afternoon, a forty-foot power cruiser burst into the cove well beyond the speed of a responsible boater. It anchored at the far end, and the boisterous party onboard intensified. Peggy was drawn to the activity and watched like an envious child at a playground. The others were irritated.

"These frickin' punks piss me off," Stosh proclaimed as the invaders' wake rocked the boat. "With all the beach-side joints, why do they have to dick with the sailors?"

Peggy stood on the bow, looking in the powerboat's direction with a big smile. She posed to put herself on display. Jimmy got a knot in his stomach. He had already begun to wonder if sailing with her was a mistake. Now he was graveled by her need to make herself the center of attention with assholes like this. Jimmy heard a distant splash, and then another. The roar of marine engines followed and increased as two jet skis, each with a pair of partiers, raced around from the cruiser's far side. Now Peggy was glaringly excited. As she jumped and clapped her hands, her breasts jiggling like a pole dancer's.

"Frickin' A," Stosh said as he went below to report the affair to the Coast Guard. Not so many years before he would have taken care of the situation himself. But he'd mellowed and with the new drinking and boating laws, the authorities had become much more aggressive. Whether a patrol boat was nearby would be the big "if."

Peggy watched the invaders weave among the anchored boats, competing to see who could make the biggest waves and draw the most protests. She looked at Jimmy. "Do you think they'd let me ride?" she asked. As they approached Stosh's boat, she waved, and one stopped for a better look.

"Nice," the driver yelled before he made a suggestive gesture. His female partner slapped his head, and he reluctantly turned and sped away. Jimmy was pissed. Peggy continued to show off. As he stood to try and reel her in, a small official boat motored into the far end of the cove. The marauders were busted. The tickets would be plentiful and the fines severe. Peggy was heartbroken, Jimmy elated, Stosh and Deb toasted.

"Why can't they just let them have fun?" Peggy said. "They weren't bothering anybody." No one responded. They had all come to realize Peggy's place on this sail.

As the evening set in, Stosh prepared to cook, Peggy changed into a sweat suit, Deb and Jimmy continued to sip, and all calmed down. Jimmy sat with his arm around Peggy. Snuggling into him, she actually joined into the conversation, and her bad fit in the afternoon seemed like a fluke. All were relaxed by the slow sunset. By the time they finished their steak, the effects of the day and drink had them sleepy and, after a stiff nightcap, the couples retreated to their berths.

Peggy was already horizontal when Jimmy closed the door. With the afternoon's irritations long gone, he was fired up for her. Nothing was better than to be anchored, feeling the slow rock from the sea and in bed with a beautiful woman, and for Jimmy it had been a long time. As he moved toward her with what had become an automatic first touch, Peggy stiffened.

"Not here Jimmy, they'll hear us and I'm really tired tonight, OK? I'm sorry, Honey."

Jimmy's passion drained. This was the first time Peggy had turned him away, and this night was to be the highlight of the trip. He lay back in frustration and disappointment. This was a feeling he knew all too well, and hated. He rationalized it was OK. She'd be right back tomorrow; she just had too much sun and booze, and she didn't know Stosh and Deb enough to be comfortable. After all, he was being selfish and wasn't thinking how she felt as the newcomer trying to fit in. It was all OK. They still had another night in the hotel, and that would be spectacular. As he calmed himself listening to water gently slap the boat, Peggy fell asleep and started snoring, another first.

In the morning, Jimmy heard Stosh banging around in the galley. Peggy was still out cold. As he left the berth, he was careful not to wake her. The morning sparkled under clear skies, and they would have most of a day before they returned to the marina. Stosh's coffee was always strong, and Jimmy winced as his first sip shocked his taste buds. They spoke quietly for a few minutes.

Jimmy went on deck for early morning time alone. As he sipped from his mug, he surveyed the cove. In the chill, a slight fog rose from the translucent green water. On shore, lines of palms and tall grass stood behind white sand, recently decorated at the shoreline with a fresh layer of shells. The sea lapped the beach with regularity. A few birds, some strolling on the sand, others diving for breakfast, composed the soundtrack. The other boats appeared vacant. Jimmy's was the only human presence.

Stosh popped through from below with Canadian bacon sandwiches and two stiff Bloody Marys. "I don't know about you, but I need a little of this," he said as he took a long sip. Jimmy joined him, more from politeness than a hangover.

"It's a beautiful morning, Stosh," Jimmy said.

"Most are down here, or did you forget?" Jimmy *had* forgotten. It had been a long time since he had peeked outside the corporate box he'd placed himself in.

"Yes, I remember some."

As they talked, Deb poked her head up. "Anyone need anything?" she asked.

"Nope, we're fine for now," Stosh responded.

Peggy came to life about ten. She did her best to doll herself up and joined the others. Her first Bloody Mary went down fast. The second, joined by coffee, she sipped. Soon she was fixed and ready to continue her mission on the foredeck.

Jimmy had another plan for himself. He'd been admiring the shore for most of the morning. A quick dive was followed by the sensation of warm saltwater lifting him to the surface. It had been some time since he swam in the sea and he'd forgotten about its buoyancy. Champlain would swallow you like a rock if you stopped working to stay on top, but this bay liked to keep things on the surface. He began a slow, steady breaststroke as he headed to the shore. The regularity of motion, the pungent smell of salt, and the warm sun on his back cleared his mind. Near shore, he touched a bottom of tiny crushed shells and then floated on his back, letting the gentle current push him into knee-deep water where he flipped over and stood.

Jimmy surveyed the beach's bright white sand decorated with clumps of seaweed in various stages of decay. Palm fronds rustled in the mild breeze. The birds ignored him. He sat in the water pawing through new shells, all small and clean. He looked at the beach. No footprints, no picnic junk, no beer cans, no yellow sand. He knew others would invade in their dinghies and explore later. But he'd let it be. He sat and absorbed the peace.

After a few more minutes, he waded out to his waist, made a shallow dive and began a slow swim back toward the boat. Everything on board seemed quiet and calm. Peggy lay in maximum tanning position while Deb and Stosh talked in the cockpit. Hearing Jimmy's approach, Peggy sat up to greet him and then stood quickly. She shaded her eyes and bent her knees straining to see. In a panic, she stood straight, pointed somewhere beyond Jimmy, started jumping up and down, and screamed, "SHARK!"

Stosh and Deb instinctively joined the warning making sure Jimmy heard. His breaststroke immediately shifted to full-speed freestyle. Deb and Stosh began frantic coaching: come on Jimmy, faster Jimmy, you're going to make it Jimmy, you're almost here Jimmy, move it Jimmy. At the platform, his foot scraped against a rogue barnacle. The bleeding intensified the pandemonium on deck. Stosh, now armed with a spear gun, extended his arm to haul Jimmy out. After an eternity, their hands joined. Stosh swung Jimmy onto the boat and stood ready with his weapon.

No attacker showed. Maybe it was submerged? Deb left the cockpit to join Peggy and asked if she could see the shark. Still jumping, she pointed to a spot about a hundred yards off, just behind Jimmy's route. Deb shook her head. In the panic, no one had thought to confirm Peggy's sighting. Now it all seemed dumb.

"Those aren't sharks," she informed Peggy and nodded toward a pair of dolphins playing in the distance.

"Oh—how can you tell?" Peggy asked.

"We'll talk about it later, but there isn't a shark."

"Oh well, better safe than sorry," Peggy declared, still proud she had tried to save the day.

Steaming, Deb returned to the cockpit where Stosh was treating Jimmy's cut, looked at her husband and, ignoring Jimmy's presence, declared, "NOW the jury is in. That girl is as dumb as a box of rocks!"

Jimmy's cut was minor, and Stosh bandaged him up quickly. Jimmy went to the foredeck to join Peggy without much to say but feeling a need to thank her for her concern, at least. He knew Deb would calm down soon. He thanked Peggy, who gave him a kiss and a light hug, careful to keep from losing much oil.

"I didn't know they weren't sharks," she said. "But I would do the same thing again if I thought you were going to be hurt."

Jimmy exhaled. Bright or not, it seemed her heart was in the right place. He suggested she catch a few more rays before lunch. Peggy nodded, and he returned to the cockpit for a drink.

Stosh put himself on the wagon until they got back to the

marina, but Jimmy put down several beers. With both girls occupied, this would be their last time to talk openly. They chuckled over the shark affair. It would be a great story for future reminiscing. Stosh was kind to Peggy, and when Deb joined them she whispered an apology to Jimmy. After all, if Peggy was going to be Jimmy's girl, they would need to fit her in.

* * *

A new wave of northern weekenders was invading the hotel lobby when Jimmy and Peggy returned. The realization set in that tomorrow their trip was over. Jimmy had planned for time in New York, maybe a nice Saturday dinner and a quiet Sunday together. He knew Peggy had not much enjoyed the sail. Tonight they would reunite as a couple without the stress of additional company. As soon as they got to the room, Peggy bee-lined for the bathroom and announced she would be in the tub awhile. Jimmy opened a beer, sat on the balcony and looked at the Gulf. As he relaxed, he saw Peggy scamper from the bathroom and rummage through her purse until she found her cell phone. She was dialing as she bounced back to her bath. He wondered who she had been calling but assumed it was a girl thing and none of his business. Still, it was annoying. He returned to the view. Dozens of boats dotted the water. He wondered how everyone out there was getting along.

After dinner, Peggy said she was tired. Jimmy had hoped to catch a band; maybe he'd even try to cut a rug again. But

Peggy didn't want to dance, so he conceded, and they returned to the room. Peggy changed, and Jimmy opened a bottle of wine. They sat on the balcony and sipped.

"Thank you for everything; this has been a wonderful trip," Peggy said.

"I hope you enjoyed yourself."

"I loved it, and your friends are nice."

"Maybe we can come back the next time we get a chance," Jimmy suggested.

"I'd like that."

Storms were beginning to form over the water as they chatted speculating on the next week in New York. When the bottle was finished, Peggy took Jimmy's hand, gave it a little squeeze, got up and went into the bedroom. Jimmy followed. Between the sheets, Peggy lay on her side with her back to him. He reached for her, and she turned. Jimmy kissed her. She allowed him to make love to her. She knew his routine and followed systematically. When they were finished, she gave him a peck on the cheek and turned back on her side. Jimmy got up and returned to the balcony. Peggy didn't respond to his leaving.

He opened a beer and watched the storms watering parts of the Gulf. He thought of how it had only been one month, the most intense sexual connection he had ever known, and it had already turned into an act of servicing. He hated gratuitous sex. Clair had mastered the technique. The memory haunted him. He was like a child under her control in those days. She would set the tone, allow the physical act from time to time, but withhold the passion. Bump-on-a-log fucking. The only thing worse was nothing at all. Like last night. And like Clair, Peggy's smile had changed. How did this happen?

The reality of their differences was settling in. What was he thinking? Maybe Deb was right. He started feeling regret. Should he try to find a graceful way out? But how and then what? Was he ready to return to his solo act of the past few years?

He thought more. Soon he started feeling hopeful again. After all, she was tired from a couple of days she didn't enjoy much and were for his benefit, not hers. The last two nights were not typical for them. Once back in New York, they would settle back into their thing, and it would all be good again. She probably had no idea he thought anything was wrong. It was ridiculous to think their hot, passionate phase would be permanent. That would come and go. That's what makes it special. Without ups and downs, it would grow stale at some point anyway. And, he had to remember how young and beautiful she was. When was a guy like him going to have a shot like this again? He was going to have to work more at it and be more understanding. Yeah, things were OK. Most of the trip had been great, and the relationship was good. Tomorrow they'd be back on their turf and things would be fine. Feeling better, Jimmy continued to watch the water. He wasn't tired yet.

CHAPTER VII

Back to Business

Peggy bounced around packing and listening to her music through her earbuds. Jimmy interrupted a few times to ask a question. She quickly answered and went back to her world. She made another phone call before the porter came for the luggage. Jimmy hadn't felt this ignored in years and the hope he'd mustered the night before faded. Peggy turned, smiled, and gave him a peck on the cheek as he helped her into the car. She popped her buds back in on the way to the airport and bopped along looking out the window. Jimmy felt abandoned.

Their plane was delayed. After a long security check, Jimmy and Peggy headed for the lounge. Jimmy ordered drinks and watched the hounds sniff Peggy. In one of her new dresses, she definitely highlighted the room. She continued her trip-long performance, encouraging attention whenever she could. This time, Jimmy didn't care.

After some drinks and idle conversation with other passengers, a couple from Iowa settled in next to them. He owned a shoe store, and she had been a stay-at-home mom until their kids were out. Her job now was to henpeck him. They were on their way home from two weeks at Disney.

"How did you like it?" Jimmy asked.

"It was fine," the woman responded. "We've been before. This time, we looked at the international things."

"I'd like to go someday," Peggy said.

"Well, why don't you get your husband to take you?" the woman asked.

"He's not my husband, and we came down this time to go sailing."

"Doesn't sound like much of a vacation to me, with Disney down the road and all."

"It was OK. How do you like my tan?"

Jimmy didn't care much for this kind of small talk, but he was grateful Peggy had found someone to entertain her.

"Where you from?" the man asked Jimmy.

"New York," Jimmy responded.

"Never been there. I'd like to see it sometime, but it's not the wife's cup of tea."

"How would you know, know-it-all?" his wife said. "And a little tea wouldn't hurt you. Did you tell him how many bottles you drank on this trip?"

"Yeah, I put down a few."

"It wasn't as much as a few; do you want people to think you're an alcoholic?"

"Well just how much is a few?" the man asked.

"Don't be wise when we're talking to strangers. Everyone knows what a few means."

"Four or five?" he taunted.

"No, it's not four or five; everyone knows a few is around six or more."

"Well, then what's four or five?"

"Four or five is four or five, and you know that perfectly well."

"So there's no term for that amount, four or five?"

"No, and you're acting like an idiot."

"So can I say a couple?"

"Are you trying to show everyone just how stupid you are? Everyone knows that a couple is two or three, not four or five." She looked at Peggy and rolled her eyes.

"So how can I say four or five?" the man continued.

"You say four or five!" His wife was now nearly screaming. "It wouldn't hurt you to be specific for a change, you moron. If you mean a couple, say a couple, but know what it means. If you mean a few, say a few. If you mean four or five, say four or five!"

The man nodded and turned to Jimmy. "I think I drank four or five."

Jimmy was trying to keep from cracking up without much success when the intercom called for the flight to Des Moines and the entertainment ended. Peggy turned to Jimmy. "She's right you know; that guy shouldn't be so wishy-washy. Do you think we could go to Disney if we come back?"

Jimmy nodded. "Sure thing," he said. "I'll get right on that Babe," he said under his breath.

On the plane, things were quiet. Jimmy looked out the window while Peggy read a book she'd found about cat-people. The few words they spoke were friendly and about nothing. The flight and the landing were smooth. Once they had their bags, Jimmy hailed a cab. As they eased into the back seat, Jimmy felt OK. They were back in New York.

Peggy turned to Jimmy and squeezed his hand. "Honey, would you mind if we took the night off and I went home? I'm really tired and kind of partied out. You know I think I might have caught some kind of bug too. I'd like to take a bath and go to bed early."

Jimmy was relieved. He hadn't been looking forward to continuing into the night. "Of course, Babe, no problem, we could both use a little down time." Jimmy directed the cabbie to Peggy's place where he unloaded her bags and took them to her door. She gave Jimmy a deep kiss and held him for a minute.

"Let's talk in the morning," she suggested. "You scoot off and let me see what shape my roommate has left this place in."

Jimmy joined the cabbie downstairs. After dropping off his luggage, he directed the cab to *Doc's*.

Gail had the night off, and none of the regular crowd was there. Jimmy had a quick beer and walked home disappointed. He wanted to talk to someone, a friend, anyone, about anything, just talk. He felt lonely but also relieved to be alone. For a second time, his mind churned over the last few days. He realized he was doing it again, trying to mold someone. Peggy was gorgeous and young, and he had wanted to show her the world. And now that he had come into her life, how could she possibly make it without him? She was barely surviving when they met. It broke his heart to think of her living like that again. He felt responsible for her happiness. But they didn't fit. Sometimes he was actually embarrassed to be with her. But, maybe there was still a way. She was a good person. All this needed was a little time. He would have to find workable common ground, other than just sex. He took comfort in knowing she was at the other end of the phone if he wanted. He wasn't really alone; things would be OK. He was overreacting and making himself miserable over nothing. He would have a few beers, listen to music, and think it over a little more. Then, a good night's sleep.

* * *

Jimmy woke at 8:00. After coffee and a glance at *The Times,* he went for a walk. A need to call Peggy hung over him, but he thought she would sleep late, and it was a lovely bright day. He hadn't taken the subway for a long time and grabbed a train up to the park. It would give him a lift, even if from underground.

As he rode, he thought about work. He wondered what surprises Gyges would have for him this week. Things were quiet when he left, but who knows what kind of crap brewed in his absence. Then there was Peggy. Time would be the key; best to slow down and see. Things had a way of working themselves out. By the weekend, things would be different.

As he ascended to the street, the sun became stronger and stronger until it forced him to shade his eyes. The park was lightly inhabited. He bought coffee and a muffin from a vendor and sat on a bench. He felt better. The weather, the park, and the strangers helped. Birds and squirrels and dogs and kids all attracted his attention. He stood and resumed his walk.

No plan, no particular direction, just a good free "stroll in the park." After about an hour and a half, he worked his way back to the street, hailed a cab, and went home. Almost time to call.

The phone rang five times before Peggy answered. "Hello?" she said in a raspy voice.

"Hi. You sound stuffy."

"Yeah, I think I have a cold."

They talked about a few little things, chit-chat, the kind Jimmy wasn't much good at. Then Jimmy asked, "I guess you'd rather rest than go out today?"

"Yeah, I'm still beat. Thank you again."

"You're welcome. I hope you feel better, and I'll call tomorrow. OK?"

"Yup, sounds good, bye."

"Bye."

Jimmy felt relieved. The obligation was met, and he had the day. He unpacked, organized and reviewed his work for the next week and left for the bar.

Gail was full of questions. Jimmy focused on the positive and kept his concerns to himself. Best not to talk about such things when they would be gone soon enough, and anything said now could return to haunt.

Gail gave gazes of envy when Jimmy talked of sailing. "Where will you go next?"

"I don't know. We haven't decided."

"Say, where is the beautiful young lady?"

"A little under the weather."

"Too bad, the day after a trip like that needs a little libation and relaxation."

"Yeah, I know, that's why I'm here."

Several regulars floated in as the afternoon passed, and Jimmy felt good. In the early evening, he grabbed pizza at the bar and went home to relax alone.

* * *

Jimmy walked into a busy office on Monday morning. He saw a message from Mike on his desk and immediately called. Mike would be right over.

Mike held his hand to his mouth, coughed several times and struggled to clear his throat. "Good to see you," he said. "Listen, a few things are piling up, and I happen to feel like shit. Here are four prospects that need to be finished by Monday. Take one, and distribute the others any way you want. I'm going home. You hold the fort. I'll be back in next week. This cold feels like I need real down time; I think I'd better ride it out and rest. No calls from anyone but you, and try to keep those to a minimum. You're in charge. I sent a memo."

"OK. I hope you feel better soon."

"Me too. Right now I feel like death warmed over. OK, I'm out." Mike dropped the folders on Jimmy's desk and left.

As Jimmy was reviewing the projects, a rare visitor walked in. "Back from sunny Florida I see. Not much of a tan." Jimmy looked up to see Barry Gyges in front of his desk. "Say, I hear you're doing Peggy Jones. I've thought of going there myself; she's a hot one. Better be careful though, might be too much for that old heart of yours. She's made stronger guys than you say uncle. They tell me she can really destroy a box spring."

Jimmy controlled the impulse to stand and swing. He took one folder and handed the other three to Gyges. "These need to be done by Monday morning."

"Why do I get them all? I'll have to work half the weekend."

"We need your expertise."

"Does Mike know about this?"

"You got the memo. You want me to call him?"

Gyges held his tongue for a change and thumbed through the stack. He stood back a moment, put his hand in his pocket and rubbed The Old Man's lighter. "OK, Doctor Eagleson, if that's the way you want to play, I'm in." He stuffed the papers under his arm and left.

Jimmy perused his folder, but his mind was on Gyges's comments. What did he know about Peggy, and from where? Must have been her friend he dated. And this was Gyges; he could create bullshit with the best of them. He was probably trying to work his way under Jimmy's skin, as usual. Jimmy was glad he didn't respond, and glad he'd poured on the work. He knew one guy who was going to be very busy.

The rest of the week went much as expected. Jimmy called Peggy a couple of times, and they talked pleasantly. The question of the weekend hadn't come up yet, but Jimmy was ready. He was now looking forward to seeing her.

On Thursday, Peggy said she still felt too achy to do anything that weekend. Jimmy was disappointed, but on Friday morning Mike called to ask if he would meet with clients from out of town. He was still very sick, and it was important. Fortunately,

Jimmy was free, and he would do anything for Mike although he wasn't crazy about the place near the theater district the visitors had requested. But the food was good, and it had beer.

Jimmy arrived about seven. A quiet, out-of-sight table had been reserved, and the three executives, two men, and a woman, were already there. In fact, they were on their second round. Jimmy introduced himself and ordered a beer, and they settled into their dinner discussion. The ice was broken when one guest told an off-color joke the woman enjoyed. The business was easily accomplished, and Jimmy soon assessed the meeting had been unnecessary. The real purpose was a company-paid trip to New York, and Jimmy was happy to be a part of it. The new companions tried to convince him to join them at a comedy club, but Jimmy graciously declined. They left about 9:00 and Jimmy decided to stay for one more drink.

The railroad-style bar had booths along a series of large windows facing the street. At this hour, the view mixed the action on the street with reflections of activity in the room. Jimmy found a stool and watched. After a few minutes, he noticed a familiar image reflecting at him from a booth a few down from his stool. It looked like Barry Gyges. It would make sense; this was his kind of place. The man was facing someone and listening intensely. Both his arms were extended across the table. Yes, it was definitely Gyges, and it was all looking very romantic.

This was Jimmy's chance to shake up his nemesis for a change. He strategically used a couple being seated as a shield as he snuck down to surprise the love birds. It felt juvenile, but he enjoyed it. Once he was in position, the couple moved on, and Jimmy had a clear view. His heart dropped. Gyges sat smiling and gazing into Peggy's wide eyes. Peggy! Gyges was with Peggy! They were holding hands across the table as she talked. She wore her new earrings and one of her Florida dresses, a red one Jimmy had told her he found especially sexy.

Jimmy stood speechless. Gyges felt the stare and turned his head. Then Peggy looked. She paled and yanked her hands away. She looked down. Gyges didn't. He stayed fixed on Jimmy and gave him the smirk.

Jimmy stood for a few more seconds. His primal side wanted to kill Gyges and ravish her, leaving whatever was left for the waiter. His romantic side wanted to sweep her away from this fraud. The problem solver looked for a fix; maybe this wasn't what it looked like. But, the sting in his gut told him to leave. He turned and forced himself to walk casually to his stool, retrieve his coat and briefcase, and exit to the street. He waited an agonizingly long time for a cab. In the back seat, he worried about his appearance at the bar. He had developed a painfully firm erection standing there and hoped it hadn't been apparent. It was only now starting to subside. His head was hot and tingling, his palms were wet, and he felt sick to his stomach. The cabbie asked him where he wanted to go three times before he finally answered—*Doc's.*

The burning sense of betrayal and jealousy throbbed. Somehow this woman he had struggled not to dump became the only one in the world he wanted. Why Gyges? Why the man he detested? Had they been to bed? Had she done the same things with him? Had he seen Tinker Bell? Jimmy was obsessed with thoughts of the two of them together, his gorgeous young lover and the world's biggest idiot. And what would Jimmy do now? Would he ever have sex again? Was Gyges the mystery caller in Florida? Had that son of a bitch ruined his trip? Over and over he came back to the question, how could this happen?

By the time he got to *Doc's*, Jimmy had regrouped some. Gail was off, but he found a spot next to Tony and Art. They greeted him warmly and returned to their never-ending debate. Jimmy tried to listen, but his mind wasn't cooperating. Things in the room sparked memories of Peggy. Jesus, it had only been a month. You'd think it was years.

Tony left for the men's room, and Art turned to Jimmy. "Where's that beautiful young lady you've become so attached to?" he asked. Jimmy didn't know how to answer and wondered how many times he would have to field this question. "Margarette isn't it? I always liked that name. You're something of a scholar, Jimmy, wasn't it in Gerota? Didn't Faust have a Margarette?"

"He probably had this one—looks like everyone else has," Jimmy snapped, startling Art. Then Jimmy smiled. "We're not seeing each other any longer."

Art nodded, understanding. "Well, we won't need to talk of her anymore."

They went on to other topics. Art made an effort to keep Jimmy in the conversation after Tony returned. Jimmy was drinking much faster than usual, and after several Crowns became opinionated and negative. His companions noticed how out-of-sorts he was. But they knew he was upset, and this was New York, so he wouldn't be driving.

By 1:30 Jimmy was a drunken puddle and the few friends who had stayed with him convinced him to take a cab home. His tie was loose and crooked, and one shirttail hung out as he stumbled outside. He pulled his suit coat on his shoulders and began to hail a cab but changed his mind. He wanted to walk. A different way though. He wanted a change.

Both his sense of direction and distance were shot. After drifting awhile, he found himself in the "Tenderloin." He was just sober enough to know he'd taken a wrong turn and stopped to check a street sign. On the far corner, an old, dirty drunk was throwing up on the street. The smell almost made Jimmy follow suit. Behind him, at a small dive with a few chairs and a bent metal table on the sidewalk, two men were ranting about something. One coughed violently enough to expel a lung. They watched Jimmy suspiciously. As they stood, he increased his pace, as much as he could in his condition. He didn't look back to see they didn't follow.

Jimmy got his bearings and wobbled down a street that would bring him back around. But it would be a few blocks. As he staggered by a rat-hole building, he saw a woman huddled in a doorway with a young girl. The woman was bandaged over half of her face; blood had seeped through part of the dressing. Both were covered in a threadbare blanket. The little girl clung to a ragged stuffed animal. Jimmy stopped. He pulled a fifty-dollar bill from his pocket, stumbled over and tapped the woman on the shoulder. As she turned her working eye to him, she grabbed her little girl tighter. "Fuck off asshole!" she said. "You trying to get me killed?"

Bewildered, Jimmy returned to his fast drunken stagger.

From an open window, a couple of teenage kids yelled at him, "HEY WINO—WINO, LOOK UP HERE." Jimmy looked up. A half-full beer can hit the side of his face, nicking his cheek and spraying his face and neck. Two more followed but missed. His taunters laughed and yelled more insults as he did his best to run.

Finally, he came into familiar territory. On the corner, a woman with short hair and a red dress paced between two doors. "PEGGY!" he yelled and waved. She turned and approached him. "What's your pleasure handsome?" It wasn't Peggy, only a common whore. She teased Jimmy about the sexual options he was passing up as he lumbered away as fast as he could. He scampered for two more blocks and was finally in his neighborhood, grateful but still shaken.

* * *

The phone woke Jimmy at about 10:00. His head ached, and he was nauseous. He pulled himself off the couch but didn't answer. Only one person had called him in the past month, and he didn't feel like talking to her. He poured leftover coffee and put it in the microwave. The phone rang again and he went to his desk to check the caller I.D. It wasn't Peggy's number, but he figured she could be calling from Gyges's place. If it were someone else, they'd leave a message. They didn't. The microwave dinged and he fumbled to get a grip on his cup. As he took a sip, the phone rang again. Now angry, he went back to the desk.

"Hello," he said sternly.

"James, this is Victor; I'm sorry to bother you at home."

"That's not a problem Victor. What's up?"

"James, I have very sad news and am sorry to have to give it to you."

"What is it, Victor?"

"James, Michael had a heart attack yesterday."

"What—how is he? Can I help?"

"Well, his cleaning person found him this morning. I'm very, very sorry to say he isn't alive any longer."

"Mike is dead?"

"Yes, James. I'm very sorry."

"Well, is there any other information? I mean I know it's early, but is there anything else?"

"Not that I know, James. I think we will have more on Monday, but I don't know any more now. I'm very sorry."

"OK, Victor. Thank you for calling me."

Jimmy was dumbfounded. Mike dead? He looked at his coffee and took another sip. The phone rang again. This time it was Peggy. He didn't answer. She didn't leave a message.

After several Excedrin and a short beer, Jimmy developed enough strength to shower. His head swam from his hangover and last night's events. Parts were blurry, but he remembered enough to be embarrassed, and grateful. He was lucky, a real irony, given everything. Now, this would be a day of thought, sorting things out, and grieving. One thing was sure; it all meant a big change.

* * *

The next day Jimmy felt better and walked down to *Doc's*. Gail was working, and the crowd was light. She set up a Molson as he walked in and gave it to him with a big grin.

"I believe this is yours," she said as she handed him his coat and briefcase.

"I figured it would be here," Jimmy said.

"I heard you tied one on Friday night."

"Best I can remember."

Gail asked why and Jimmy filled her in. She looked at him with fury in her eyes. "Well, I apologize for hooking you up with that bitch. If I'd had any idea—"

"All you did was what I asked you to. It's OK."

After a moment of silence, Gail calmed down and cautiously asked, "Why do you do this?"

"What?"

"Well, you live here, you work here, and when you're here, you spend most of your time alone. But you have the place up north, you love it there, your friends are there, you don't need money—I'm just wondering why."

Jimmy didn't have an answer. Things weren't as easy and straightforward as Gail had summarized. "I don't think I can explain right now."

Gail didn't push and pulled him another beer from the tap. "What will you do tomorrow? You know you'll run into him."

He thought for a second and raised his eyebrows. "Play it by ear."

"Well, if you decide to kick him in the balls, give him one for me."

Jimmy stayed for several hours. A baseball game was on, and though he rarely watched, today he appreciated the diversion. He talked to Gail and a few others and left the stress of the past days for a little while. For now, all of that seemed long ago and far away. He found himself actually cheering at one point. Tomorrow might be different. But today things were OK.

* * *

The office looked like a middle school class waiting for the substitute teacher. Mike had been more than a leader; he was the corporation's conscience. People came back to the same work they left on Friday but with no one to keep them on task. Jimmy walked straight to his desk and returned to his unfinished project. He knew it wouldn't be long before a new boss was named, and the best way to make it through the uncertain period was to work.

At mid-morning, Victor came in. "James, I have heard our board will decide on a new head person by the week's end. My friend, their secretary, thinks they will choose someone from the inside of our organization."

Jimmy was concerned. He had hoped for new blood. While

there were some good lawyers in the group, there were too many pinheads, and he feared the worse from an inside search.

"Some of my colleagues and I were hoping they would pick you. We know you would be an excellent person for the position."

Jimmy's mind whirled. He had come to the office to work with Mike, not replace him. He knew what that job required and the time it would take from him. But what was the alternative? If he didn't get it, the place could become a hellhole in no time. And there was Gyges. He was junior, and his incompetence nearly destroyed dozens of deals. But, like so many others, he had some board members beguiled. And now, with the Peggy thing, how could Jimmy stay if the asshole were chosen?

"We are hoping you will accept the position if you are offered," Victor said. "And we will support you in the interviews."

"What interviews?" A board like theirs was more apt to make a decision quickly and on their own. It had no obligation to conduct any interviews.

"We have been told there will be interviews with members of our staff."

This will be interesting, Jimmy thought. "If I am offered the position, I will seriously consider it, Victor, and I thank you for your faith in me."

"Thank you James; I will tell the others."

At lunch time, Jimmy walked by the main reception area. There he was, Gyges, gabbing idly. The buddy he was talking to nudged him. He turned to see Jimmy and slowly formed the smirk. Jimmy had had enough. He turned to face the little smartass, stared him in the eyes, clenched his fists, and moved toward him. The smirk flashed to fear, and Gyges scampered off toward his office while his buddy chuckled. One look, two fists, and three steps. Problem solved.

With his door cracked open, Gyges watched to be sure Jimmy left and pulled out The Old Man's lighter. He looked at it and grinned. The embarrassment of Jimmy's standoff fizzled away. If "Dr. Eagleson" only knew. Now, not only did he have the lighter, he'd nailed his girl. And "Dr. Eagleson" did know about that. He was on a roll. The next step would be to work his way up. He snickered as he thought of how it would be when he became "Dr. Eagleson's" boss. He'd begin his campaign immediately.

* * *

Mike would have a small private funeral in Atlanta, so the company organized a short memorial in his honor on Tuesday. Jimmy was disgusted watching the same people who feverous-ly plotted for advancements putting on an act for the board. Gyges led the pack looking particularly mournful. Annie stood next to him also displaying insincere grief.

As soon as the bosses left, the place returned to discord with much laughing and joking. Jimmy had to leave. He decided to stop at St. Patrick's Cathedral and pay his respects on his own.

He sat for a while in a back pew, before kneeling. As he looked up at the magnificent ceiling and forward to the equally impressive altar, he thought of his friend and offered his best reference for Mike's redemption. No canned prayers, just straight-forward communication, personal and genuine. After a few minutes, he was disturbed by a group of noisy tourists who had gathered at the gift area to buy souvenir novena cards. He was finished anyway; it was time to leave.

For the next several days, the organization was sloppy. Many managers, including Gyges, were taking three-martini lunches and barking orders like drill sergeants while most of the support staff sat at their desks reading magazines. The place needed a new rudder quickly. The board had announced it would select a director by Monday. Jimmy was relieved. It didn't seem like it, but given the interviews, this was moving fast. The weekend would be suspenseful.

Saturday went slowly. Jimmy had much to think about and, except for a long swim at the pool, stayed close to home. On Sunday, Victor called. He had been told the board was still undecided but was leaning toward Jimmy. Jimmy didn't know whether to be pleased or worried. He had found himself in competition for a job he didn't want. But a decision wouldn't be coming tomorrow. The board had determined more interviews were necessary. The new boss would be announced by Friday.

The week crept by with continued anarchy, much like the last one. On Friday afternoon, a secretary delivered two sealed envelopes to Jimmy's office. Jimmy was alarmed. Having had no direct contact with the board he feared the worst. He opened the first envelope.

TO: All senior staff
FROM: Carlos Clark, Chair
RE: Appointment of New Corporate Director

After careful consideration, the board has offered the position of Corporate Director to Mr. Barry Gyges. While others were seriously considered, Mr. Gyges's commitment to innovation and forward thinking were recognized as invaluable for the future success and expansion of our organization. We congratulate Mr. Gyges on his achievement and ask that all welcome and support him in his new challenges. We also recognize the excellence of our other senior staff and know their acumen and continued hard work, along with the new leadership they can depend on, will make what is already an outstanding corporation even more superlative.

So there it was. Jimmy wasn't surprised but felt passed over and belittled. He knew the forward thinking and innovation the board thought they had found in Gyges would probably bring the place to bankruptcy. In two weeks, this little shithead had taken Jimmy's girlfriend and Mike's job. Jimmy knew he would have to resign. He had no idea what might be in the second envelope. Maybe he was being cut loose anyway. This one had a large red stamp across the seal that read "Personal and Confidential." This couldn't be good.

TO: James Eagleson
FROM: Carlos Clark, Chair
RE: New Position

After careful consideration of information obtained in recent interviews and a thorough review of your performance evaluations prepared by Michael Patton, the board is prepared to offer you the position of executive assistant to the chair. In this capacity, you would handle the final review of all contracts and recommendations on the viability of all new projects and would report directly to the board of director's chairperson. Other details will be worked out to our mutual satisfaction should you agree to accept the appointment. We have for some time been most impressed by your skills and business savvy, and sincerely hope you will seriously consider this offer which would represent a significant change in the existing corporate structure. We would also ask you to keep this offer in strict confidence until a formal decision has been made, as only the board has knowledge of this possible change. I have reviewed your current file and am aware you have accumulated at least two weeks of personal leave. I would consider now to be an appropriate use of that time, should you wish. Mr. Gyges will not require an explanation. We thank you for your outstanding service and hope you will accept the many challenges this new position will present.

Jimmy was stunned. The board had found a way to split the baby. He would be Gyges's de facto boss without any responsibility for the daily bullshit. Now he was flattered and gratified. But he still didn't know if he wanted to stay.

He lingered in his office until after 5:00, figuring everyone would be gone. He was surprised to see Gyges with a few others near the reception area, thinking by now they would have moved on to a high-end bar. They drank champagne and celebrated. The new leader's back was being repeatedly slapped as he received insincere praise from his new subordinates. He caught Jimmy's eye, and feeling safe with his troops, delivered the smirk. He reached into his pocket and rubbed The Old Man's lighter. If he only knew, he thought. "Would you like a drink, Dr. Eagleson?" he said. Jimmy just walked by. If the shit-head only knew, Jimmy thought.

* * *

That weekend Jimmy's mind swung back and forth. Should he leave and let well enough alone or stay and battle it out with Gyges? It wouldn't be much of a fight, and the little snake surely had it coming. But was revenge a reason to commit to this new job? The satisfaction would wear off eventually, and he might be stuck in a loathsome position. And he could count on Gyges to try to sabotage his every move. But he could also count on Gyges to be bad at it and to be so poor at his own work that he might be fired. Should he even care about Gyges? What about this new job? What was it? How much could he customize it? What about his time and freedom? What happens if the board changes chairs?

By Sunday, Jimmy's mind still spun. *Doc's* seemed the ideal solution; he wouldn't be able to talk about it, so maybe he could turn it off temporarily. He arrived as Gail was opening. It would be just the two of them for a while. She drew him a Molson and scampered to turn things on and move things around. She finished in record time and sat next to him at the bar, sipping coffee.

"A guy from your office was in. He was talking about a new boss? Could that be you?"

"He's talking about Barry Gyges."

"The guy the bitch was with?"

"Yup, the same."

"Jesus, Jimmy, you're on a roll."

"I'm OK."

"You sure? I'm a little worried about you. How you doing with this break-up anyway? I know how sensitive you are. This can't be easy."

"Just one problem."

"What?"

"I'm really horny." They both laughed.

"Don't look at me," Gail said. "We both know how things worked out for us."

"What went wrong with us anyway? Were we really so bad?"

"Not bad, just incompatible."

"Incompatible? I thought we were good together. You never seemed to complain?"

"I'm not talking about the sex; there was more to it."

"You know," Jimmy said, "I felt the stress. I knew things were tense, and I knew we weren't going to make it. But I never understood why. I mean what was it?"

Gail took Jimmy's hand, exhaled, and spoke with gentle sternness. "Do you remember when I got behind on my car?"

"Yeah."

"And the one time I had problems with the rent?"

"Uh huh."

"And when I was in a pissing match down here with Mr. Taylor over my hours?"

"Yeah, I remember all of that. So?"

"And what did you do— then and how many other times? What did you do?"

"I helped you out. I told you at the time not to worry about it. I did it because I wanted to. I never expected anything."

"That's the problem; you don't even know when you're doing it. Jimmy, you needed to let me take care of those things. You just stepped in, and at the time I appreciated it. But I should have done it myself. After a while, I felt like you were becoming more of a sugar daddy than a partner. Sometimes when we were in bed, it felt like I was paying you back rather than making love. You know, when you wanted me to move in with you, I knew I wouldn't have to worry about anything ever again. But that scared the shit out of me. I know you never asked for anything in return, but that almost made it worse, like I owed something to someone who wouldn't let me give back. In a way, that gave you all the cards. I couldn't do it. If we'd kept going, my feelings for you would have been destroyed. You would have become nothing but a provider, and I would have been your sponge."

Jimmy tapped his free hand on the bar and looked down. Gail held his hand tighter and continued. "Please, Honey, the last thing I want to do is hurt you, especially now. You're the most gentle and generous man I've ever known. But I need to say this because I think you need to hear it. You've got to let us do it on our own. If you're always bailing us out, we never get the satisfaction of fixing things for ourselves. We need to make our own way. I know you do it out of love, but it blocks us from having any way to love back. I know there are plenty of women who would be happy to take advantage of you. You are such a good man; you deserve much better than you've had. But you're your own worst enemy sometimes. Jimmy, remember the song 'God Bless the Child'?"

Jimmy felt drubbed. But he knew he'd heard the truth. Gail hugged him with great affection for many seconds. He felt better, then OK.

"Hey you two, break it up," a customer yelled, swaggering in. Gail looked up, interest on her face. Jimmy glanced in the mirror behind the bar. A big smile nearly touched his ears. Salvatore Esposito was in the house.

Sal headed for Jimmy, gave him a man hug, and sat beside him. "I thought I'd find you here. My plane was delayed. Seven fucking hours. Oh well, turned out to be a good thing. What's new?"

Jimmy and Gail looked at each other and laughed. "Must be some shit's happened around here," Sal assessed. "Want to fill me in?"

A ripple of customers pulled Gail away as Jimmy summarized. Good fortune had provided someone he could talk to about everything. Strict confidence didn't apply in attorney-to-attorney consultations. But first, Jimmy tried to explain Peggy. Not easy with a guy like Sal.

"Let me ask you this," Sal inquired. "Did you get your dick wet?"

"There was more to it than that."

"A month with a hot young chick, you're getting laid, she's getting jewelry I assume, knowing your style. Then just as it's going bad, a dick-head who you despise takes her off your hands. Is this essentially what you just told me?" Sal had a way of cutting to the chase.

"Yes, but—"

"But you got too close too fast—as usual, I might interject—and your feelings got stomped. Is that the rest?" Jimmy grinned and nodded. "Besides, looks like you're doing just fine." Sal gestured at Gail. "Who's she?"

"She's a good friend."

"That all?"

"Well, it is now. You interested? I think she likes you."

"No, no, no. You know I'd never go someplace you've been. She is a doll though. So getting back to this Peggy chick, how are you now, a couple of weeks later?"

"I'm fine now. But let me tell you the rest. Let me tell you about work, lawyer to lawyer."

"Oh, this sounds serious. Please continue, Counselor."

Sal paid close attention as Jimmy explained. "This is good shit. You should have pounded that fucker in the office."

"That never solves anything."

"Does for me. Can I?" They both snickered. "Well, what are you going to do?"

"I don't know yet."

"And why should you? Listen, my friend, if they're cutting you that much time you'd be crazy not to take it even if you did know. If you decide to stay, you want them to think it was hard for them to get you, a better position for negotiation. If not, you want them to think you had a hard time leaving, a good parting, better for future references, and all that happy horseshit. You never know; you might want back in the game. Take the time. Besides, it's early May. You could go up north—or stay here. Either way, it's a good time of year."

Jimmy sat back nodding. Sal was right. He'd seen exactly what Jimmy would have known immediately if he were advising someone else.

After a couple of beers and talk about Sal's Phoenix deal, Sal leaned back. "Whatever happened with that shit Gordo sent you about The Old Man?"

Jimmy took a deep breath and filled Sal in on the stories he'd discovered and told him what Stosh had said. Sal's eyes widened and he broke into laughter as Jimmy talked. "I always liked the old guy. Now I think I love him. Anything else? This is all too good."

"I stopped reading; it got to be all the same."

"Let me get this straight. You, James Eagleson, didn't finish reading something, especially something like this? You finish everything. You'd better get back to it. I want to hear more." Sal paused. "You know, it seems to me there must be more to this shit anyway. Gordo wouldn't have been so serious about it if it were only about The Old Man's fucking around. Well anyway, finish it. It's too good not to. You know you're on a lucky streak. A new job offer, time off, and some of the best reading you could ask for—shit, you're almost on top of the world."

Gail was able to rejoin the conversation after some customers left. Following a real introduction, the three joked and told old stories. After a half-hour, Gail looked toward the door; her face turned sour. In staggered Barry Gyges with two of his cronies. As they stumbled to the bar, Gail reluctantly left to serve them. Jimmy looked over and whispered in Sal's ear. "Can I pound him now?" Sal said. "After all, he came to me."

"What would you like?" Gail asked.

"Three of those," Gyges said and pointed to a bottle of single malt. Gyges turned his head and for the first time noticed Jimmy.

"How the hell are you, Dr. Eagleson? Jesus, your friend is big enough to run two backhoes at once. Is he another plowboy from Plattsville or wherever the fuck you're from?"

Jimmy had never seen Gyges this drunk and chose to ignore him. Sal looked at Jimmy. "Does this guy have a death wish?"

"He's drunk and isn't worth the effort even when he's coherent. Shit, coherent, he's never coherent." Jimmy and Sal cracked up.

"Something funny?" Gyges said. "Don't you think you should let your new boss in on it? I love a good laugh. I've been laughing a lot lately, Dr. Eagleson. Yeah, there's been lots to laugh about lately."

Jimmy smirked. "Just ignore him, Sal. He's not worth the shit he's full of."

Gail served Gyges and his friends their drinks and returned to Jimmy and Sal. "What a total asshole," she said.

Jimmy stood. "I'll be right back," he said and left for the men's room.

Sal watched as Gyges partied with his fellow clowns. They quickly downed their drinks, and Gyges pulled a pack of cigarettes and The Old Man's lighter from his coat pocket. Sal squinted to get a good look. Where the fuck did he get that? Sal grinned and sat back. He'd always said The Old Man wanted that crest to be seen from across the room.

"Hey put those out. You know you can't smoke in the bars anymore!" Gail yelled. Gyges smirked, crushed the cigarette, and yelled back for three more drinks. "You're done here," she said. "I don't serve sloppy drunks."

"Fuck this place," Gyges said. "The new bar around the corner beats this shit hole, Babe." He and his friends stood, and as they ambled to the door, Gyges turned back to Gail and grinned. "Hey," he said, flipping her off and walking out. Sal stood, but Gail shook her head. Sal nodded and sat back down.

"Where's shit for brains?" Jimmy asked walking back from the men's room.

"Just left, said to say goodbye, love and kisses, all that shit," Sal said.

"Well, good. Let's get back to business," Jimmy said.

Gail served a round of fresh beers, and the three chatted for over an hour until Sal announced he had to leave for the airport. "All right you guys; this was the best delay I can remember. Gail, it was wonderful meeting you. And you, my friend, get back to that good reading, and I'll see you soon."

"When?"

"Soon, and Jimmy, step carefully. You've got the world by the balls, just stand back and think it all out carefully."

"Yeah, you've got it, Sal. Have a safe flight. Soon, my friend."

After a parting group hug, Sal looked at his watch, tipped his hat, and hurried out to catch a cab.

"Wow, that guy will take your breath away," Gail said.

"He sure will."

"And Jesus, what a build."

"Shoulders like Detroit," Jimmy mumbled.

"What?"

"Shoulders like Detroit. Just something we used to say."

After one more beer and a little more time with Gail, Jimmy headed home. As he walked, he remembered what Gail said, and processed Sal's advice. He laughed at Gyges's drunken stupidity; the idiot had no idea Jimmy would be choosing who called the shots. This had been a fortuitous day, maybe a turning point. He had much to think about. But one thing was decided. First thing in the morning he would call the office and inform them he was on personal leave.

* * *

Gyges stood at the curb in front of the bar smoking a cigarette too drunk to notice when Salvatore walked up.

"Give me the lighter," Sal said.

Gyges turned his head and smirked, "Oh, it's the plowboy. Fuck off."

Sal put his arm around Gyges's back, placed his hand on his far shoulder, and slammed his fist into Gyges's ribs. Grabbing his side Gyges bent forward and threw up in the street. A couple leaving the bar looked over, concerned.

"What's the matter," the man yelled.

"Just a little too much to drink," Sal said still with his arm around Gyges's back. "He'll be fine."

"Yeah I'm not surprised, he's been partying hard all weekend," the man said. "Said he got a big promotion."

The couple walked off, and Sal returned his attention to Gyges. "Now you should know this plowboy graduated from medical school. If I hit the right spot—and I'm quite sure I did—you'll find you have fractures in your thoracic cage, most likely ribs seven and eight. As a physician, I can tell you it will be very painful to laugh for several weeks, so you should try to forget the things you've found so amusing lately. Now, let's try this again. Give me the lighter."

Still bent over and now groaning Gyges struggled to get his hand in his pocket. He worked The Old Man's lighter out and held it up. Sal snatched it and examined the crest.

"I don't know how you got this, and I don't have time for an explanation, but if you mention one detail of our little chat here, I'll be back to finish the conversation." Gyges nodded and again threw up. Sal stood back. "You're one lucky little fuck; I have a plane to catch."

CHAPTER VIII

The Old Man

After breakfast, errands, and a swim, Jimmy settled at his desk. He looked at the bulletin board and saw his note, READ THE LETTERS. "That's what I'm here for" he whispered. He cleared the desktop, took the envelopes from the drawer, and arranged them as Aunt Lucy had. He felt apprehensive but thought there couldn't be much left to stir his pot, especially after the past few weeks. He'd probably just find a few new stories to share with Stosh and Sal.

As he browsed through the early letters and reacquainted himself, he thought of how his life had changed since Gord sent this stuff. How minor and distant the recent drama seemed. The Old Man had been at war. Now Jimmy, over 60 years later, was living the irony of his inheritance. Feeling worried and stressed while basking in paradise. What would it be like to be in the army—told when and how to do everything with no objective other than to win a war? The Old Man had been lucky. He never left England. But what about the guys in combat—what would that be like with real guns and real killing? Not the chicken shit jostling of Jimmy's world.

He thumbed to the first unread letter and dove in. One after another the letters were like the first batch, lots of bragging about misbehaving. Then one revealed a long kept secret.

> November 10, 1941
> Dear Frank.
> . . . We're still bored as hell. One lieutenant has spent more time on pep talks than training. He comes into the barracks and spews out all of this shit that's supposed to motivate us. He hasn't a clue how we laugh at him. And the dumb bastard always ends his sermons the same way, "Chins up lads. Keep those chins up." He is a hoot. Last week at a nearby pub Jimmy got drunk and started impersonating him. He was hilarious. At the end of every line of crazy shit Jimmy was making up, he said "Chins up," and took a gulp of beer. He got us all doing it. It's the company toast now. The lieutenant has no idea how truly inspirational his shit turned out to be. . . .

After a lifetime of hearing The Old Man's toast, Jimmy finally knew its source. Somehow he felt closer to The Old Man, having his first "inside" information. He read several more letters. Then, he came on one different and disturbing.

February 14, 1942

Dear Frank,

Happy Valentine's Day. Things here are, unfortunately, much the same, bad food, too much drilling, too many orders, no action. Most of us have had it. We came here to kill Germans. It's been a year and a half, and nothing. If not for the occasional bombing in our area we wouldn't know there was a war. That is except for the constant orders from our fat officers. I don't know where they get the food, but they can't be eating the same shit they feed us. If we could, most of us would just go home. The Brits just can't get off their asses and do something in Europe. Hell, they're not even much fun to fight with anymore, although we do. Jimmy and I both took up chess. We're not much good at it, but it helps to keep us from losing our fucking minds stuck in these barracks.

I should tell you I've met somebody. Not one of the barflies I've written about, a nice girl from a farm around here. I guess I don't need to tell you this is a secret from anyone back home, except for you of course. I'm still writing Lil, but I've changed and I think she has too. Maybe it's just the war and the separation and all of that. I hope so. But this girl is very nice and I very much enjoy her company, although we don't get much time together. It's almost frightening how much she looks like Lil.

Jimmy is fine and sends his regards. He's still

full of piss and vinegar and said to tell you "chins up." But even he has had it. I'm telling you if we don't get some action soon it won't be pretty. We all hate the army. Morale stinks and the assholes in charge don't seem to give a shit. We're told General McNaughton won't let the limeys break us up so we have to wait for a chance to fight together. Maybe that's good. But when will we get a chance? At least I can see Rose once in a while. That's a lot more than most guys have. Well, not much more to complain about today. I hope all is OK with you and I will write again soon.

Warmest regards,

Gerret

Who was Rose? The Old Man had a girlfriend, and Mum didn't know? This was more than just sleeping around and getting his rocks off. This looked serious. Jimmy's pot was stirred.

Many of the next letters continued the new theme, Rose. And who was this other Jimmy? The Old Man always mentioned him. Jimmy got up to get a cup of coffee. He knew he wouldn't be leaving until he had read everything. This was developing into a complicated story.

April 15, 1942

Dear Frank,

Hello from jolly old England, otherwise known as hell for most Canadian soldiers. I'm doing fine because of Rose, but the rest of the guys are ready to desert. Jimmy has talked openly about it. He's really fed up.

Things with Rose have developed to more than I had figured on. I can't stop thinking of her and I have snuck off the base to be with her several times. I believe I am in love and I think she is too. Her parents seem OK with me as I help out around the farm when I can. I even brought Jimmy over once, but it just made him more homesick and down on the army. I must tell you I have written to Lil about it. I don't think it is fair to keep her waiting when I don't plan on coming back to her. Rose and I have talked about getting married someday. I thought we might go to Western Canada. She's willing. Or we might stay here. Whatever we decide, I can't imagine a future without her. I hope you will not think the less of me for not telling Lil earlier. She is a wonderful girl and I truly wish the best for her. The letter to her was the most difficult I have ever written. We have so much history. But she doesn't know me anymore. We are approaching two years of separation and everything has changed.

The company has been drilling on new tactics, mostly on the beach, making some guys think we might be up for some kind of action. I hope they're right and they're not just trying to keep us busy like with all the other training they've pushed us through. I came here two years ago to be an engineer.

What a laugh, all I do is shoot. So much for the army's promises.

It's time to get this war finished so we can all get on with our lives. I for one have much to look forward to. But I hate the army as much as anyone, even if for different reasons. I hope everything is fine in Ottawa. The spring is so lovely there. I've told Rose about it and promised to show her someday. I miss Canada. And I miss my freedom, being able to go and do what I want when I want. This glorified summer camp they have us in is going to explode soon if they don't get us fighting.

Well, enough of that. I hope you are well. Please give my regards to all and do what you can to support Lil. She always liked you and there is no need for your friendship to end because of me. I never wanted to hurt her and hope for her understanding, along with yours. Take care. I'll write again soon.

Warmest regards,

Gerret

Jimmy found it increasingly difficult to read about The Old Man's private life with this strange woman for whom he abandoned Jimmy's mother. The little trips, the gifts, the way he felt, all made Jimmy slightly nauseous. This was The Old Man acting like a pussy-whipped schoolboy in puppy-love, acting too much like his son. A part of one letter particularly hit a nerve.

. . . I've heard from Lil. She wrote me a beautiful

letter saying she understood and wishing both of
us great happiness. She spoke of all the good times,
but she had also seen what the separation had done
to us. She ended by giving us her blessing. She is
a wonderful person and I almost wish she had just
told me to fuck off and die. I feel like a heel hurting
someone so good. . . .

"You should, you fucking asshole," Jimmy said out loud.
Then the theme changed. The war came alive.

June 5, 1942
Dear Frank,

Our training has changed again. We have been
in boats for a month. I can't tell you more, but I
hope this means we will be in action soon. It's time
to kill Germans and get this stupid thing settled
once and for all. Everyone has hope now. Jimmy is
particularly restless and has been spending extra
time on the rifle range. He has become a crack shot
and has been teased by some guys for the insults
he yells at his targets. He's learned to say "Die you
fucking kraut" in German. It's a gas to watch him.

Things are good with me. Rose is wonderful, as
always. I was due for a short leave and was going to
spend it with her. But it has been canceled. At first
I was hot. But, now I figure it's a sign something is
up. I can't wait to see action and get this thing done.
Well, I have to go. We're on double drills now. I might
not be able to write for a while so don't worry if you

don't hear from me. Take care of yourself and give
my regards to all.

    With warmest regards,

    Gerret

After a few more short and guarded letters, The Old Man
didn't write for more than two months. He'd found his action.

September 14, 1942

Dear Frank,

By now you have already heard of the disaster
my division was part of and of the death of my best
friend, Jimmy. It has taken me this long to be able to
sit and write about it. But now, I will try to tell you
what has happened, as best I can.

On July 5 we were herded onto several ships.
We knew it was for real; no drill could be this
complicated. Within a couple of hours, the Germans
must have got wind of us and started to bomb. It
was terrifying. All we could do was sweat and listen
as the compression from the bombs rolled through
us, over and over. Once it was over, they took us off
the boats, sent us back to the barracks and scuttled
the whole fucking thing. We were supposed to have
made a raid on a French port called Dieppe. We were
going to hit the place for a few hours, destroy some
guns and other shit, take prisoners and then get out.
A hit and run, maybe just to show the Germans we

could do it. We wanted to go, to fight and get this thing done. But it was canned.

For the next few weeks, we trained more and then found out we were going to try again. The same fucking place. Mountbatten figured the Germans would never expect us to try the same thing. In his stupid limey head, he thought the idea was brilliant. On the night of August 18, they loaded us. Same port, same boats, same plan. The three nights before some bartender wished me luck in Dieppe. A fucking bartender knew what we were doing. They should have just put the plans on the bloody BBC.

When we left that night, we ran into a German convoy and got into a fight that slowed everything down. A lot of landing boats were hit. But we went on. Then the real shit flew. It is very hard for me to write this. I will probably be broken up over it for the rest of my life. And anything I say will fall far short of what it was really like. But I'll tell you what I can as you should know and I will write to Jimmy's folks too. They deserve to get the straight story.

The Germans were plastering the landing boats on the way in. We were late. It was supposed to happen in the dark, but it was morning and they could see everything we were doing. When the doors opened, seven or eight guys, including the captain, were killed right away. None of us had ever seen somebody actually get killed, but we were so scared we got off as fast as we could. Once we were on shore, we didn't know what to do. The Germans were nailing us with artillery and machine guns, and sniping at will. The sergeants took over and got some of us behind shelter near a sea wall. Jimmy was right next to me. He had moved out to try and help a guy who had his foot shot off when he was hit. Most of his face was shredded and the top of his head was sliced off. I could see his brains. When I pulled him back, he was yelling at the Germans, making no sense at all and his head was squirting blood like a leaking hose. A medic bandaged him and gave him morphine, but he just got worse. At some point he asked me to kill him. My best friend was begging me to kill him. He was so bad I actually thought about it. What the fuck would that be like, to kill your best friend, for any reason, and just go on with it all? But his pain must have stopped because the next time he looked at me his face was calm. I held his head, he smiled and said "Chins up Eagleson." He died a few seconds later. I became too hysterical and scared to know if anything that was going on was really happening anymore.

We were stuck there for three hours waiting for the fucking boats to come back. We just sat, under constant fire, losing a guy here and there. We were helpless and petrified and surrounded by dead bodies, including Jimmy's. The beach was full of them. A few had been piled up to protect guys who were pinned down. Nobody figured they'd mind and we all thought if the fucking boats didn't come soon the Germans would be tossing the rest of us right on top of them. The sounds of guns and shells and the screaming Stuka dive bombers scared the shit out of us. And the smell; gunpowder, burned flesh, salt. We were all pumped up and wanted to just run, just get the fuck away. But all we could do was wait there, standing in mud at the side of the cliffs waiting to be shot.

When the boats finally came, we were numb. A lot of guys were killed trying to get on board. I was lucky, I was hit twice, but neither was bad. I was never so happy to be on a boat, even though several were blown out of the water on the way out. At least we were going in the right direction. When we got back to the ship, the reality of the whole thing set in. Jimmy was gone and I had to leave him there. I feel so guilty. Why him? It's been several weeks and I'm still fucked up about the whole thing.

You should know, Jimmy died a hero trying to save another guy. I'm OK. My wounds weren't bad and they are healing well. I'm not sure what bullshit the papers there are saying but, best I can tell, of the 6,000 who went in about 1,100 were killed, maybe 300 wounded, and nearly 2,500 were captured. Almost all losses were Canadians. The Brits set us up. There's no way the Germans didn't know we were coming. General Roberts told us it would be a piece of cake. Well, fuck him. Now Mountbatten is playing up all the positives. Well, I was there and I didn't see anything positive for anyone but the Germans. The thing was FUBAR from the beginning.

I do have the consolation of having Rose. She has been a great comfort to me. And they are much less stringent about leave and rules now. If you were at Dieppe, you're on a long leash around here. There isn't much left of the division so I don't know what's next, but I will try to keep you informed as best I can. I hope all is well with you. Please give my regards to all and let them know I'm alright. And please tell everyone Jimmy died a hero.

Warmest regards,

Gerret

Dieppe? Holy shit! The Old Man was actually there? Just about every Canadian of Jimmy's generation knew all about it. He was raised on the story, but not by The Old Man. The Old Man never talked about it. What was all the bullshit about combat engineering? Why all of these secrets? Jimmy was overloading. Gord was right; this wasn't easy. He sat back and took a sip from his coffee. Who was this guy, The Old Man? And who was this Jimmy, The Old Man's best friend who died in his arms? The letters never even mentioned a last name. All the folks and their friends must have known him. How was it he didn't? How could it be Jimmy Eagleson never heard of this guy, this other Jimmy? If it had been so carefully kept from him, why?

Jimmy thought of taking a break from the letters but

couldn't. His whole world was being re-written. He felt shaken and confused. A hook was set deeply, and he was being reeled in. He had to keep going.

The next letters were shorter. No more bragging and bravado. These were humble and almost apologetic. The Old Man wrote of the division's rebuilding and much on Rose, much more on Rose than Jimmy cared for. Reading about The Old Man's affections and intimacies made him uncomfortable. The parts about future hopes and dreams made him angry. Then, near the holidays, The Old Man sent one confirming one of Jimmy's worst fears.

December 18, 1942

Dear Frank,

I am pleased to be able to tell you that as of last night, Rose and I are married. We decided to just to do it, with only a few friends and her family. It was very quiet and very graceful. I'm sorry I didn't tell you before but I knew your attendance wouldn't be possible and it really did come together quickly. She is a wonderful girl, and with all we've seen with the war, waiting didn't make sense. We felt it best to be together when we can, although we plan for that to be a very long time.

Rose's family has been wonderful. She has an uncle who is a silversmith. He made us matching rings with a custom crest of folded eagle's wings cradling a rose bloom. I was stunned but even more surprised when Rose's father gave me a solid, silver lighter with the same crest. I was worried he might disapprove of our marriage. He's been very protective of her. But he told me he's proud of my service and gives us his blessing.

I still live on the base, although we now have a room of our own at the farm too. The captain has been good about it. I'm at the farm a lot, even though I'm a sergeant now. Oh, I haven't told you yet. Last month I was made sergeant of my group. I'll be spending most of my time on the range, training. The place is flooding with new recruits and some of them are going to make good shots. The promotion will give me a little more money too. And I am now officially at the highest level of sharpshooter, a sniper in fact.

I've spent much time talking to Rose about Dieppe and Jimmy. She has been a Godsend for me. She listens and understands. We've heard of good things that came from the raid. At some point, there's going to be an invasion and we now know what to expect and what it will take. It helps to think Jimmy and the other guys died for something. But it's still hard. I think of him every day and keep a picture of us with me to look at when I see his shot up head in my mind. He was so smart and could have done so much with his life.

Not much more to say from here. I hope all is well

with you and that things in Ottawa are safe and sound. I'll write soon. Please give my regards to all.

Warmest regards,

Gerret

Jimmy sat back and looked at his hand. "Folded Eagle's wings cradling a rose bloom." What the fuck? No wonder The Old Man hadn't been able to tell him. And The Old Man had done it. He got married. Not much of a surprise the way things were going. And he did seem different in the letters. His manner was polite and positive, and his swearing was absent. This was much more the tone of The Old Man Jimmy knew. But it still sucked, and Jimmy felt the sting of seeing it confirmed in writing. He twisted off the ring and tossed it in his desk drawer.

The letters continued to be about Rose and the war, always in that order. The Old Man's division was to stay in England until further notice. Others were sent to North Africa and Italy, but the 2nd stayed put while they rebuilt and trained. The Old Man seemed to be settled in, although his men were itching to fight. He'd earned a couple of bottom stripes over the next year. Letter after letter seemed routine with maybe a tad bit of something new. Jimmy was getting tired and thought about putting them away for the night when another special one turned up.

October 11, 1944

Dear Frank,

I am very pleased to be able to tell you Rose is pregnant. We had not planned on a family at this

time, but we are both delighted. The doctor says all is
well. I can't believe I'm going to be a father. It is all
so new, and both exciting and frightening. She is
due in June, and if it's a boy we both thought we will
name him James. . . .

The rest of the letter went on about family hopes and plans.
Where was this story going? He had heard of wartime marriages of passion that ended with the war and figured that was
probably what The Old Man had gotten himself into. After
all, he had been an emotional wreck after Dieppe. It wasn't
surprising he would latch on to this girl. But now this? Jimmy
knew for sure he had been raised by two people named Lil and
Gerret Eagleson. He knew their wedding date. So The Old
Man came back well before, presumably alone and available.
Now, on top of a wife was a child. Did Jimmy have a sibling
out there somewhere?

He read on about the family and the war. The Americans
were flooding the island in preparation for an invasion. No
one knew where or when, just that it was inevitable. The Old
Man talked about the new heavy equipment and about a new
precision rifle he was mastering. Finally, D-Day came. But,
the Canadian Second Division wouldn't be part of the initial
invasion. The Old Man was relieved.

. . . Rose is popped out and feeling the baby's
movements. She is due to deliver any day. While
my men are angry and demanding to fight, I know
what to expect and am very glad to be on this side of
the channel. We will be involved soon enough and

every day I am here with her is a good one. She is
having minor complications and will have to see a
doctor in London. I'm told there's nothing to worry
about. She will be staying with her cousin for a few
days. It's a good time to go as we now own the skies
and the German bombing has been quieted. . . .

Then, two letters later:

June 24, 1944
Dear Frank,
I apologize for not writing in the last week. I am
in a bad way. Rose and the baby are dead. There is
no subtle way to say this kind of thing anymore.
She was killed by a V1 rocket while in London. The
Brits call them doodlebugs. Only the limeys could
call a fucking bomb something like a doodlebug.
One asshole actually tried to console me by saying
"nasty things those doodlebugs." The fucking idiot.
It should have been me who died. I was on top of the
world, now I feel totally alone. I'm told the baby was
a boy. That doesn't make much difference now.

Tonight, my captain told me to send the guys into
town. Then he told me in confidence no one would
be leaving the base after tomorrow morning. This
could only mean one thing. We're going over soon.
I will deliver this letter to Rose's mum to be sent to
you in a few days. It's not likely you'll hear much
from me for a while. I'll fill you in if I get back.

I'm glad to be going now. I've been here for four

years. Four fucking years. Now I'm going to kill Germans, every damned one I see. That's all I care about anymore. I thank you again for always being there for me. My sounding board, the one who always understood and put up with all of my shit. If I should not see you again, I want you to know I hold you deepest in my heart with much love and respect. Please take care of yourself. You're all I have left.

    Warmest regards,

    Gerret

Jimmy felt small. This woman he scorned was blown up, the part of The Old Man's life he'd resented and feared, obliterated. He wanted it all to go away, and it did. Now he couldn't bring it back. Tears came as he felt The Old Man's pain. He felt ashamed of himself. He couldn't read any more right now.

* * *

Jimmy woke from a short, restless sleep, made coffee, and showered. A concoction of dream fragments swirled in his head. The coffee helped. Opening the window and sticking his head into the fresh May air helped more. Three levels of reality shrunk to two as the dream parts faded away. Now, right in front of him, was New York, loud and in his face. And on his desk lay 1944 Europe, just as real, and demanding his attention.

He picked up the next letter. As The Old Man had predicted,

he sent nothing in July or August. But the gaps would be filled in.

September 5, 1944

Dear Frank,

I am now able to write you again and there is much to tell. By now you should have been informed of my wounds. Three machine-gun bullets shattered bones and caused much infection. At one point, a surgeon was planning to amputate. But I was put aside while he worked on worse guys and when they got back to me, a second doctor saved the leg. I'm back in England and they still don't know if I will be able to use the thing again. The bones were really bad and some muscles were removed, so, right now it's just there, still attached but quite useless. It's better than being gone and much better than a lot of the shit I've seen. I'm not sure how long I will be staying here. I can't go back into combat, but I might be able to train on the rifle range. They just don't know.

Trying to retrace what has happened in the past couple of months is very hard. I saw and did many things. This combat was very different from Dieppe. We were there to stay this time and fought nearly every day. While I worked with my guys for a long time, I never got close to anyone, not like the guys who were with Jimmy and me. Many of them were killed or hit much worse than I was. I'm proud of them all. They were brave heroes and we killed more than our fair share of Germans.

We landed on July 7. I have never seen so much equipment and so many troops, all headed south. The Third Division went in on D-Day and was cut up badly. They had been fighting ever since and were shit to us. We were the clean, fresh, little boys who missed all the shit at Juno and got to walk into France over their backs. They were at Caen when we got there. I killed my first German there. He was trying to surrender, but I nailed him between the eyes before his hands got above his shoulders. It felt good. We had just heard the Germans were killing prisoners. A Canadian lieutenant had been executed by the SS in a nearby Abbey, shot in the back of the head. They think they'll find a lot more. Fuck taking prisoners.

Caen was rough. We were up against a couple of Panzer divisions that had been in a lot of combat and knew how to fight. Those fucking tanks are enormous, much bigger than ours. Monty was supposed to take the place on D-Day, but the Yanks say he moved his troops like a herd of turtles and gave the SS just enough time. We fought there for about ten days. There was no letup, no showers or latrines, and not much food. But we killed lots of Germans.

I was pulled from my unit and assigned to take out German snipers near the town. In one kill I was in a cellar for nearly 12 hours, ankle deep in mucky shit from a broken sewer, just waiting. Another guy, a Brit, was with me but silence is essential in my business and I didn't even get his name. We had to shit and piss only when there was enough noise from moving tanks. We both knew approximately where the target was, but that fucker was good and stuck to the rules. Right near sunset, a rat climbed the Brit's leg and bit his thigh. When he yelled the German nailed him. But I saw the son of a bitch and took him out while he was still exposed. The Brit did his job. So did I and I got out of that fucking cellar.

All in all, I had over 20 confirmed kills before we took the city. By then the place had been bombed to rubble. There were a few civilians rummaging around, and a few German holdouts popping off an occasional shot. Engineers were trying to clear the roads of destroyed tanks and trucks and every other kind of shit you can imagine. It was totally destroyed. And there were bodies and body parts all over the place, pieces of kids and dogs and women. I don't know who killed them. But I know who started this fucking thing.

Next, they sent us to this place called Verrières Ridge. We were told this was the key to breaking out of the stalemate we were in. This was almost as big a fuck-up as Dieppe. The place overlooked the road to Falaise, which was what we really needed. But I think every German that had left Caen was there, and more. We were delayed for two days by real bad rain. The roads were nothing but mud and none of the big equipment could move. By the time we got to it, the Germans had moved hundreds of tanks and guns up there. In the first couple of days, things were slow and a lot of guys were killed. Then they sent in the Black Watch. Those fuckers are as tough as it gets, but only ten of them got back. We finally took the place with a night tank attack. But most of the Panzers had pulled out. As it turned out, we didn't need it that bad anyway. We lost over a thousand guys. But we killed a lot of them too.

When we left, we headed south to try and connect with the Yanks near Falaise. Battlefield fighting is a lot different from the city. I could take a position in a tree and pick off targets at will. The trick is not to be too greedy in any one place. Then they figure out where you are, and that's all she wrote. I hit a tank commander rolling along with the top of his body sticking up like a jack out of his box. One shot. The tank turret turned willy-nilly and they shot into the woods far from me. But there'd be no more shooting from that tree for me. I wasn't going to be stupid for them.

I was hit one morning on the way back to camp with another guy. Out of nowhere, a machine gun opened up on us. We never saw it. He was killed and I was shot up. In a few seconds, the nest blew up. Some other guys took it out using us as a diversion.

They got me back to camp. From there I eventually got here. And that, in a nutshell, is the story of the last two months.

I didn't have time to think much about Rose and the baby over there. There was so much action so fast. But when I did, I was furious. Who are these fucking people? They just send a few bombs anytime they feel like it to kill a few civilians here and there? I know we are bombing the shit out of them ourselves and I think they deserve everything we can throw at them. I've come to hate them. For four years I've been stuck in this war because of some little out-of-control cocksucker who somebody should have taken out years ago. My wife and son are dead. Now I think about that constantly. Why? They didn't do anything to anyone. I regret I couldn't kill more of those demons.

Rose's mum was here to see me. She has done much better with it all than I have, but not so with her dad. He blames me. She brought me the few things I left with them and I've been told it's best for me not to go back to the farm again. I won't. I just can't understand it. Now I'm hated for loving someone. He's let the Germans off the hook and made me her murderer. It's all fucked up.

I'm not sure when I will be out of the hospital. I hope soon, they need the bed and I can manage now. There are wires and pins and other shit in my leg and it's in a cast. But I can still make it around OK on the crutches.

Not much more to tell you right now. I'm not in the best frame of mind. I'll write again soon. I hope all is well there. Please give my regards to all.

With warmest regards,

Gerret

Jimmy was no longer surprised by what he read; he was getting to know The Old Man. His criticism was gone, replaced by pure empathy. The Old Man was not the man in the boring myth Jimmy had grown up on. There had never been the combat engineer who had an accident and never saw action. What incredible service. What an incredible story. But he still couldn't understand why he was never told. The stack was thinning and he hoped he'd find an answer before he finished.

September 30, 1944

Dear Frank,

I was released from the hospital two weeks ago. The cast is off and I have started physical therapy. Not much progress yet but I can stand on both legs and the docs think I'll get some use from the bum one after all.

I saw a report about a camp the Russians say they found. It was like a factory for killing Jews and Gypsies. Our brass thinks it's all exaggerated. I don't. I think those sons of bitches could do anything. They say they also found mass graves from executions. I don't think we've scratched the surface of what the bastards have done. There will be real hell to pay when this is over. Some say it will be done by Christmas. I hope they're right.

Life is boring for me now. Other than therapy, I hang around a lot. I read, play a little chess here and there and drink a few beers with the guys. They haven't said anything about getting me back to the range. I'd like that. If I can't kill Germans myself at least I could train other guys who can. But the war might end before they need me and that would be OK too.

Well, that's that all on this side of the pond. I hope all is well and I'll write again soon. I thank you again for always being there. Give my regards to all.

Warmest regards,

Gerret

Jimmy could feel The Old Man's hatred and confusion as he read on.

October 18, 1944

Dear Frank,

I'm in my fifth year now. It doesn't seem possible. I've been thinking of Canada in the fall, there's nothing like that here.

The leg is coming along well. I get around on the crutches and can put some weight on it. I've been able to move my toes and can feel tension in my calf muscles too. The docs are hopeful.

This week I visited the shore area we used to guard.

It looks much the same, but I was nervous. When I first got there, there were no boats to be seen. I felt anxious and trapped and almost asked my buddy to get me out of there. Then patrol boats came by. My relief was unbelievable. I felt safe. I figure it's from Dieppe. It's the strangest fucking thing and I don't know if it will go away.

My division is fighting near Antwerp now. The Brits took the city, but it's useless until we clear out some islands the Germans hold. Last Friday we lost over 200 guys. What I would give to be there with a machine gun killing every German I could find. God I hate those fuckers. I feel useless here just hanging around.

I must tell you I'm still buried in thoughts of Rose and the baby. I'll never understand her father. Fuck him, I did everything I could for her and her family. He's got me wondering if I am responsible and I can't stand that. I didn't send that fucking bomb. Everything here reminds me of her and of the bombing and killing. I'd be better off in combat where I could make them pay. All I do here is think about it all.

I thank you again for always understanding. Your letters are my only connection to home now and you'll never know how much I appreciate them.

I have nothing here. I'll write soon. Please give my best to all.

Warmest regards,

Gerret

The same themes repeated themselves—hatred, loneliness, betrayal, boredom, and fear. In between, The Old Man wrote about the war. The failure at Arnhem, the Christmas offensive at the Bulge, Russians finding more camps, and The Old Man, stuck on the sidelines. His leg was getting better. He was getting some real use back and was looking forward to graduating from crutches to a cane. Then, in a long letter, something new surfaced.

. . . I've talked to some wounded fellas back from the front. One guy who lost an arm and an eye said the Germans are only doing their job, just like us, it's not personal, in another place and time these guys might be our friends. Well fuck that. He didn't lose a wife and kid. But it's still strange. How can he let it all go like that? I hate those people. I don't seem to be able to come to terms with any of it. Maybe if I'd stayed on track with Lil and kept the war away from my world? But even most Brits don't burn like me and they're the ones who were bombed out. I don't know. I think I need to deal with this somehow. Sometimes it helps to think of you and

Lil and the times before the war. Five years ago. Five fucking years. . . .

The Old Man's confusion was increasing. In the next few letters he repeated his wish to go back in time and said over and over how obsessed he was with hate. Then, in March, the circle seemed to be coming around.

. . . I received a letter from Lil last week. At first I was angry with you. I'm not anymore. I'm glad you talked with her now. I actually hoped something like that would happen. It was wonderful to see her handwriting again. She spoke of things in Ottawa and filled me in on our old friends. I don't know how to explain myself to her now. So much has happened. But I'm working on a letter. Maybe if I take it slow, we might try again. I hope so but will understand if that's not possible. . . .

. . . I wrote to Lil and she has written back. This letter was more personal than the first. She has left the door open. I hope I can keep from giving her a reason to slam it shut. . . .

. . . Lil and I have decided to try again. As soon as I get back I will ask her to marry me. Knowing she is back in my life has helped me a great deal. I'm not as afraid or obsessed with the Germans. I still think of Rose and the baby. I always will. But she would want me to move on and I have to. While Lil never probed, I've told her everything about Rose and some of what I've written to you. I also told her

many things are best kept between brothers and she understands. And Lil is no consolation prize. She's the best. If she can live with my ghosts, I'll give her a wonderful life. . . .

In early May, The Old Man sent his last letter.

May 3, 1945
Dear Frank,

By now you've heard Hitler is dead. Most guys are celebrating and toasting to his damnation. I don't know how I feel. Maybe it hasn't sunk in yet, but right now there's almost a letdown. The guy has been the focus of everything for so long and now, in a finger snap, he's gone. I wonder what we'll find to fill the space.

But the real news I have is I'm coming home. They expect a full surrender any day now and I'll be sent out before the rush. I wrote to Mr. Brown last month and he's got a job for me back in his business. This time he'll find me the hardest working and most reliable man he's ever had.

I'm very happy to be leaving here, but it makes me really think about the last five years. I would not be able to live with the person I have been over here. I don't like him much. But he was what he was, and maybe had to be, and I can't change any of that. And I can't honestly regret any of what I went through. Years ago when we talked about the school of hard knocks, I never had any idea what I would learn there. What

I've seen will always be in my mind. That's where it has to stay.

I must ask you to make a promise. You and Jimmy were the only ones I could really talk to. Now that it's just you and me, I need to know what we have shared will always stay between us. I can't and won't spend any time reliving this. When I get back, any talk of this war from me will be just the general chitchat, just enough to be polite. The truth is only for you and me. Sergeant Gerret Eagleson, marksman first class from the second Canadian division, will not be leaving England. He must stay here, or I will not be able to live with myself. Thanks to you, I have a chance at the kind of life I have always wanted. If Lil and I are lucky enough to have a family, they will never want for anything and they will know nothing of the man who fought in this war. They could never understand anyway. I don't think I do. I only hope I can learn to be close again. Not with you or Lil, we've been that way. But over here it's a curse. You get close, you get hurt—badly. I've not made a real friend since Rose. I don't know how anymore. When things start to get at all personal, I move away. It's instinct now. I doubt I can change it. Well, that will be my burden, and after all, having two people like you and Lil is more than one guy deserves.

I've written to Lil about this, but she has asked I never forget Rose or the baby I never saw. She thinks it would be a big mistake to try and they deserve my ongoing love. Lil is a fantastic person to see things like that. She insists I wear my silver ring and carry my lighter. She says the crest will be a reminder of the good there was despite five years of hate and killing. But, as these memories are mine alone, I've asked that the crest's meaning be kept a secret among the three of us, and she agrees. I know you will understand too.

My ship leaves in a few days. I can't wait to see you and Lil and Ottawa. May is always so beautiful there. And one more favor, I'll phone you when I arrive and let you know what day to expect me. If you can find one, pick up a pork loin. I'll cook it for us all the first night. Oh, and good beer, as if you didn't know that already. No need to give my regards to anyone, I'll do that myself soon. And Frank, thank you again for all you've done for me. It will never be forgotten.

With warmest regards,

Gerret

Jimmy had completed the journey. He breathed in deeply and cleansed his chest with a long exhale. He sat thinking in his favorite chair. He had an urge to re-read parts of letters. Did The Old Man really mean this or that? How did he say it? He wondered what had happened to Uncle Frank's letters. They must be out there somewhere. And who was this other Jimmy, the man Jimmy Eagleson was named for? His head buzzed. Now that he'd been through all The Old Man wrote, he didn't want the story to end. And it was a story he was never supposed to know. His life wouldn't be the same now. Gord was right; this was incredible.

Jimmy looked at his watch—two o'clock in his second day of immersion. He needed to get out of his apartment and walk. A bright sky and a light breeze made the weather perfect. At first, Jimmy didn't notice the weather. He'd brought his obsession with him. But when he got to the village, he sat on a bench in Washington Square Park and let the day in. He watched a young man with a pink Mohawk and a face riddled with piercings. His teeth had been filed to sharp points and his body covered with satanic tattoos, all contrasting with his Bermuda shorts and floral tropical-shirt. As the young man sat on a bench and rummaged through his lunch sack, a large crow swept down, stole a sandwich he'd placed on the bench, and perched comfortably in a tree across from him. The young man stood and yelled. All eyes turned as he stomped and waved and hollered profanities and racial insults. The crow looked at him unconcerned as it picked the baloney and cheese apart. Eventually, the defeated victim sat and sulked and crunched his baby carrots while still glaring into the tree and mumbling to the bird. In the quiet, things returned to normal and the spectators turned to other things.

Jimmy faced the sun and for a second absorbed some rays. Then he noticed a man standing next to him in a three-piece suit, his face buried in the *Wall Street Journal*. Farther away, he saw kids arguing near the swings, people sitting and reading, two gang types hanging near the corner sidewalk, and scores of others, each a story.

As he walked to a corner bar, he saw three girls in tank tops, each walking two dogs. The dogs panted happily and wore sweaters asking for someone to adopt them. One girl smiled at him. She was on a mission. But there wouldn't be any money in it. There wasn't any money in The Old Man's mission either. He remembered what Gail had said about the satisfaction of just doing it, whatever "it" was. Lately, Jimmy's missions had been solving meaningless puzzles so rich people could get more from other rich people while the little folks who worked for them fell by the wayside. There was money in that. And Sal, his true friend, loved it. It couldn't be all bad. Maybe none of it was bad. Maybe "it" wasn't any more than simply what "it" was, all just OK.

Jimmy walked in, approached the bar, and cheerfully ordered. The beer came ice cold in frosted mugs. It was happy hour, and they were two for one. Happy hour, what a concept, and beer, an even better one. Right now, Jimmy had no concerns and felt good.

After a couple of rounds, he decided to walk to *Doc's*. He strolled slowly acutely aware of everything, paying unusual attention to the simplest activities. He felt as if his brain had been scrubbed clean and clear. When he reached the bar, he felt like no time had passed. Somehow he was just there. Gail was on. Why? This wasn't her shift. She was just filling in, but why now? She told him one of the regulars had dropped dead, a guy he often talked to. She mentioned how young he was and what a shame. She referred to him as "poor Allen, that poor man, the poor guy." Jimmy simply nodded. He remembered their talks about business and family and worry after worry. But recently he'd said he was doing well. Jimmy got the feeling he was on top of things. Maybe Sal was right, maybe that's the time to go, on top of it all when there's nowhere to go but down. Either way, now it was over for him. Jimmy wondered what that was like, the end of a life, a finished story, like The Old Man's. They all must have an ending. He felt no sorrow. He just wondered.

"You all right Jimmy?" Gail asked. "You look a little spaced out?"

"I'm fine."

"Where's your ring?"

Jimmy looked at his hand and for a second panicked. Then he remembered. "It's at home, safe. I forgot to put it back on." He thought of the lighter and felt the loss. Now he knew its importance.

Her question nudged him back to the present. They gossiped. She filled him in on the last two days' news. He enjoyed the chit chat, not caring at all about the content. He enjoyed the voices and the laughs and the connection. And he enjoyed the beer. Today it tasted better than ever.

At home that night he still felt good. He continued to wonder about many things, but he wasn't obsessed for answers anymore. That need had left him, maybe helped along by the magnitude of his discovery. He felt proud of The Old Man and accepted his need for secrecy though he was glad he now knew. He put the ring back on.

He decided to call Gordon. Gord was the only one Jimmy could talk to about the whole story. He'd have a few new tales to add to the Gerret Eagleson saga he'd started with Stosh and Sal, but only of the times before Dieppe. There'd be no mention of the rest. Only Gord and he would know it all.

"Hello," Gord answered after one ring.

"Hi Gord, this is Jimmy."

"Jimmy, how are you, eh? I was wondering when you might call. I'll guess you've read the letters."

"Yes, now two of us know the story."

"Yeah. Now, before you ask, let me tell you a couple of things. My dad's letters are gone. I couldn't find anything more. And, I went to the Royal Legion Hall in Ottawa. No one knew who Jimmy might have been. Actually, a couple of guys went off on long stories they thought would help. But they were dead-ends. I guess the folks stuck to your dad's wishes. Well, with one exception, eh? So I don't have any answers for you, my friend. I guess there are things we will never know."

"I figured. And maybe that's the way it should be. I already know more of The Old Man's 'inside' than my kids will ever know about me. And I think it's enough just to know there was another Jimmy and how much he meant."

"You OK?"

"Good, actually really good."

"When did you read the stuff?"

"Over the last couple of days."

"Great. Then they were good for you right off the bat. I'd hoped for that. They were good for me too, but he was your dad. I was worried about it all with you."

"You know, it's a whole new thing for me now, even though nothing's changed. I feel kind of clearheaded, and just good. I don't know why. The initial shock of it all—I mean The Old

Man I knew wasn't anything like the guy in the letters—well, it smacked me."

"I figured it would. Shook me up too. But I know what you mean about feeling good. I kind of like young Gerret. Reminds me of my favorite cousin. A lot of gaps are filled now. Your dad was one hell of a character."

"Yes, he was."

"You know, Jimmy, I think your dad was kind of a symbol, eh?"

"Of what?"

"Oh, that time, his bunch, the ones that lived the depression and the war and all. They gave us a lot, except one thing."

"What's that?"

"Their experiences. You know? The real context. You and I never lived a war. To us, they're abstract. A few veterans try to tell us, but we never really understand. And the letters woke us up, but we still can't 'know.' Maybe it can't be done—put someone in another's world.

"I know what you mean."

"And I wonder how well we've done with what they did give us. In my world, their values took a trip to the outhouse, eh? There's lots of money but not much worth anything. Oh well, we are who we are, I guess."

"Yeah, I guess."

The conversation continued for some time. They talked about the kids and wives and old times and laughed. It was good for each of them to have the other as a partner in keeping The Old Man's secrets. Gord vowed to visit Camp in the spring.

When they finally hung up, it was after midnight. Tonight, Jimmy would sleep well.

* * *

For the rest of the week, Jimmy did the kind of touristy things New Yorkers avoid. He went to the top of the Empire State Building. On Thursday, Gail accompanied him to the Statue of Liberty and Ellis Island. He went to museums he'd never seen and a few where he was a regular. Somewhere in the back of his mind were thoughts about work and his next steps. He'd deal with all of that soon enough. For now, his time was his own, and he was going to enjoy it.

By Sunday, he knew he would not be returning to work. He felt no need to. He missed Camp and was looking forward to being back at the lake. He would call Mr. Clark in the morning.

He was up early. After a walk and a stop for breakfast, he returned to his place and started to pack. At around 9:00 he sat down to end his employment with the company he had been with for seven years. He felt no remorse. With Mike gone, he had no good reason to stay. Mr. Clark's secretary answered the phone and immediately pushed the call through. "Yes, this is Carlos Clark."

"Mr. Clark, this is James Eagleson."

"Yes, James. It's good to hear from you. Have you decided on our offer?"

"I have, and I'm afraid I must most respectfully decline. Your offer was very generous, and it's very hard to turn down.

But I think it's time for me to move on. You know, I came here to work with Mike, and now, well, things are different for me."

"You know the conditions are negotiable; we are willing to stretch to keep you."

"I thank you for that. But it's not the conditions. It's just time for me to go."

"Let me ask you a question in confidence."

"Yes."

"Does your decision have anything to do with Mr. Gyges?"

"I thought it might when you first extended the offer, but no, he's not the reason."

"Is there anything we can do to change your mind?"

"No sir, I have to leave."

"Then I want to tell you something, again in confidence."

"Understood."

"Several of us thought you were clearly the best candidate to take over the operation. Your reviews from Michael were always outstanding, and we were well aware of your work. But a few of your colleagues, a Miss Anne Young in particular, were adamant you wouldn't be an effective manager on a day-to-day basis. They insisted Mr. Gyges had more vision and superior leadership skills, and these people were persuasive with some younger board members. Many of us disagreed, but when I proposed the new structure we thought we would have the best of both worlds. I fear we've made a mistake. I don't have the confidence in Mr. Gyges that Miss Young expressed and now I think we've lost our ace.

"I know you will do well wherever you decide to go, and I wish you all the success in the world. You've done a great deal for this company, more than most will ever know. I'll prepare a letter of reference for your vita and will have it placed on your desk for you. I'm not happy you're leaving us, but I think I understand. Should you decide at any time you'd like to return, you'll be welcome; please call me directly. James, we will miss you."

"Thank you, Sir, I feel honored."

"You deserve much recognition. Goodbye, James."

"Goodbye, Sir."

It was done. And with a little sadness, Jimmy felt free of it all. But he worried for Annie. Poor Annie Young, who thought she had made a good deal by doing Jimmy in, had cut herself the worse bargain of her life. Gyges would have her out in no time. But that wasn't Jimmy's problem. He was going home.

The next afternoon, Jimmy went to the company complex for the last time. Things were not much different—still a sense of disorder, and Gyges was still at lunch. Jimmy looked around his office. He had never kept much there, a few mugs and the like, and a silver pen The Old Man gave him when he started in the family business. It had been on his desk at every job he'd ever had. He wondered where it would be next.

As he was ready to leave, Victor came in.

"I thought I saw you in here, James. How are you?"

"Victor I'm fine. Just picking up a few things. How are you?"

"I'm quite good. Barry has held several meetings with us, and I think he has many good ideas. He has said a lot of things I think make sense, although I don't know his part of this business well."

"Victor, you're talking about a guy who can't wipe his ass without getting shit under his fingernails."

"Please James, Mr. Gyges is my boss now, and this is my job. He deserves my support, and I'm not going to be criticizing him."

"Victor, listen, my friend; not everything that comes out of a little worm's mouth is silk. Please be careful." Victor smiled and nodded. "You'll do well wherever you go. You're one of the best, my friend. If a good offer comes up—I think one will—don't hesitate to take it. And if you ever need something from me, you've got the number."

"Thank you James; I will miss you."

"I will miss you too."

Jimmy put his pen in his briefcase and left everything else on the desk. He walked through the wing one last time. Near the door, Gyges was standing over his secretary's desk frantically waving a piece of paper as he scolded her. Gyges looked up, saw Jimmy, tried to laugh and grabbed his side in pain.

"What happened to him?" Jimmy asked another secretary.

"Cracked a couple of ribs. Probably fell off a curb the way he's been drinking lately." Jimmy looked back at Gyges and waved goodbye. "Maybe staying would have been fun," he whispered as he walked out the door.

Jimmy arrived back at his place just in time to catch his cleaning lady. She told him she would be back on Friday to empty the trashcans and refrigerator and to deep clean the bathrooms and kitchen. She blushed and said she'd found something under his bed and left it on the counter. Jimmy thanked her and gave her a generous tip. It had been a good day's work.

Now Jimmy had closure and time for a beer. As he approached the bar, he saw the housekeeper's find, a pair of women's underwear. He walked over and picked them up. Peggy, what would happen to poor little Peggy? He wondered if she was still with her new beau. Maybe she had already moved on. Peggy would be just fine. After all, she had a new wardrobe, and she could always sell her diamonds if she were short of cash. Oh Peggy. He gazed at them a moment, then stepped on the trashcan's lever, popped it open and dropped them in. He smiled. Three days' coffee grounds, one banana peel, and Peggy's panties. He removed his foot and the lid slapped shut.

CHAPTER IX

The Fix

The mirror showed no signs of the tractor trailer's kiss. Jimmy was picking up a Lincoln that looked better than ever. Sal was in Phoenix, but his boys had it detailed and gassed. Jimmy drove north on Route 87 into the bright, green Adirondack Mountains. He gazed into the blue sky decorated with just a few cumulus clouds, then lowered the windows and let the fresh air flow on his face. It was spring in the North Country as the postcards promised, and he was driving his favorite car to his favorite place. He clicked on the radio and dialed-in an oldies station. Blood Sweat and Tears played "And When I Die." Jimmy recalled Sal's proclamation on death that winter at the Sagamore, "If there is such a thing as a blessing, going out on top is it." He snickered and remembered what Stosh shouted on the last day of December when the sandman nearly killed them, "NOT TODAY." He laughed and sang along.

Jimmy exhaled. No more wallowing in worry or planning someone else's next move. Now the moves would be his own. As he passed each town, he remembered the hardware stores he used to visit with The Old Man. He thought of the back roads he'd take whenever he had time. He stopped briefly at the High Peaks rest area and admired its familiar view. It became noticeably colder as he traveled north. He closed the windows and watched for patches of ice. Passing the base of Poke-O-Moonshine, he looked up at the high cliffs of the 2,180-foot crag and remembered how the winter ice would cascade in long sculpted formations. He could still see traces. He remembered his promise to join Ray and Kate on a trip to the ideal view.

Jimmy looked forward to Camp. He would sit on the porch and visit Turtle Rock. Maybe that night Ray and Kate would go with him to the little Italian place. He wondered if the boat was back in the water; in his rush to leave he forgot to ask Ray to take care of that. Ray would have known anyway. Maybe he should get a new boat; it had been a while, a long while, and he would be on the water much more now. Of course, he'd never sell The Old Man's Lyman. But why not have another, maybe one with a cabin? Not too big, just enough to feel like camping. He could even sleep out, right there in the bay if he felt like it. This deserved further consideration.

Near Cumberland Head, he stopped for a hot dog. He hadn't had a "Michigan hot" since the last summer and craved one. He sat at the counter and asked for two Michigans with onions, an order of fries, and a Labatt Blue. They came quickly. German franks in freshly steamed buns covered in a thick, spicy meat sauce and smothered with onions. With a hot Michigan dripping sauce on his hand, he was home.

Jimmy chatted with his waitress. She asked him where he

was from and was surprised he lived on the lake, remarking that living on the lake was so expensive, but she still hoped to one day. Maybe she would, Jimmy thought.

At Camp, he turned into his driveway and noticed the pickup was gone. He'd be alone for a while. Good, he thought. Once inside, he poured a cold beer from a freshly tapped keg and planted himself in a rocker on the porch. Champlain was calm. A few surface blemishes appeared from place to place as a light breeze traveled around, and The Sister Islands looked near enough to touch with an oar. A few birds were busy with spring chores. In the morning, there would be loons.

Jimmy's mind went to The Old Man. How many times did he stand atop that bank and look out on the same scene, always with a boat resting in its hoist. For a moment, he missed him and his mother. They were different people to him now. He knew them, and they were better. No need for questions anymore. After all, he'd never questioned his other friends. He heard a truck coming down the drive.

Jimmy was refilling his beer when Ray came in the great room. They stood and looked at each other. Ray could see Jimmy was unusually peaceful. "You look good," he said.

"Yeah, I got some things sorted out."

"That's good, yeah, that's good."

Ray filled a mug and sat across from Jimmy. "I didn't put the boat in yet. I wanted to talk to you about it first. The ice was rough this winter. The usual spot got beat up pretty bad. We'll need to dig out a lot of stone or move the hoist where it used to be on the other side of the turtle. You know, it won't block as much view from the beach if we move it, but you'll see a lot more of it from the bank again. I know you don't care for that."

"We'll move it," Jimmy said. "Yeah, we'll put it back where it was. It's good to be able to see it from the bank."

"Good then. I'll get on it in the morning. You know, you really do look good."

"Thanks, Ray."

Ray filled Jimmy in on the affairs of Camp. Jimmy filled Ray in on the basics of Peggy. He told him about leaving his job, all the details. He figured his confidentiality had a geographic statute of limitations. And Jimmy told Ray he would be staying, staying indefinitely this time. Ray smiled broadly. They went on about other things for more than an hour when Ray said, "Shit, Jimmy. I forgot to tell you Kate called. She said she has something she wanted to talk to you about as soon as you got home."

"How did she sound?"

"OK, I think. She didn't seem upset or anything, just anxious to talk to you. I mean right away."

Jimmy's eyebrows lifted, he took a sip with one hand and reached for his phone with the other.

"Hi," Kate answered, knowing it was him.

"How are you? Ray said you wanted me to call. I just got in." Jimmy winked at Ray.

"Yeah, I'd like to talk to you about something but not on the phone. Soon, if you can."

"I can. I'll be here. I'm not going anywhere."

"OK, I'll be out in a little while."

"Hey Kate, before you hang up, do you want me to make

reservations for tonight?" Jimmy turned to Ray. "Ray you good for tonight?"

"Sure," Kate said as Ray nodded.

"Great. I'll see you soon. I'll probably be down on the beach."

"I'll meet you there."

They hung up, and the boys filled their mugs knowing that for Kate a little while could be some time. Jimmy leaned back and looked at the mantel. His eyes popped and he hurried over. "Jesus, Ray, look," he said as he pointed to The Old Man's lighter sitting proudly in its case. "Did you find it?"

"No, I had no idea it was there."

Jimmy picked up a piece of paper lying near. "Chins up, Fins," it read. Jimmy grinned ear to ear as he crushed the note. "Never underestimate the magic of Salvatore Esposito," he whispered.

* * *

Jimmy hopped on the back of turtle rock, his favorite perch. Ray had cleaned some beach, but deposits of driftwood and debris still dominated the shoreline. Champlain's waves rhythmically lapped over the rocks. Jimmy looked up into the bright cloudless sky to watch a great blue heron drift by. No hurry. The bank and steps were still spotted with ice in places where the sun couldn't penetrate. As Kate ambled down, she slipped and fell on her rear end.

"Watch that step," Jimmy said.

"I could have hurt myself you know," Kate said as she carefully stood and whisked herself off.

"Sorry."

Jimmy shifted to make room as she maneuvered around him and sat. Kate gave Jimmy a kiss and hugged him awhile.

"I heard about that little bitch in New York. You OK?"

"I'm fine."

"You know, I can see that. I thought you might still be hurt, but you sure don't look it."

"I'm fine. Look." Jimmy pointed. The winter freeze had fixed Turtle Rock. For the first time in decades, it had an attached head.

"An omen?" Kate asked smiling.

"I doubt it, just the work of some ice. So, what's up? You sounded like you have important news."

"Maybe not all that important, but I wanted you to hear it from me for a change. Well, now it's official: Steve and I are getting a divorce. Not much more to say about it, I guess."

"And David?"

"Long gone. I told you he was on the way out."

"Well, that was a while back."

"Anyway, you know Steve and I have been something of a joke from the beginning. I've had enough. We barely see each other. This would have happened years ago if not for the assets—his precious assets. I'm giving him most of the stuff. There are a few things I want, but not much. You know it still feels weird. We've been married a long time, and even bad history is history, I guess."

"Yeah, he's been a big part of your life. It's not going to be easy."

"Yup, I hear you." Kate latched on to Jimmy and started to cry. "I've just wasted so much time."

"There's still more."

"Not much though."

"Enough."

They looked at the lake together. Jimmy's arm was around her and her head on his shoulder. Kate broke the silence. "Why didn't we ever, you know?"

"I don't know, too dangerous I guess."

"Dangerous?"

Jimmy was quiet. "I could always live with you, the way you were, and me, the way I've been. But I wouldn't be able to ... after us."

Kate hesitated. "Why would there have to be an 'after us'?"

"Because, for me, there's always been an after us."

Kate sat quietly a minute, then wiggled to get closer and kissed Jimmy. "There really isn't much time."

As she gave him another kiss and exhaled, Jimmy took in a deep breath through his nose. There it was, that smell, that wonderful calming scent he'd thought only Clair had. He'd never let himself inhale Kate before, but there it was. Jimmy wondered if it had always been there. He basked in it awhile.

"Listen, I'm back to stay," he said. "I left my job—I'll tell you about that sometime. I plan on being here, well I don't know, at least for the summer, maybe for good. You're going to be going through more shit than you might think, especially with Steve. But we can spend real time together. Where are you staying?"

"I'm not sure. We're selling the house, so I'll be moving. I thought I might look for a little place on the lake; you know I love it out here."

"Why not stay here? There's plenty of room, and hell, you've spent more time here than I have, for Christ's sake."

"I didn't come out here to ask you for a place to live, and I don't want you to be in the middle of the shit, as you have so accurately put it. You know what a bastard Steve can be."

"I know he won't fuck with me."

"You've got that one right, Eagleson. But I don't want any handouts, Jimmy. I have my own money, and unlike your highness, I still have a job."

"No handouts; you take the room you always have. If you recall, you decorated it for yourself. No strings."

"I'm not worried about strings, I'm not even sure I know what they are. OK … I'll think about it."

"But you'll stay tonight?"

"Yes, I'll stay tonight." They hugged again and kissed until Kate said, "Let's go up, my ass is getting flat." Jimmy helped her to her feet. They looked at the lake and then carefully made their way up the stairs.

Jimmy poured beers and joined Kate on the porch. They felt warmer, and the lake looked just as magnificent from their new perspective. Jimmy filled her in on his time since St. Patrick's Day. Kate winced when she heard of the gifts he'd bought Peggy. "You've really got to stop that shit you know."

"Yeah, I suppose."

She thought the shark incident was hysterical and laughed so hard her stomach hurt. She filled Jimmy in on her breakup with David and the particulars of her decision to leave Steve. Jimmy thought she was remarkably clearheaded given all she'd dealt with. She continued to pry about what might have happened to put Jimmy at such peace. He told her he'd come to understand The Old Man and after a great deal of thought, he was good with everything. He didn't mention the letters. They were private territory, even for her.

In the late afternoon, Ray joined them. The talk changed to North Country news and even the wars. A son of one of Jimmy's friends had been killed in Afghanistan. Jimmy stared off at Champlain. He couldn't help but think of The Old Man. At about 6:00 both Kate and Ray left to change. She would meet the guys at the restaurant. Jimmy sat alone mulling the conversation at the rock. After several minutes, the sound of a motorboat racing across the bay brought him back to the present. He left the porch to clean up.

* * *

The marinara tasted delicious, as Jimmy expected. Kate and Ray showed their culinary contentment too. The table sat next to a window that looked out on the little city. The sights brought back old memories, though the old buildings were long gone. Jimmy and Kate sat next to each other like a long-time happy couple. Ray talked a lot about the mountains. He'd been on the trails throughout the winter and early spring and raved about the changes. The eastern woods had reinvented themselves since his summer visits.

Jimmy's interest was piqued. He'd been thinking about old Poke-O-Moonshine all winter. He'd always loved it up there. For the second time that day he remembered their plan. "Hey, Ray. You still want to hit that spot you were talking about?"

"Oh, yeah," Ray said. He suggested they go soon before the season starts. After Memorial Day, it would be too crowded. "How about the day after tomorrow?" Jimmy and Kate looked at each other, nodded, and that was that: time for an adventure.

Back at Camp, they sat at the bar for a couple of rounds. Then Ray instinctively left Kate and Jimmy alone. They relocated to a couch where they cuddled, chatting between kisses. Then Jimmy nervously suggested it was time for bed. Kate nodded.

"Are you sure you want to do this?" he asked.

"Yes." She gave him a long, deep kiss before taking his hand and leading him to her room. The smell of fresh linen, clean air, and the newly found scent of Kate intensified Jimmy's passion as they modestly undressed and slipped between the sheets. Their skin touched for the first time as they explored each other, each discovering a brand new body they had known for many, many years. They went slowly and with great concern for the other—no rush or aggression, just a gentle and patient connection. They were in no hurry; they had all night.

Jimmy woke early and quietly left the bed. Kate was sleeping soundly, and he didn't want to disturb her. He put on his robe and walked to the porch to catch the sunrise. Soon a bright outline filled the Vermont side of the lake. The edge of a large red circle crept up over the green mountains. On the lake, loons were diving and cooing. A woodpecker began making tat-tat-tat-tat-tats on a nearby oak.

Jimmy thought of his night with Kate. Maybe they'd crossed a line. It could be dangerous. But he was where he always wanted to be with the woman he should have been with all along. It couldn't be better. Maybe it was time to get used to being happy.

A hand on his shoulder and Kate's voice startled him. "You were going to do this without me?"

"Good morning. Here, I'll make coffee."

"Let's just sit here; there's plenty of time for coffee."

They watched the spectacle until the light hurt their eyes. Kate took Jimmy's hand and led him back to the bedroom. She's right, Jimmy thought, the coffee could wait.

* * *

Jimmy knew Kate would take her time in the bathroom, and why not? After a simple breakfast and fresh hot coffee to start the new day, she could take all the time she wanted. He watched the sailboats from Turtle Rock, munched on a Nutter Butter and thought. He wished Kate had been with him in Florida. He wished Kate had been with him a lot of places. Well, the matchmakers will celebrate this one for sure. And this time, he knew what The Old Man would think. He heard the porch door slam; Kate was on her way down to the beach.

She carefully managed the stairs this time and handed him

a tall Bloody Mary complete with a properly trimmed celery stalk. "Could you hold this please?" she asked. She handed him her glass and used both hands to sit on the turtle's still slippery back. They sat quietly. Then Kate spoke. "It is beautiful out here."

"Yup."

A ski boat sped around the corner of the bay pulling a girl in a custom-fit wetsuit, riding on a large round tube. Bouncing off the wake, she screamed and belly-laughed in excitement almost drowning out the loud droning of the outboard motor.

"Ever do that when you were a kid?" Kate asked.

"Nope; The Old Man's boat wasn't for pulling me around."

"Too bad. She's having a ball. I bet you would have enjoyed it."

"I had something better." Kate gave him a questioning look. "One day in July I think—I don't know, I must have been seven or eight—The Old Man came home with an old inner tube he'd picked up at that Sunoco station that used to be on the corner near the state park—you remember that place?" Kate nodded. "Well, I was in that thing for the whole summer. I figured I could go anywhere in it. I remember sitting on the old porch planning an adventure. I'd go up the lake to the Richelieu River and then catch the St. Lawrence out to the Atlantic. From there, who knew? In that thing, I could flutter kick to any place I wanted. My mother would yell out at me sometimes when I was in it. 'Jimmy you've gone far enough, Jimmy it's getting rough you need to come in, Jimmy, there's an offshore wind, you'll float off to who knows where if you don't come in now.' But not The Old Man. He wasn't home much, but when he was, he'd stand on the bank, watch me, and smile. My mum would yell out to him too. 'Gerret, do you see where he is? Don't you think he should come closer to shore? He might drown you know.' But he'd just holler back 'He's fine, Lillian, he'll be just fine.'"

"What happened to it?"

"I don't know. I looked everywhere for it one spring and couldn't find it. I asked if anyone had seen it. It just disappeared. By that time I was probably beyond it anyway."

"Well, now you've got your boat. You can go wherever you want, and much more safely."

"Safely wasn't part of the plan back then."

"Have you thought about moving in here?" Jimmy asked.

"I haven't exactly had a lot of time. I'm thinking about it. But I'm not staying tonight, OK? I have to take care of some things and—Jimmy last night was incredible. I want to savor it for a little while. OK?"

"OK. What time do you want to leave tomorrow?"

"I'll be out by 8:00. Ray is really excited about this, you know. We haven't done anything like this in so long."

"Yeah, he's a good guy. I'll enjoy being around him more often."

"Come on, let's go up. I think I could do one more Bloody Mary. How 'bout you?"

"Oh yeah."

Kate stood carefully, took Jimmy's hand, and pulled him to his feet. Jimmy looked far down the shoreline. A panting dog bolted from the beach, leaped from a dock, smacked onto the water, and swam frantically to retrieve a stick.

Snatching the prize in his mouth, he began a casual paddle back to shore. "Look at that," Jimmy said. "Can you imagine anything happier?"

Kate smiled. "Maybe in the next life."

* * *

Ray said nothing. Jimmy broached the subject once to give him an opportunity, but Ray didn't bite. Jimmy always liked that about Ray, his ability to mind his own business. But clearly he was pleased; his face was a public announcement. They spent a lazy afternoon. Kate had left, and they had nothing urgent to do. They rocked and sipped on the porch with an occasional comment on something of no real importance as the afternoon slowly passed.

In the early evening, they went for Michigans. Once back, Ray lit a fire with applewood, The Old Man's favorite. The roaring flames created a comfortable, warm zone extending through half the great room, and the aroma reminded Jimmy of more times in his childhood. They watched the flicker and random illumination until the fire faded. Then Ray turned in, and Jimmy was left with his thoughts. It had been quite a homecoming. Hell, it had been quite a year. So much change so quickly. How did he ever survive the boring times?

Out of beer, he got up for a refill. But he had a sudden impulse to put his mug down on the bar and visit his study. The room was just as he'd left it. He sat and looked around. All the books and his prize stick were in the same place, safe and sound. Even a pencil he'd used at New Year was where he left it, next to an unfinished note about nothing important. He remembered his pen set and went for his briefcase. He took out the old gift and placed it on his desk. He looked in his case at the stacks of The Old Man's letters neatly bundled, just as he'd received them. He hesitated and then carefully took them out. He looked around his room full of books. He'd read hundreds of them and files and letters. But nothing had ever had the effect of the paper he held in his hands. He sat fidgeting with the string and then decided to move back to the bar.

Jimmy laid down the letters and drew the beer slowly, as The Old Man had taught him. He sipped the head, picked up the letters, and returned to his chair by the dying fire. Tomorrow he'd visit one of his favorite places with some of his favorite people. He didn't know what after; he didn't need to. And right now, it was just him and The Old Man.

Jimmy tugged one bow knot loose, stopped, paused to think, and retied it. This was an unintended gift. Not like the desk set, which was meant to stay. This wasn't. This was secret and personal, and The Old Man had made clear what he wanted done with it. Jimmy walked slowly to the mantel and took The Old Man's lighter from its case. He lit the corner of the old paper. "Chins up, Eagleson," he whispered. He laid the burning stack on top of the applewood embers. He watched the flames grow around it, turning the outside to ashes as they worked their way to the heart. He sat quietly, watching the blaze finish its mission, and said goodbye to Sergeant Gerret Eagleson, marksman first class from the Second Canadian Division.

* * *

Jimmy woke to a brisk morning with dark gray skies. It felt like a fall day. The mountain awaited and the adventurers would soon be on their way. Kate arrived for breakfast and cooked a pile of eggs, Canadian bacon, and rye toast. They needed to fill up. There wouldn't be a hot dog stand on the trail, and nobody cared to haul a soggy lunch around. He looked out onto Lake Champlain covered with white caps. Cedars near the bank bent backward in a gust of wind. The Sister Islands were invisible, hiding behind dense fog.

"Nice day for a walk," Jimmy said.

"Come on now; it'll be fine up there," Ray replied. "You know how things can be so different just a few miles apart up here. Besides, the weather will keep the amateurs off the mountain. So it's Poko today?"

"What do you think Kate?" Jimmy asked.

"I don't know. Even the roads are slick. It's not a very nice day."

"Yeah, but Ray has a point. That could change quickly, and there won't be many of us up there."

"I would vote to wait," Kate said. "I think it could be too dangerous. But, I'm a wimp about these things—whatever you want."

"OK, nothing ventured nothing gained—or some bullshit like that," Jimmy said.

"Good," Ray said. "I'm telling you guys; this view's incredible."

"We might not be able to see very far today," Kate said.

"We'll see plenty," Ray replied.

They quickly cleaned up, changed into hiking gear, slipped on temporary shoes, and climbed into the pickup. Without the new truck, the three would pass for North Country hicks. Ray drove. Jimmy kept his arm around Kate. She'd filled three travel mugs with coffee, and they sipped at random intervals and talked about past climbs. They calculated it had been more than ten years since they had hiked together. In fact, it had been over ten years since the three had done much of anything together.

Ray turned off Route 87 onto a backroad. They passed new ranches, a few log homes, and several older trailers, all snug in the trees. Most were well kept, but a few properties looked like junkyards. They were in the Adirondack Park now and would be at their base point soon.

Kate whispered, "This is wonderful, Jimmy."

"Oh, yeah," Jimmy whispered back.

"I just hope it's OK up there," she added.

At the foot of the trail, they pulled on their boots, carefully tightened and tied the laces, and stretched their legs. A light cover of new needles and cones lay on the path. The taller pines swayed freely in time with the brisk wind filling the woods with their scent. At the path's side, mossed rocks served as natural compasses. Curious chipmunks popped up to see what was breaking the wildlife code of silence.

"Here we go," Jimmy said.

"I'll lead," Ray suggested.

"How far is it?" Kate asked.

"Maybe a couple of hours, it's pretty close to the top of the east side. I can't wait for you guys to see this view."

"Let's do it," Jimmy said.

The trail's incline began gently. Soon it steepened. Although Jimmy had walked a lot in New York, his calves tightened. Kate commented on her aches too. For Ray, this was a stroll in the park.

They stopped near the top. Ray went off to check his secret path while Jimmy and Kate rested on a rock.

"Wow, I didn't realize how out-of-shape I am," Kate said.

"Yeah, me too. It's a good thing it's all downhill from here, I don't have any vertical climb left in me. Hey, give me a kiss."

"Right now?"

"Yeah, right now, and make it a good one."

"Oh, you can count on that," she said sliding over.

Ray returned to find them in an embrace. He waited. "Come on you two, break it up. Let's go."

They snaked their way to the east side, moving carefully between multiple obstacles on a trail only Ray seemed able to identify. Branches scraped their clothes, and the uneven ground twisted their ankles.

"I wouldn't want to be doing this in shorts," Jimmy said.

"I'm not sure we should be doing this at all," Kate replied. "It's terribly slippery."

"Come on you guys," Ray said. "It's not much longer."

At the eastern face, the tree density diminished, and Ray's perfect view appeared. He hadn't exaggerated; it was extraordinary. The sky had cleared revealing a panorama of Champlain lying between the Adirondack and Green Mountain ranges.

"This is breathtaking," Kate said. The others nodded.

Ray led them to a clearing near the edge where they stood atop a cliff, hundreds of feet above the valley and absorbed the view. The wind nipped their faces and made their wide eyes tear. The elevation made Kate dizzy, and she kept well away from the edge.

"This is perfect, Ray," Jimmy said taking a long deep breath and grinning.

"Yeah, best view I've ever found."

"Not just the view, Ray. Everything. It's all perfect."

"Come on over here," Ray said as he approached the drop-point.

"Ray, let's not tempt fate," Kate said. "There's still ice up here."

"I think it's OK," Ray replied.

"Well, I'll stay here if you don't mind. I think I'm close enough."

Jimmy and Ray carefully stepped over. The mountain's steep decline intensified the rush. They both felt like kids who'd snuck off to a place they were told not to go. Jimmy surveyed the ground carefully before stepping back. As Ray turned to join him, he slipped on hidden ice, fell backward, and couldn't find a foothold. His face contorting, he gasped and looked at Jimmy. Jimmy grabbed him by the arm and pulled. Ray stabilized in euphoric thankfulness. He stood by himself, smiled at Jimmy, and shook his head. But before he could speak, Jimmy turned and stepped on another ice patch. Ray quickly reached out for him but missed. Jimmy slipped backward, stumbled over the cliff's edge, and became airborne. All of Ray's helpless terror was now Jimmy's. His arms spun like a helicopter tailpiece. As he screamed in pure fear, he could hear Kate yelling, "JIMMY! NO! JIMMY!" Then nothing.

On her hands and knees, Kate crept to the edge to look. Jimmy was on his back, motionless, caught by a ledge fifty or sixty feet below. Ray was nearly in shock.

"He can't be dead! He can't be dead!" Kate yelled at Ray. Then she regrouped. "All right, we've got to get it together. We've got to get him out of there. Did you bring a cell phone?"

Ray shook and started to cry. "Jimmy's got it."

"All right. You've got to get down as fast as you can and call for help. I'll stay here."

"What the hell will you do here?"

"Stay. He'll need to know somebody's here when he wakes up. Now get going!"

Ray scampered through the woods to the trail and ran for help. Kate yelled down cheering Jimmy on. "Hang in, Jimmy. Stay with me, Jimmy. It's all going to be fine. Ray's gone for help. You're going to be OK. Please, Jimmy, stay with me. ... "

* * *

"Any change?"

"No."

"Philip, you said you were surprised about this one."

"Yeah. This guy's no dummy, and he's been around the North Country all his life, and he was hiking with Raymond LaFleur."

"Who's that?"

"He's a sort of recluse who's a legend up there. One guy told me he's the best climber to come along in a generation. It doesn't make sense they were where they were. That kind of wandering around is for the amateurs."

"Is there any hope?"

"Ah, the ultimate question my dear, 'Is there any hope.' Hope for who? Hope for him? Hope for his people? Yeah, the ultimate question, 'Is there any hope?'"

"You don't have to be sarcastic."

"You know the prognosis, no recovery. The only question is will he live as he is, or die? Either way, somebody benefits and somebody loses. Now, let's talk about a little hope for us. Have you thought about our getaway?"

"Philip, I told you we are trying hard to put things back together; my marriage means a lot to me. I don't think so."

"Listen, you said he'll be gone anyway—doing who knows what. What'll you do while he's out prowling? You going to just watch TV? Maybe knit him a sweater? Come on, it's Lake Placid. You love it there. And it's just between the two of us."

"He's going on business and to play a little golf with his buddies."

"And the three *nights* in Vegas? What kind of business then?"

"I don't know ... when would we leave?"

"We're out of here on Friday afternoon, back late Sunday night."

"Well ... OK ... but just this one last time."

* * *

The sounds from life-support apparatus filled the hospital room. The rescue and Medevac had been difficult, and no one knew how many injuries it may have added to Jimmy's condition. Except for voices drifting in and out, he laid unconscious, much the same as when he arrived the week before. His neck and spine were broken in several places, and a breathing machine and intravenous feeding kept him alive. The doctors told Stosh little could be done. One more honest doctor said nothing. Stosh had become Jimmy's advocate, and the doctors talked to him freely. He was the executor of Jimmy's will and had emergency power of attorney. Kate had been with Jimmy since his arrival and took a room next to Stosh's at an Albany hotel. Ray was in and out. He felt responsible for the whole thing.

Clair had arrived. She was no longer related, but Jimmy Eagleson, the meticulous lawyer, had made a mistake. He had written an airtight living will for himself years ago, but he never thought to change her authority. Only she could pull the plug.

Jimmy could hear sounds as Kate and Stosh talked.

"Stosh, I know you never cared much for Ray. But you don't know him. He's a good person, and he's been more help to Jimmy than you seem to understand."

"Yeah, for as many bucks as Jimmy could line his pockets with. He's been a leech for years. I don't know why you guys can't see that."

"Maybe, just maybe, it's you not seeing something. Not everybody works the way you do. I've never met someone whose nose is to the grindstone like yours. You've done very, very well for yourself, and we all admire that. But Ray ... Ray is a different sort. He just doesn't think your way. He's not lazy, you know. Whatever Jimmy asks, he does right away and well. You haven't seen Camp in a long time. It's immaculate, and that's due to Ray. And Stosh ... Jimmy really loves him. Maybe you could cut him some slack for that reason alone."

"Why did he have to go on that frickin' path? What was that bone-brain thinking?"

"We all went. We all wanted to go. It's not his fault. It's nobody's fault." Stosh stared blankly into the distance. Kate couldn't tell if she'd made a dent. Both were exhausted and stressed to their last nerve. She realized continuing now was futile.

Jimmy's brain was badly bruised from the fall and awash with morphine. The voices mingled with dreams and fantasies and left him with no real comprehension. But he was alive, at least technically, and seemed to be comforted by the tone of a familiar voice, or the music Kate played for him. The doctors insisted he couldn't possibly be responding to anything.

Still, the important conversations, particularly about his condition, were taken outside the room. Stosh motioned for Kate to join him. "Listen, all I know is I'm here with my best friend figuring I'm gonna have to find a way to kill him. You and me both know he didn't wanna live on like this. Yeah, Jimmy said what you said about Ray. But, to me, he's the frickin' craphead who put me in this spot."

"You're wrong, Stosh. Jimmy put you here. Ray or no Ray, Jimmy trusted you to take care of things. That's why you're here. And Jimmy wanted you to try and understand Ray too, or at least to back off. He never expected you to like him. But he always wanted you to end the grind you've got for him. Look at what it's doing to you right now."

Stosh went silent again. Kate paused before returning to the room. She looked at Jimmy lying in his bed, pathetically hanging on and wondered how life might have been for them. But this was the reality. If he somehow survived, he'd be as he was right there in front of her. Stosh had hit the nail on the head. How strange to be looking at someone you want so much, wishing for him to die.

As she left the room, she saw Clair coming up the hall. What a surprise, she thought. The gracious ex-wife had only once been to see her suffering past love in her four days in town. The two silently passed each other smiling politely. Clair had made it clear to Stosh she would not allow the life support removed. Her lawyer had informed her Jimmy's death would result in a major reduction in her income because of a provision in the divorce agreement Jimmy had inserted. At the time, his death was the last thing on Clair's mind, and thinking she would soon be hooked to an equally lucrative provider anyway, she overlooked it. Now she faced her mistake. The big checks would continue to flow only as long as Jimmy lived.

She made it clear he wouldn't be changing her mind but had agreed to meet with Stosh and at least talk about the situation. She entered the room, walked to the bed, and looked over Jimmy's nearly lifeless body. "Well, how are you today, Honey?" she said.

* * *

A somber Stosh left the doctor's conference. The consensus was if Jimmy made it for two more weeks, he would probably go on for years with no hope of improvement. He would be moved to an intensive care facility where he would spend the rest of his life. The good news was his living will was valid and he met the conditions for termination of life support. Damned if you do, damned if you don't, Stosh thought as he walked down the hall. He couldn't do anything anyway other than advocate for his best friend's wishes by begging for his death. The hospital had a private area where he and Clair would meet. He considered lying to her. The long-term prognosis was good for her plans. Maybe if he didn't tell her that part she'd be less hard-nosed. But he figured she'd find out before anything could be done anyway and end discussions.

Clair entered in style. "Like my new outfit, Stosh? I got it here in Albany. Who'd have thought they'd have such good shopping here? Well, what have you got to say? If it's only about Jimmy, the answer is still no."

"It is about Jimmy." Stosh filled her in on the results of the conference somehow hoping it would soften her.

"Well then, sounds to me like he has a good chance of living. I'm glad to hear that."

"Not much of a life, Clair. No life at all 'cept for the breathin'. Clair, you read his will; you know what he wants done. It's the right thing to do. For God's sake, end it now."

"God has nothing to do with this, Stosh. Nope, we're right back to square one with the fantastic Jimmy Eagleson. What Jimmy wants, Jimmy gets. Not this time. What I want matters now. No."

"Look, he gave you one heck of a life, and you don't need the extra money. You'll still have more than most. Listen, if you don't want to do it, I mean make the decision, sign it over to me; I'll take the heat on it. But, let him have what he wants this time."

"This time? Do you have any idea what it was like living with him? He called all the shots. Sure, I got anything I wanted, but only with his approval. It was always his way. And 'more than most,' Stosh, you think that's enough? I was taken way beyond that—by him I might add. He made that happen. I know what you and your friends think of me, the asshole monster from Miami. Well, he's the fucking Dr. Frankenstein who put me together. And I know you wonder about the kids. Don't worry, Stosh, they're both his; my screwing around didn't include babies. And the completely unavailable Mr. Eagleson can thank himself for that too. He made no time for Clair and even less for the girls. On the rare occasion he was home, and we were actually in bed, his mind was still on some fucking case somewhere. So don't lay your shit on me, Stosh. You want me to feel sorry and compassionate and feel the pain like the rest of you? Don't hold your fucking breath."

Stosh was becoming livid and paused to contain himself. He knew the other side of the story and was infuriated by the twist Clair put on it. He also knew a rebuttal would do more harm than good.

"Look, he made a lotta mistakes, and I know what he was like when he was workin'. But he still gave you everythin'. Can't you let him go?"

"I've got two girls who expect things. I live in a very expensive place, and I like it. I won't let him go, Stosh. You get it?"

"Can't you see what you're doing to those girls? You're raising a couple a spoiled brats who won't ever be happy. All this stuff you give 'em makes none of it matter. They never earn nothing on their own. Don't you know how good it feels to earn your own way? You're wreckin' that for 'em."

"What a preacher you've become, Stosh. Did you go to the Eagleson School of oratory? You sound just like someone I used to know. My girls like their lives and are perfectly happy. And I intend to keep it that way. That fucking provision in the divorce would change everything, Stosh, and that's not going to happen."

"Clair, don't you want to get married again anyway?"

"Remarry? Look at me Stosh, you see a spring chicken?

When Jimmy and I split, I thought I'd remarry. I thought the guy I was with was serious. And as soon as the ink on my divorce was dry, so was he. I'm lots of fun, Stosh, until the next cougar comes along. Remarry, my ass."

Clair picked up her purse to leave. "I think we're done here."

"Wait a minute, Clair. Look, if he lives he'll be nothin' but a vegetable, no feelin', no sensation, just a breathin' corpse. Clair, can you really live with that?"

"Yes, Stosh. The way I see it, if he's in the condition you have so dramatically portrayed, then he won't mind, will he?"

She let the automatic door close itself behind her. Stosh was fuming and knew there would be no changing her mind.

* * *

The days passed routinely, with regular visits during authorized hours followed by repetitious discussions about the absurdity. The sounds of the machines and the hospital's smell became nearly intolerable. Occasionally, they were asked to wait in the lounge while an orderly changed him. Often the orderly would still be holding the plastic bag containing Jimmy's soiled diaper as they were called back in. Ray had managed to avoid Stosh, mostly for Stosh's sake. But both had seen enough to agree on one thing: this was wrong. Kate's leave of absence was ending, and Stosh had several contracts to deal with in Florida. He felt guilty about leaving but knew he wasn't doing any good. Besides, Jimmy had made it past two weeks and would be moved soon.

"I'm flying out tomorrow," Stosh said.

"Well, I can't thank you enough for all you've done," Kate answered.

"I ain't done fuckin' shit."

"Stosh, is that you talking? I haven't heard you use a word like that in years."

"Yeah, well tonight I'm off the fuckin' wagon. This really sucks, Kate. And it's all due to that fuckin' c—"

Kate raised her hand to cut him short, "Not that one Stosh, I don't like that one."

"Sorry. I'm just so fuckin' frustrated. But we're not doin' no good here. I wonder if we're even stayin' around for Jimmy anymore. Seems like it's more for us. We can't do this shit forever. We know he's gone; hell, he checked out back on Poko."

"You're right. We have to come to grips with it. We've done all we can. I need to get back to work too."

"Listen, I met with Ken about the will. He's got everythin', just in case, you know... Fuck it, just in case Jimmy dies, like we all want. I signed all the paperwork. Shit, I don't know what half of it was, but he did. And if Jimmy trusted him, so do I. I do know one thing: if Clair ever saw it, she'd figure there was other reasons we all want to pull the plug."

"Why?"

"Well ... Shit, Kate, Ken will tell you when it's time—if it's ever time. I don't figure talking about it now is good. Ah fuck, I should'n'a said nothing about it. I'm not good with that kind a shit."

Stosh walked over to the bed and looked at his friend.

"What do you figure he'd done, I mean with all the time he was gonna have?"

"Don't know. He always said he wanted to teach."

"Teach what?"

"Philosophy."

"Philosophy? Shit he can do that right now."

Kate and Stosh burst into laughter, tried to contain themselves, and burst out again. "I needed that," Kate said.

"Yup, me too." Stosh left the bedside. "I just wish I could do what he wants, right here and now."

Ray walked in and saw Stosh. "Sorry, I'll come back later," he said.

"Nah, I'll be goin' in a minute anyway," Stosh answered.

Kate caught Stosh's eye and gave him a pleading look. Stosh walked over to look at Jimmy one more time. He returned to Kate and gave her a long hug. They nodded to each other. Stosh shook his head as he turned toward Ray, reached out to shake Ray's hand, and then wrapped an arm around him. "Come here you fucking bum," Stosh said. "Take care of things 'til I can get back, will you? And Ray … thanks for all you done for Jimmy." A little embarrassed, Ray nodded. As he walked out Stosh said, "I'll be in touch."

Kate looked at Ray and smiled. At least one wish had been granted. "I guess we should leave soon too," she said. "Visiting hours are over."

"OK, in a minute," Ray said standing at the bedside. "You know, I never thought anything like this could happen. Never meant to put any of us in danger. I fucked up."

"No … you didn't, and we all know that."

Ray was quiet. Kate took his hand and led him out of the room.

* * *

A scanty staff settled in for the graveyard shift, busy with paperwork and charts. Alone in his room illuminated only by a dim light and machine monitors, Jimmy was nearly invisible in the shadows. The door opened quietly, bathing Jimmy in the bright light from the deserted hall, and shut, returning the room to darkness. A figure in a hospital coat crept to the bedside, removed a vial and syringe from a pocket, held them in the dim light and filled the hypodermic, carefully tapping the cylinder and squirting out excess fluid to reach an exact measure.

"Fell off a fucking cliff," he said as he inserted the needle into an intravenous port and slowly pushed the plunger. "You always were the dramatic type." He slipped the kit back in his pocket and watched a monitor a few seconds. Satisfied, he took Jimmy's hand and gently squeezed.

"So long you clumsy fuck. I'll be seeing you soon enough."

He quietly headed to the exit. As he opened the door, bright light shone again on Jimmy's face and cast the silhouette of a tall, well-cut man with shoulders like Detroit.

CHAPTER X

The Gang

Stosh postponed his flight when he got the news. He planned to stay a few days more to help Kate with the arrangements. They knew Jimmy would want his body cremated, but that was the extent of any wishes they were aware of. They planned a small memorial at Camp in a few weeks. Guests would need time for travel, and there was no hurry anyway. Now, three days after Jimmy's death, Stosh was packing again. He heard a knock on the door and thinking it was Kate, he opened it smiling. His smile disappeared. "Well, Clair, how are you? Thought you went back last week. You must have heard."

"Yes, Stosh."

"Come in. What's new? I mean—"

"I know what you mean, Stosh."

"What brings you back?"

"I needed to talk to you."

"Here?"

"I thought of writing a letter, but I needed to see you face to face. And this is where we talked before. This is where Jimmy died." Stosh grew apprehensive. "Stosh, things got very complicated for me very fast."

"They been screwed up for us all."

"But you have each other. You're all part of Jimmy's circle. I'm not. I'm alone."

"Clair—"

"Just let me talk, OK? Look, I've got two girls you most graciously have defined as spoiled, although I prefer calling them 'well cared for.' And that's it, Stosh. I know lots of people, but I don't have any real friends, not like you. It wasn't that way when I was with Jimmy—at least at first. But that's the way it is now."

"Clair, is this about the will?"

Clair looked away for a second. "Yes, Stosh, it's about the will."

"You know, Ken says it's airtight. We figured you might want to contest it, but it don't look to me like it would do no good. But it's up to you; you can tie everythin' up for a while if you want."

"I don't want to tie it up, Stosh. I'm not going to contest it. We both know the chances of Jimmy making a second mistake are next to nothing. And I don't want to fuck with it anyway. Not anymore. In the real world, it's more than fair."

Clair's eyes teared; Stosh handed her a tissue. "Stosh, I don't know how it all got so fucked up. You know things just go along day to day, and you don't really think about anything but keeping it as it is, and then something happens, and you see how truly fucked up it is, and there's no going back. I don't know what went wrong—too much money, too much work, too much partying, maybe too fucking much of everything. When we were first together, we'd go down to the Keys with a tent, a couple cases of beer, and some hot dogs and have the best time. We didn't need to spend a lot. You know, I didn't even know he was rich until we were about six months in. And I didn't care then. And sometimes you were there and some of the others and we had so much fun, remember?" Clair smiled—a smile Stosh hadn't seen in many years.

"Stosh, what I needed to tell you was I really did care for him. I need for you to know that. It wasn't an act. But he worked so much. I was always alone. He changed; he started throwing money at our problems rather than just being with me like he had at first. Jesus, I missed him, Stosh. But that's no excuse for what I did. I changed too. I admit I got to like the money, and if he wasn't going to pay attention, I'd find someone who would—you know where that got me. Well, there's no fixing any of it now. Jimmy's gone."

Stosh put his arms around her as she openly cried. Then she stepped back and composed herself. "And the will is fine, Stosh. I needed to tell you that too. Well, I guess that's that."

"You have any plans?"

"I don't know exactly what I'm going to do. I'll have to sell the house now and get out of the Gables. Might be good for the girls anyway. They aren't doing well in school, and I don't like the friends they're choosing. I need to get off my ass too. I'd like to get a job. In all these years, I've never used my degree. Work would be good for me although I know it would be tough, especially at first. I don't really know. I've got a lot going through my head. But there has to be a change. I know that."

"You know where I am if you need somethin'."

Clair hugged Stosh again. "Well, I need to get back to the airport. Thanks for listening, Stosh."

"You know, Kate's comin' in just a few minutes to take me. Like to ride with us?"

"I'd love to Stosh. But I'm not part of your world anymore. Thanks anyway. I'll get a cab."

Clair walked to the door. "Clair, thanks," Stosh blurted. "You'll be at the service, won't you? I mean you and the girls should be there, Clair."

"Maybe, I don't know. I'll ask them."

"Can I ask you a tough question?"

"Go ahead."

"Would you have ever let us—well, you know—let him go?"

"I've thought a lot about that, Stosh. I don't know. I guess that's something we'll never find out. But he's at peace, and we're all grateful for that. Now we're each left to sort it all out and move on ourselves. OK, I have to get going. Stosh ... thank you."

* * *

Kate knew the way to Ken's office well. He was representing her in her divorce and was now executing the details of Jimmy's will. Ray was also asked to come but declined. This kind of thing "wasn't his bag" he said. Kate understood.

"I think I have most of this in order," Ken said, "But I have a few questions, Kate. First, I want you to know this isn't easy for me. I didn't know Jimmy like you did. We met only a few years ago and would grab a drink from time to time. I really liked him. When he wanted me to handle his personal affairs, I was surprised. He was twice the lawyer I am. He said he wanted someone objective who did the day-to-day nitty-gritty stuff. He wrote most of the will himself, but said if push ever came to shove, he knew I'd take care of everything just as he would. That meant a lot to me. Well, here we are."

"I hope I can help."

"Let's start with you. I need some signatures, actually many signatures to get your part transferred."

"My part?"

"Mr. Stoshowicz didn't tell you?"

"He said you would explain everything."

"Oh, well, OK. To start, Jimmy had quite a bit of money. You know he didn't spend much, I mean compared to his income, and it piled up. Let me show you."

Ken took a ruler, placed it under the line with Kate's name. Kate looked. Her eyes opened wide and she folded her hands. "Why? I don't deserve anything, but that much?"

"Don't feel bad. He left similar amounts to several others. I hoped to discuss Mr. Lafleur's sum with him today, but that can wait a bit."

Hearing Ray's inclusion made Kate smile. "What about Stosh? He's the one who really kept things going."

"I suppose I can talk about this. I told Mr. Stoshowicz as

executor he should inform everyone anyway. I wonder why he didn't."

"I guess it's hard to mourn your best friend and give all of his stuff away at the same time."

"Yes, I could see Mr. Stoshowicz is one emotional man. Well, the company is now solely his, with no debt to the estate. In real money, he received the most, by far." Kate smiled and nodded.

"Now maybe you can help me with one person here. I don't remember ever meeting her. Yes, here it is, a Ms. Gail Smith? Can you tell me how to contact her?"

Kate smiled again. "Yes."

"Good, the real estate is always the most complicated. There are a lot of documents for each of you to sign."

"Each of us?"

"You know, I wish Mr. Stoshowicz had at least told people a little about this. If I'd known no one knew the general information, I would have called a meeting last week. Jimmy left you Camp, with a condition."

Kate was stunned. After a moment, she shook her head. "A condition?"

"Yes, right now Camp and the guest house share a common egress. A separate drive to the guest house will have to be constructed. I've looked into it, and the land meets all the requirements, but it may have to cross a slight part of your property which we'll have to transfer. We'll have to do a full survey and finish the legal details before we can get a permit. You will need to sign off on all of this."

"Why a separate drive?"

"Mr. Lafleur will be receiving the guest house and Jimmy didn't want any right-of-way complications with either deed in case of future sales. Mr. Lafleur will also be receiving a pickup truck and a boat. The New York City property is much less complicated. It goes to Ms. Smith, no strings attached."

"There'll be no strings on Camp either; I'll be more than pleased to sign."

"Now two items, a silver ring and cigarette lighter, are to go to Mr. Gordon Eagleson. I assume this is a relative?"

"Yes, Gord is Jimmy's cousin."

"Good. Jimmy was quite concerned about this. He said— I'll put it the way he did—'The Old Man insisted these things stay in the line of Eagleson males.' Jimmy was adamant this be the case."

"I'll let Gord know; he'll be honored." Kate sat back in tears. "I can't believe Jimmy's generosity. He had the biggest heart." She wiped her eyes and smiled.

"Well, I'm glad you're pleased with the arrangements. There's one more item I don't know how to pin down. I hope you can help me with this one. Have you been in contact with Mr. Esposito?"

"Not recently. He hasn't been around for any of this."

"Jimmy left him something he called 'the stick.' Know what that means?"

Kate started to laugh. "It's something they found when they were kids. It looks like a rifle. I'll see Sal gets it."

"Oh good. I must admit, that one was confusing. Mr. Esposito will also receive a 1966 Lincoln Continental. Jimmy said it was 'the only thing the fleet was missing.'"

Kate smiled. "Yes, Sal has many cars, but nothing like the Lincoln."

"All right, I think that's everything. If you could make yourself comfortable at the table, you can start signing; I'll notarize as you go. This shouldn't take more than an hour or so."

Kate took out a pen, and they began the assembly line process. When they finished, she asked Ken about the divorce proceedings. He assured her none of her inheritance was accessible to Steve. He added that Steve had been quite reasonable at their last meeting, and the separation agreement should be finalized soon. She was relieved but still shaken by her new, instant security. As she left, she looked forward to telling Ray. He hadn't said anything, but she could tell he was worried about having to find a new place and a job. He would have to get in to see Ken right away. There were important things for him to sign too.

* * *

Camp was booked to capacity, except for one room. Kate wasn't ready to invade Jimmy's space. She knew that would have to come, but not now. She stayed in the wing. Gail had arrived for her first visit ever; the others were due that day. Right now, they had no time for gloom. Everyone focused on preparations for a grand party. Ray had fine-tuned the grounds while Gail and Kate cleaned inside. The great room was sparkling from the lake view and proudly displayed a new addition to the mantel, a carved oak urn holding Jimmy's ashes. Now that the chores were finished, Gail and Kate sat at the bar chatting.

"Something to drink, Gail?" Kate asked.

"Sure. Is Chardonnay OK?"

"Around here? Anything you want, girlfriend." Kate opened a bottle and poured two glasses.

"Kate, how do you feel, I mean, about all of this?"

"I'm not sure what you mean."

"Well, you know, with me ... I never wanted anything from Jimmy. I'm a little embarrassed; the last time we talked I kind of chewed him out about always giving too much, and now ... well ..."

"I know. I'm instantly well off and feeling shitty about it. Doesn't make any sense. But it must have been important to him for us to be comfortable. That's the best I can do with it right now. But I feel guilty. Don't know why exactly. Maybe survivor guilt. God, I miss him." Kate paused and sipped her wine, "Although I know *Jimmy* is just fine. After all, he's the one who moved on. *He's* the one who left *us* behind. *He* finished *his* race in style and on top of the world, and is enjoying the after party. I don't know if there's a better way to go. But *we're* left behind to figure out our next moves—and miss the hell out of him."

They were silent a moment. Then Gail said, "You know, I always thought you two would be the best couple."

"A lot of people did. But things are what they are." Kate paused. "Oh, who the hell do I think I'm kidding? I think about that all the time. Damn it. Why did this fucking thing have to happen?" Kate sipped again. "It is what it is." Gail nodded. They stayed quiet a moment. Then Kate asked, "Say, whatever happened to that little bitch, you know, the one who cheated on Jimmy with that Gyges asshole?"

"The last I saw of her was just after Jimmy died. She was in the bar with that very asshole. Kind of a funny story actually. He was shitfaced drunk. I couldn't hear what she was saying, but she was real upset, and he looked at her with this sarcastic smile that begged to be slapped. Then he announced at the top of his lungs, 'Here's to Dr. Eagleson, the man who could do anything, except fly.' She threw her drink at him and walked out in tears."

Gail started to laugh.

"What's so funny?"

"Well, it just hit me. That's almost witty for a dumb bastard like him."

Gail's laughter became infectious and Kate joined. They wailed uncontrollably for nearly a minute. Then Kate asked, "What did he do?"

"He just stood there; then I cut him off. Told him to find another place to drink. He told me to fuck off. Our bouncer grabbed him by the collar and belt and threw him out." Gail laughed again. "I can still see that pompous little shit wearing that beautiful, white, silk shirt splattered with cranberry juice, being tossed out the door. He was grabbing his side and screaming 'don't, my ribs!' but the bouncer didn't care. You know, he can't fly either." Both Gail and Kate broke back into hysteria.

Gail looked at a pile of sympathy cards on the bar. "Jimmy had a lot of friends."

"Yes he did," Kate said. "Say look at this." Kate sorted through the stack and found a printed sheet of paper. "Our lawyer found this when he cleaned out Jimmy's laptop."

Gail read aloud. " 'I chanced upon an obit in *The Times*. Maybe it's not yours. Either way, I wish you peace, Jimmy Eagleson. And I hope your flight was wonderful.' Wow, that's strange."

"Yeah it is."

"Who's Susan Fort?"

"I have no idea."

Kate filled their glasses; they finished the bottle and opened another.

* * *

Stosh and Deb arrived at about three. They hadn't seen the place in years. Ray stood by the garage as they pulled in.

"This place looks fantastic, Ray," Stosh said, squirming his way out of his rental car.

"Thanks, Stosh."

"No, I mean frickin' fantastic."

One by one, Stosh pointed out to Deb the many changes he recognized as Ray stood by smiling and looking down. Then they joined the others inside.

"Stosh, Deb, this is Gail," Kate said.

"Ah, so this is the New York girl I used to hear so much about." Stosh grinned and gave Gail a hug.

"It's great to finally meet you," Deb added, smiling and nodding.

The few preparations left could wait. Gail insisted on performing her familiar role as bartender, and after serving the beer, she whipped up some exotic drinks to go with it. "I've never seen a bar this well stocked," she commented.

"You know Jimmy," Stosh said. Everyone paused in response to Stosh's use of present tense.

Deb raised her mug. "To Jimmy Eagleson, simply the best. Chins up."

They all laughed, clicked their glasses, and loudly responded, "Chins up!" The gang continued to drink, chat, laugh, and occasionally drift off into a memory.

At about 5:00, came a knock on the porch door. Kate approached, struggling to recognize a figure through the screen. "Is that Gordon?"

"Sure is, eh?"

She pulled opened the door and welcomed him. "It's been so long I didn't recognize you." Kate started a handshake, then changed her mind and hugged him.

"Yup, guess I lost track of some time. Should have come more. ... Ya know, I hear there's beer here and figured I'd better stop by and see."

"Oh, you came to the right place. Let's go to the bar."

"Gord, how the heck are you?" Stosh yelled.

"I'm great, Stosh," Gordon said as he shook Stosh's hand, then Deb's, and finally Ray's. Turning to Gail, Gordon said, "I don't think we've met." He shook Gail's hand, joined the party, gulped down two beers and announced, "There, now I'm ready to drink, eh?"

"Hey, Gord," Stosh said. "Jimmy told us about some a The Old Man's gallivantin' in England." Gord silently sipped his beer. "Who'd a thought the guy was such a frickin' wild man?" Stosh recounted the stories Jimmy had told him on the sailboat. The others were stunned by young Gerret Eagleson's behavior and laughed heartily. Gord smiled, waiting to see how much Stosh knew. Soon he suspected Stosh didn't know it all—he was far too jovial.

"Oh, that reminds me," Kate said. She walked to the mantel and picked up a small gift bag lying next to Jimmy. "Jimmy wanted to make sure you got these, Gord. His will stated they were to stay in the Eagleson male line. Jimmy's lawyer said those were The Old Man's wishes."

Gord reached in the bag, fumbled with colored tissue paper and lifted out The Old Man's ring and lighter. He gazed at them somberly, cracked a grin, and slipped the ring onto his finger. "Hey look, it fits, eh?" He looked at his hand and rubbed the crest with his thumb.

"Hey Gord," Stosh said. "Maybe you'd know. What's the meaning of that crest? And maybe you know where The Old Man picked up the 'chins up' toast."

Gordon shrugged. "Best I know, The Old Man never spoke of either." Now Gordon was sure; the important secrets were his alone.

After a few more rounds, the group dispersed to get ready for dinner. Kate had reservations at the little Italian place, and, as usual, they were running late. She and Stosh were the first back at the bar. She poured two fresh beers and asked, "Are Clair and the girls coming?"

"I called, but she didn't know."

"I hope so if just for the girls' sake."

"Yeah."

"And Sal?"

"Called him too. Said he didn't know but not to figure on him. Somethin' 'bout some deal in New Mexico. All about timing or some frickin' crap like that. He said Jimmy'd understand. You get that? Jimmy'd understand? Frickin' Sal, he's never around when ya need him."

"Too bad; he'll be the only one missing."

"Screw that."

The others started returning to the bar. Tonight they were on their way to dinner, then back for more drinks and stories. Tomorrow they would say goodbye.

* * *

Ray rose at dawn. Only a table was needed for the gathering. But he puttered around making sure the yards were pristine. The lakeside lawn was Jimmy's favorite place for an outside party. Most of the festivities would be on the porch, but everyone agreed this was the place for the testimonial. When he finished his work, he went to the shore and sat on Jimmy's rock.

"Ray, come in and have breakfast," Kate called out.

"Yeah, in a minute," he yelled back. Ray wasn't as

comfortable with it all as the others seemed to be. He always found life's adjustments difficult. This was the biggest he'd ever faced, and he still felt responsible. He looked out onto Lake Champlain. That night he'd do his last favor for his best friend. In confidence, Jimmy had told him he wanted his ashes spread over the bay. In between fixing details on the lawn, Ray had been preparing the boat.

Ray wasn't sure Jimmy would have wanted the gang's tribute. He liked things done quietly. Ray wouldn't have even been involved in a memorial if he could have done it himself. But he knew Jimmy hadn't planned on dying so young with so many friends needing closure. And he knew Jimmy would approve of the party that was to follow.

"Come on, Ray; it's getting cold," Kate chirped. Ray reluctantly hopped off Turtle Rock, climbed the stairs, and joined the early festivities.

The gang hovered around the bar. A few had Bloody Marys. Most drank coffee. They'd tied one on the night before, and heads were thumping. Breakfast looked great as always, more Canadian bacon, eggs, and rye toast. Ray half-filled a plate and took a stool.

"That all?" Stosh ribbed.

"For now," Ray said.

Everyone would be there in an hour or so. They were shooting for a ten o'clock start, but plans were flexible. No one felt the pre-service panic that usually came with these things. There would be a small group from town, the core of the old partiers. All those invited were asked to keep it quiet. This bash wasn't for just anybody.

"You going to change?" Deb asked Stosh, who wore jeans and a flannel shirt.

"Why?"

"Yeah, you're right."

The guests started trickling in at 9:30; they all knew to come in through the garage door and go to the bar. Ray watched everyone laugh and tell stories and wondered when it would settle in for them. Right now, everyone felt relieved, but it was so new. Jimmy didn't seem really gone. But he was, and one by one that would hit each of them. Ray was glad for the joy around him now but was already feeling the loss intensely. He knew Kate was hurting too. For both, Camp was a place of many good memories, almost all with Jimmy. It would take time before they could be themselves there again.

"OK, I'm thinkin' it's time," Stosh announced. "Will you all join me on the side lawn?"

Ray hurried out through the porch to put the table in place as Stosh took the guest of honor from his perch on the mantle. Jimmy was positioned in the middle of the lawn, and the group formed a circle around him. Just as they were ready to begin, the sound of a car coming down the drive turned everyone's head.

"Clair, I'm so glad!" Kate yelled as Jimmy's ex and two daughters wiggled out.

"Thank you for calling again, Kate," Clair said, approaching. "You were right. We all should be here." Several of the gang greeted them warmly. The others were introduced in turn. Then Stosh asked everyone to re-form the circle.

"I knew Jimmy wouldn't want no formal service or nothing

like that. And he wasn't much on sermons or preachers and the like. Jesum, we used to whisper smart-ass stuff to each other when we'd have to listen to that kind of crap. So I figured we'd do it all ourselves. Go around the circle and everybody says something or tells a story or, well you know, do it like that. OK, who wants to start?"

Everyone looked at each other chuckling nervously, urging someone else to go first. Finally, Stosh began, but the gang's attention was drawn to an oversized gaggle of Canada geese flying north and unusually low. They grew louder and louder eventually drowning Stosh out. He stopped to watch. They headed for the circle. Ray smiled broadly, put his hands together and reverently faced Jimmy's box. One by one the others did the same. The honking reached a deafening crescendo directly overhead, slowly fading as they passed and continued their journey out of sight. Laughter began, and Gord started everyone cheering and whistling. All eyes were wet. Stosh pointed at the table. "I figured that sucker would find a way to show us all up. If nobody objects, I figure we're done here." Everyone nodded and dispersed to the porch.

"Will you join us?" Kate asked Clair.

"No, I don't think so. The kids want to get back to Montreal. We've only got a couple of days, and we might not be traveling much after this. But thanks, Kate. I'm glad we came. Maybe we'll see each other again sometime."

"I hope so," Kate said and they hugged. Kate walked them back to the car.

Stosh approached Ray and shook his hand. "I'm going with you tonight," he said.

"How did you—"

"You been playin' with the boat all morning. I don't figure you're going water skiin'. Besides, we both know he didn't wanna be planted in no box on no mantel. Naw, he loved the water. That's where he belongs."

"Best if it's just the two of us."

"Yup, agreed."

"The others might be pissed."

"They'll understand." Stosh looked back at the table. They'd let Jimmy sit on his favorite lawn for a little while before escorting him inside to the party.

"Time for a beer, Stosh?" Ray asked.

Stosh instinctively looked at his watch—10:30. He slowly raised his head and looked at Jimmy's urn. He remembered the ride to the airport just before the New Year, the last time it was just the two of them. He could hear the last thing Jimmy said, "You finish the beer." He smiled, wiped the corner of his eye and looked out onto Lake Champlain. "Yeah," he said. "Let's have a beer."

To the reader,

Thank you for joining Jimmy Eagleson on his flight. Your Amazon review would be much appreciated.

The story continues in

Salvatore

COMING IN 2017

Chins up,

Jeff Delbel

ACKNOWLEDGEMENTS

Those to whom I owe my gratitude are many.

David Connelly, my editor mentor and coach. David shared a Pulitzer prize leading a team covering the eruptions of Mount St. Helens in 1980. His keen sense of story and editorial acumen were invaluable. Without his drive, this book might never have been finished.

Elizabeth Haydon, a famous author of over fifteen superb novels who took the time to teach me the ropes.

Bill Canale, a man with a clever understanding of plot whose creative ideas added action and zest.

Glenn Dalton, **Maryanne Felter**, **David Henry**, **Rich Kavanaugh**, **Mitch Pajonas**, **John Rury** whose careful content analysis led to heartfelt revisions and enhancements.

Laurie Bertonica, **Aggie Crothers**, **Mary DeCavallas**, **Karen Henry**, and **Tess Personius** whose astute proof reading saved much pain.

Moreen Austin, Barbara Batman, Keith Batman, Judi Campagna, Amy Casella, Tom Casella, Kathleen Connelly, Lonnie DeCavallas, Carol Keeler, Steve Keeler and **David Raymond,** the rest of my diligent readers whose input and clear criticism led to much improvement.

Tom Casella, who lent his artistic eye to the cover design.

Natalie, Rachael and **Zack** at the turtle bar in P-burgh who advised on the "North Country twang."

Each of those listed contributed to making *The Flight of Jimmy Eagleson* a much better book.

Two additional recognitions are paramount.

The late **Rev. James A. Delbel** who on a summer day in the late 1950s snapped a photo of a boy in an inner tube on Lake Champlain. Jim taught us all how to care.

And most, to **Flight Officer James Lyman Eagleson** who gave his life flying a mission over France in the last days of the battle for Normandy. He, and thousands of others like him, made it possible for guys like me to write books like this.